Hidden

Tales of Ryca, Volume 1

Shereen Vedam

Published by Shereen Vedam, 2017.

HIDDEN

First edition. October 10, 2017.

ISBN: 978-0995344730

Written by Shereen Vedam.

Also by Shereen Vedam

Harrington Bay Mystery
Sage It Out
Missing You

Outside the Circle Mystery
To Capture Love
Death Takes a Detour
Death Shifts Gears
Death Smells Disaster
Death Swipes Right
Death Comes Up Short

Tales of Ryca
Hidden
Hushed

The Cauldron Effect
Coven at Callington
Warlock from Wales
Love Spell in London

Standalone
Tales of Ryca: The Complete Series
Torn
The Cauldron Effect: The Complete Series
Believe
Innocent

Watch for more at www.shereenvedam.com.

Chapter 1

Gilly's goats grazed on the dry grass and thicket, their occasional "maa" a soothing melody on this hot summer day. She leaned on her walking stick to take pressure off her aching left leg. This open flat section northeast of the village stretched far across the horizon. From here, she could see strangers approach from miles away. A defense tactic that had become ingrained after years spent on self-imposed guard duty.

Divided by terrain and cultures and ruled by King Ywen and his Horsemen, Ryca was a dangerous land for her kind, ones who knew how to wield *Light*, to weave magic. She had been on guard since the King's Horsemen tracked her family down in a far off woods, over two decades ago now. Along with her goats, she had run then, carrying her baby sister south across the breadth of the western edge of the Land of Ryca. Weeks later, heart sore, feet torn, lame leg throbbing and red straggly hair plastered to her wet cheeks, she reached this little forgotten corner of Ryca. A pastoral village named Nadym.

Gilly had stayed hidden on the village's outskirts, enviously watching smiling farmers go about their daily tasks in blissful ignorance of any danger. They didn't picture Horsemen hiding behind every bush. Or imagine a sword striking down each time they closed their eyes.

Her ever-present fear of discovery, one she hadn't been able to shake in the two decades she'd spent here, kept Gilly from spending much time with the people of Nadym.

The bright sun rising high in a clear blue sky hinted at yet another scorching day. Perspiration trickled off her forehead and droplets slid down her back beneath her long brown gown and linen underskirt. She was looking forward to sitting in the shade and taking off shoes and stockings to cool her hot toes. To the right, near a hilly terrain, large oaks promised cover. She herded the goats that way.

"Gilly!" The light singsong voice came from a distance.

Her heart skipped a beat in acute pleasure even before her niece ran up to her. The girl wore a pretty blue gown cinched at the waist. The material had intricate embroidery sown at the hems by her mother, Anna.

Skye came to a breathless halt, a small replica of her mother with sunshine hair, pert nose, and inquisitive eyes.

In contrast, Gilly had sun-flecked red hair, hazel eyes and a face dusky from years spent under the sun. At thirty-three summers, she considered herself past the age of "pretty."

Gilly planted a disapproving expression on her face that belied her bubbling happiness at seeing Skye. "What did your mam say about trailing after me?"

Skye shrugged and tugged a tall blade of grass to chew. "My mama's always angry with me for one reason or another. Besides, she doesn't understand."

"Understand what?"

The eight-year-old kicked at a mole mound. "All Mama wants me to do is chores. With you, I get to roam the plains." Arms spread wide, she twirled with abandon.

Gilly viewed the knobs of hills breaking up the flat surface from Skye's perspective. Patterns of purple, gold, red and silver wildflowers waved in the wind while tawny grass stretched far across the horizon. Land that usually seemed shaded with melancholy now shouted, *freedom*.

Such a rare emotion. Fear she was familiar with. Sadness. Even loneliness. This sense of well-being, in a land that posed no threat, no sense of doom? She wanted to embrace this sensation, cherish it, if only for a few moments. What harm if Skye stayed for a while?

"You go farther than anyone else," her niece said. "I'm not allowed to wander this far without someone by me."

"You're not allowed to wander at all, with me." The reprimand, aimed at Skye, generated spasms of guilt in Gilly. She wasn't on intimate terms with her sister. In fact, Anna was unaware that Gilly was her sister.

After escaping the King's Horsemen, believing they would search for two children, Gilly, then a ten-year-old girl, had decided she and her baby sister would have a better chance at survival if they separated. So, shortly after reaching this isolated village, she left the baby on a temple's doorstep, hoping someone would adopt her.

To her delight, a couple took her sister and named her Anna. Gilly should have left then. It was the sensible thing to do. The safe thing to do for both of them. She just couldn't do it.

No matter how lonely it was to watch others love her sister, she couldn't bring herself to leave Anna. What if her sister needed her? What if the Horsemen tracked Anna down and Gilly wasn't around to save her? Those questions kept Gilly Nadym-bound. So, living alone in the woods, she secretly checked on the baby's welfare.

A few months later, when the couple who adopted Anna conceived a child, they passed the "orphan" to another childless couple. Months later, Anna was passed along again, and then again. Seeing her sister shunted among families like an unwanted puppy broke her heart.

Needing to do something to help her sister, she "officially" moved to Nadym. Calling herself Gilly, a goat herder, she attempted to befriend Anna, even offered to watch her. The plan was easier imagined than accomplished. The villagers had apparently grown fiercely protective of the orphan child. Anna was indeed loved, if not intensely and personally, certainly as a member of Nadym's close-knit community. They refused to allow strangers anywhere near the child.

Still, as she grew up, Anna must have felt disconnected because she spent her childhood trying to prove she belonged in the village. That included following all village customs and rejecting everything she deemed out of place.

She didn't understand why Gilly lived alone. Couldn't conceive why anyone would shun communal activities. She saw Gilly's tendency to talk to her goats as "crazy."

Despite Anna's aversion to her, Gilly adored the woman her sister grew up to be. The day Anna married was Gilly's happiest and loneliest day of her life. Her sister had finally established a safe, secure home, but one that excluded Gilly. If Anna had her way, she would never let either of her children anywhere near Gilly, whom her sister had long ago nicknamed the *Madwoman of Nadym*.

Anna's daughter, however, had an independent streak as wide as these plains. One her mother couldn't control. One Gilly should discourage. Turning Skye away was a bittersweet task she had yet to master.

She tucked a strand of Skye's blond hair behind her ear. Despite her misbehavior, this child had a good heart. Anna should be proud of her.

The goats, which had been grazing peacefully until now, moved toward a rocky outcrop. Skye and Gilly followed. In the distance, melodious voices floated. It was harvest time, when villagers gathered on the southern fields to apply their scythes and reap in rye and oats. A community effort that seemed to require much joyful singing.

"Why do you come so far?" Skye asked.

Gilly stumbled over a rock and cursed her left leg for lagging instead of lifting. Skye's personal question intruded in places best left undisturbed. How to answer? "Guess I like the sense of vastness. Seems I've been staring out onto open fields most of my life."

"Even when you were little, as little as Bevan?"

Bevan. Skye's little brother of four summers. Now there was a quiet, lonely soul. Anna kept him close, so Gilly could only study his behavior at the market, the temple and the public well.

Skye asked again, "Did you stare off into the fields when you were little?"

"Since I was a touch older than your age, anyhow."

"What about before then?"

"Don't remember much before that."

"Why not?"

Too close! A mental warning shot out, sharp and shrill.

Normally Gilly would end the conversation here, but Skye's innocent blue eyes pleaded for a confidant, a friend. Friendship meant sharing and talking, not running away.

"Just the way I am. My mam said I'd had an accident, a fall that knocked my memories out and broke my leg."

"How did it happen?"

"Don't remember that, now, do I?"

"Does your mam?"

The question ripped open the old wound and Gilly swallowed hard to keep the pain from flooding out. Her throat clogged and her eyes filled. She looked away, searching for control. Once her throat loosened its fierce grip, she spoke softly, serenely. "She died long ago."

The ancient pain turned over like a bony old dog and returned to its pit for another nap.

"Oh." Skye's eyes softened with compassion. As quickly, her mood shifted. With a shout, she ran toward the goats.

Bleating, they scattered. Skye chased after the youngest. As she lunged for him, the kid skittered away, and Skye fumbled to the ground, empty-handed.

With a tolerant laugh, Gilly allowed her niece's play, glad the uncomfortable conversation had ended. The girl scrambled up and chased after the kid, which took off up a hill.

Skye waved to indicate she would meet her at the top and tore off at a run before Gilly could argue. That girl had too much energy. Skye scooted up a rocky portion as if she were a goat herself, her gaze firmly planted on the kid that watched her with cool insolence from the top.

Gilly forced her lame leg to move faster as she climbed after them.

A scream sliced the still air.

Skye! Gilly jerked her gaze upward. The kid was on the hill but not her niece. She cursed her leg as she hurried up the rise. "I'm coming."

The moment she reached the top, the kid raced off toward the rest of the herd. On the other side was a sharp drop some forty feet to the ground. The girl clung to a branch of a dead oak. That weak branch wouldn't hold her long. She must have slipped, unprepared for the hill to abruptly drop off.

"Help!" Skye cried.

"I'm here." Fear for Skye's safety, combined with her fear of heights, made Gilly nauseous. The contents of her stomach roiled. *Calm down!* This was no time to be ill. Skye needed her. The girl was too far down from this crest for Gilly to reach, even with her walking stick. She looked for other means of getting to the girl.

If she tried to go down, she would probably fall, as Skye had. If she went back to the village, it might be too late by the time she returned with help.

"My hands are slipping." Panic was clear in Skye's high-pitched voice.

"Hold on." Gilly's stomach did another turn, threatening to empty her breakfast over the ledge. Her head swam. As if in a bizarre nightmare, she pictured Skye smashing into the rocks below, limbs twisting and cracking.

Breathe! Think! She must save Skye. Can't let her fall.

The dry branch cracked. Skye screamed and fell.

Instinctively, Gilly reached out. "Halt that fall! Come wind, come leaves, cradle my girl, lift her up and bring her back to me."

Shimmering Light surrounded Skye. She hovered midair, her body limp. Slowly a breeze stirred the droplets of Light surrounding the child. Fallen leaves rose from the ground to cradle Skye and then lifted her higher to gently place her on Gilly's outstretched arms.

"Gilly," Skye said, awakening. "What happened?"

"I have you. You're safe."

Skye stared at Gilly quizzically and then said, "You can put me down, now."

Startled, she realized she stood carrying her niece's weight *equally* on both her legs. She knelt to set Skye down. Her lame leg felt as strong as the other. Before she could ponder that physical oddity, Gilly heard the sound she dreaded most. Hooves pounded. Swords clashed. Horses snorted. She swung around expecting to see the King's Horsemen.

The plains were empty of riders. Her goats watched from below, curious but unconcerned. Despite the evidence of her eyes, Gilly was worried. She had performed magic. *High Magic.*

The signs were everywhere. The grass looked greener. A glance over the cliff showed the old oak in full leaf, as if it had never died. The air itself thrummed with excitement. How could this not be detected? The Horsemen would come. They always did when someone wielded High Magic in Ryca. How much time did her family have to escape? She must warn Anna. Time for them to flee again.

Gilly's sides were aching from running back to the village, but her niece looked as if nothing were the matter. As if she hadn't dropped off a cliff and almost died. As if she hadn't raced ahead and sped back a dozen times to hurry Gilly along.

Worried Skye might tell someone Gilly had saved her life, she had warned the girl to keep mum. Skye had reluctantly agreed. The fact Gilly planned to return to the village with her seemed to make up for that disappointment.

Thankfully, the goats, too, obeyed Gilly and ran without argument or need for coaxing. However, the race to the village gave time for other worries to poke at Gilly. The change in her surroundings for a start.

Where use of High Magic had blossomed the area around Skye's fall, the closer they drew to Nadym, the worse the countryside looked, as if a wave of dark magic had swept the land. Everywhere there was charred grass, dead trees and overhead, thunderclouds gathered.

If that wasn't enough for concern, she was also anxious about what to tell Anna. She couldn't talk about the magic she'd performed. Use of any kind of magic was forbidden all across Ryca and her sister was more likely to turn her in than run away with her. Nor was Gilly comfortable revealing their true relationship to her sister. Anna simply wouldn't believe her. Somehow, she had to convince her sister and her family to leave Nadym.

When Gilly and Skye arrived at the village, the first drops of rain splashed her cheeks.

"Look at everyone," Skye said. "Wonder what's going on?"

The place teemed with not only villagers, but also men on horseback. Gilly's worst nightmare had come to life.

In green capes and black armor, the King's Horsemen were in Nadym.

Breathless, Gilly stumbled to a halt. Her face went icy cold as if blood had drained off in a rush. Despite spending years being careful, avoiding people, refusing to use any hint of High Magic, the King's Horsemen were here. They had come to this backwater village because she had used magic.

She absently touched Skye's head. How else could she have saved Skye?

I should have watched her better. Told her to be careful. Made her go home. This happened because I let down my guard. Allowed people to get close. I knew better!

Gilly couldn't shut off the self-recriminations, but she did pull Skye behind a house before either of them was spotted.

Turning to the goats, she spoke firmly. "Home! Go. Go. Go."

The goats scampered away toward her shack.

"Look, there's my mama!" Skye pointed.

Pulse racing, Gilly peered around the corner.

At the far edge of the crowd, Anna's blond head bobbed up as she repeatedly leaped, trying to see past everyone.

Foolish woman, stay down! Gilly took hold of Skye's arm, and they worked their way into the heart of the village, hiding in alleyways and between animal pens at the back of houses. Every time Gilly checked on Anna, her sister seemed to have made more headway, working through the crowd. Ignoring grunts and curses, her sister finally broke into a central clearing and came face-to-face with a Horseman.

Gilly groaned and shut her eyes. She couldn't watch.

Skye found a crate to stand on for a better view.

Gilly joined her on another. If she was to save Anna, she needed to know exactly what was happening. Just their luck that was not any Horseman Anna had stumbled into. His darker green cape indicated he was the captain. A black metal patch covered one eye. He gazed at Anna with disdain.

"What's going on?" Skye sounded more animated than alarmed.

"Those are King's Horsemen, and they're here for your mam."

"What do you mean?"

"Shhh! Not now."

The rain had started to fall in earnest but the street remained crowded. The villagers probably had never seen this much activity and they weren't about to miss any of it because of an inconvenient summer shower.

Anna, apologizing, stepped away from the captain and onto the toes of Vyan, the village chief. He stoically moved her behind him and with an ingratiating smile to the captain, said, "Perhaps we should conduct our business indoors? Away from the um, rain, yes?"

His backwards glance at Anna suggested she should be avoided as much as the downpour.

Gilly could have kissed the man for separating Anna from the captain but she was also worried. Vyan wasn't Anna's closest ally in Nadym. Ever since her sister rejected his marriage offer and instead chose Marton, the village blacksmith, Vyan had held a grudge against her. Gilly didn't care for the idea of him speaking privately with a King's Horseman who'd no doubt ask about children who might have come here twenty odd years ago.

The captain frowned at Anna over Vyan's short stout shoulders, pausing long enough to make Gilly gulp with fear. Finally, he nodded assent.

Air rushed out of Gilly's lungs in profound relief.

Vyan led the captain away while the Horsemen dismounted in a clatter of metal on metal.

"We have to get your mam out of this village," Gilly whispered to Skye and then stepped off the crate. Her leg began to ache. Curse the rain.

"She won't like that," Skye said. "This is something mama knows that Lissa doesn't. She'll want to stop and tell her."

Lissa, her sister's confidant and fellow gossip-monger. "There is no more time for village chit chat. Run home and tell your papa that I said all of you must leave Nadym."

"Leave? To go where?"

"Anywhere but here, Skye. These Horsemen mean to harm your family. Run home and tell your papa your family must escape." She gave instructions to get her father and brother packed and to a secluded cowshed north of the village. "I'll bring your mam. Hurry!"

Gilly then wove her way into the crowd until she came up behind Anna. Her niece might be easy to convince, but Anna not so much. Deciding to go the no-explanation route, Gilly took an iron-fisted hold on her sister's wrist and pulled her behind her.

Villagers scrambled aside as she dragged her sister to the outskirts of the crowd. Luckily, Anna was at first too stunned to make a fuss. Soon enough though, she dug in her heels and pulled back, hard, and their headlong rush came to a jarring halt.

"How dare you!"

Gilly checked her surroundings. They were well past the Horsemen. Still, she stepped closer before whispering, "We have to leave. Now."

Anna pushed her back, incensed. "First, you lure my daughter from her family—I know she was with you today, Lissa told me Skye was headed in your direction—and now you drag me through the village when I have important business to attend. This is the last time you'll interfere with me or mine, Gilly, I promise you."

Skye ran up to her mother and tugged at her sleeve. "Mama, you have to listen to Gilly. You're in danger."

Gilly could have cried. Why hadn't the child gone home to start packing?

"Don't talk to me about danger. You're in enough trouble." With heat rising up her face, Anna looked like a pot boiling over. "Go home and start on the vegetables."

"Mama, please. It's important."

Anna cut her off. "Enough, Skye."

"Your mother's right," Gilly said with a sigh and nodded to Skye. "Time she and I talked. Go home. You know what to do."

Skye glanced from her mother to Gilly, and then, with a frustrated cry, sped off.

Gilly turned back to Anna only to find her sister was even more livid. *Now what?*

"That will be the last time you tell my daughter what to do." Thunder rumbled overhead.

The wind, which had subsided, picked up, blowing Gilly's red hair about her face. The coincidence between Anna's temper and the worsening weather wasn't lost on Gilly. Unconscious magic was more powerful and uncontrollable than manipulating Light. She hoped it was less traceable. Then a way to get Anna to listen became clear. "You have your papa's temper."

Her sister looked shocked and confused.

Anna hated her label of "illegitimate," given to her long before she'd learned to milk a cow. So, hearing she had her papa's temper, which suggested Gilly knew who that man was, wouldn't be overlooked. Gaining information about her parentage could erase the label and give Anna the finest accolade possible in a village where lineage was highly prized – a family tree.

Leaving her sister sputtering in shock, Gilly spun and headed home. She had a small cottage on the outskirts of the village, located halfway between Nadym and where Anna and Marton lived. Sooner they were out of sight from these Horsemen the better. She had lots to do and little time to waste. A check over her shoulder confirmed Anna followed. *Good.*

Once inside her home, Gilly stuffed clothing and food into an old knapsack, the same one she had carried when she left her mam's cottage with baby Anna in her arms. Long ago, she'd lost too many loved ones. This time, they would either all escape together, or perish together.

"Maa." One of her goats cried the warning. Her sister had arrived. Took her long enough.

Anna lingered by Gilly's open doorway as if afraid to step into the Madwoman of Nadym's home. "For someone with a gimpy leg, you move pretty quick."

"I've learned that allowing my deformity to slow me can cost lives."

"Why must you say such outlandish things?" Her sister's voice was peppered with frustration. "I've known you all my life. You've never been in danger. The villagers treat you well. When have you ever had to run for your life?"

"I had a life before Nadym."

Anna strolled around the room, her gaze following Gilly's movements.

"That pack will split before you're done," Anna said.

The sack did look ready to fall apart at the slightest wind, but it would have to do. Gilly bent by the fireplace, lifted a loose stone and dug within for the coins she'd squirreled away for this emergency. She'd expected the Horsemen to find her every day for the last twenty odd years.

Jingling bag in hand, she faced her sister and was taken aback. Anna looked so grown up. Straight blond hair, strong determined face, brooding eyes full of worries, and a no-nonsense manner.

Anna gave up on small talk. "What did you mean about my papa's temper?"

"Exactly what I said." Gilly tucked the money in a belt under her dress and picked up the knapsack. She avoided looking straight at Anna in case she was tempted to hug her. That would surely spell disaster.

Anna ran to bar the doorway. "You're leaving the village?"

"We're leaving."

"I'm not going anywhere, Gilly. Now, what makes you think you know my papa?"

Gilly took a breath brimming with dread. She'd known this day would come. She had expected to feel a little intimidated. Not have her guts twist like a washerwoman wringing out clothes. *Spit it out.* "Your mam used to say your papa had quite a temper. This once you must put aside your animosity and think about what's best for your family."

"How could you possibly know any of this?"

"I was the one who left you at the temple. It had been my job and privilege to watch over you and keep you safe."

She cringed at the half-truth. Safer this way. Less chance she'd blame Gilly for deserting her. Better demeaned as a servant than hated as a sibling who abandoned her.

"Why not say this before?" Anna demanded with suspicion. "Explain yourself!"

Gilly gazed past her sister and out the open door. Any moment a Horseman could appear there. "I left you to keep you safe. Admitting our connection would have put you in danger from the King's Horsemen. They've tracked us down anyway." She shied from mentioning magic. Like the other villagers, Anna would condemn the practice of the ancient craft as illegal. She probably didn't even realize she was capable of shaping Light. *Finish this.*

Gilly spoke tersely; getting the words out before her throat closed too tight or a Horseman came by to slit it. "Your family is the enemy of King Ywen. A blood feud. I was your...keeper, charged with your safety. The king had your father killed first and then one summer later, the Horsemen discovered your mother, brother, and sister." Her voice cracked and her next words came out in a hoarse whisper. "Only we escaped because I didn't return to help the others."

Anna sucked in her breath.

Gilly avoided her sister's critical gaze. The haunting deed was etched in blood in Gilly's soul, one she wasn't ready to elaborate.

"Maybe they're still alive." Hope vibrated in Anna's voice.

Gilly looked up then, and spoke with authority, slaughtering that particular idea in its path. She wasn't about to let hope fester in Anna like an open wound that never healed. How many nights had she lain awake hoping her mother hadn't perished? That she was out there looking for her and Anna? Hope was for fools.

"They're dead, Anna. Your mam loved you very much. If she were alive, she would never have stopped looking for you." For us. She finished with, "Now the Horsemen have come to Nadym, we must leave."

"No." Anna crossed her arms.

Gilly's mind rocked at her sister's adamant stance. "But..."

Anna waved a dismissive hand. "I only have your word for any of this."

Gilly leaned forward. "The Horsemen are real enough. You've seen them yourself."

"So what? I'm not afraid of them." Anna stared directly at her. "I'm not a coward. I have nothing to be ashamed of. I was a baby at the time. What could the king possibly hold against a newborn?"

Terrible unease built up in Gilly at Anna's cool reasoning. She didn't care what sins she was responsible for; she would not sanction another family tragedy. What would it take to make Anna listen to sense?

"Maybe the king isn't looking to finish me off," Anna said. "Maybe he's searching because he knew my family and they were friends. Perhaps he wants to offer a grant in memory of my parents. You've simply prevented him from finding me for all these years."

Finding her jaw hanging open in stunned disbelief, Gilly shut her mouth with a snap. Frustration burned a hole in her midsection and she spoke through clenched teeth. "Anna, he wants to kill you, not give you a present."

Then dread raced up her back as one of her perimeter spells activated. Someone was coming.

A woman's voice called Anna's name.

"It's Lissa," Anna said with joy.

Gilly grabbed for her and missed as her sister hurried out the door. She had no choice but to follow, searching the area for any sign of a green cape.

Lissa, a plump young woman of Anna's age, grabbed her friend by her shoulders. "You'll never believe this. I came straight away to find you." She spotted Gilly then, and her flow of words halted. "What are you doing here with her? I almost didn't believe it when a villager said they'd seen you come this way."

"I was telling Gilly to stay away from Skye."

"Oh! Of course. Anyway, I've got news. There are King's Horsemen in the village."

Anna casually straightened a metal brooch that held her shawl in place over her blue dress. "I saw them talking to Vyan. I meant to tell you, but I've been busy. You finally heard, did you?"

Lissa's cheerful expression fell. "You knew?"

"I also know who they're looking for. I was on my way to speak to them when you interrupted. You can come with me, if you like." Arm-in-arm, Anna led her friend down the lane toward the village.

"Don't be foolish, Anna," Gilly said as her control of the situation slipped away.

"You stay away from my family," Anna said over her shoulder. "Let's go Lissa."

"All right." Lissa looked backward at Gilly, eyes wide and curious.

Under that intent, unwavering stare, the hairs on Gilly's neck quivered.

"When I left the village, the Horsemen were asking who had come to Nadym as children." Lissa said. "You were found as a baby, weren't you, Anna?"

Gilly clutched her knotted stomach and ordered herself to breathe. "Anna!"

Ignoring her call, her sister marched down the lane and out of sight.

Chapter 2

Gilly had a quiet word with her goats, telling them to go into the woods to live if she didn't return by sundown. Then, with her legs shifting in a rhythm uniquely their own, she followed the two women back to the village.

Anna was fast, but Gilly knew where she was headed, and why. Her sister was filled with uncertainty, about her family, the king's intentions, and her future in Nadym. That uncertainty made her rash.

Gilly increased her pace, pushing her game leg to its limit. A flame built in her left hip and knee and soared into an inferno by the time she reached the edge of the village.

The crowd was still there. The Horsemen had spread out to surround them. She blended into the outbuildings and inhaled deep, painful gulps, and willed her legs to stop shaking.

A Horseman, his green cloak draping his back and covering the hindquarters of his roan mount, waited not two feet from her. They were facing inward, toward the village. Probably posted on the outside of the crowd to keep villagers from fleeing. Anna would have had no trouble entering. The silly twit probably announced she was the one they wanted.

A commotion up ahead distracted the Horseman beside her. People cried out, and then a strident whistle sounded. A signal? The one near her rode forward.

Gilly worked her way to the village center.

Recognizing the cobbler, she stole up to him and whispered. "What's happening, Jimmy?"

"Vyan's dead. They've got Tom strung upside down like a wood pigeon ready for market day. They say he killed Vyan but that man's never hurt anyone since I've known him. What's happening, Gilly?"

Tom? Her head swam for a moment and she shut her eyes. *Focus!* "Did you see Anna?"

"She pushed her way in with Lissa. Said something 'bout important business with Vyan. They moved up 'fore I could tell 'em he'd be interested in nothing no more."

Gilly left him with a comforting pat on his shoulder and advice to go home. She then headed toward Vyan's house, the largest in the village. Constructed of timber, its front room faced the porch where Tom's interrogation took place.

Gilly had known Tom most of her life, since shortly after she arrived in Nadym. The tall slender boy with dark hair and intense brown eyes had been a few years her elder. Over the years, he had grown into a loner, almost as much as Gilly. He cared for his cattle but had never married, and rarely spoke. Anna often scoffed that he preferred brew to banter.

He may have been quiet, but Gilly had gained the impression that he was also kind. Perhaps from the gentle way he treated his animals. Tom couldn't have killed Vyan; she was as certain of that as she was that the Horsemen had killed her family. She couldn't worry about him right now. He wasn't her responsibility. Anna and her family were counting on her to save them.

She scooted to the back and entered the shed behind Vyan's house, slipping past the sheep and into the back room. Wailing came from the front room. There, she found Vyan's wife and daughters huddled together beside the central hearth, looking like a heap of colorful, expensive material on the floor. Past their skirts, Vyan's motionless legs protruded.

Tom was visible through the front window, strung up by his feet on the house's front porch. His tunic had been stripped off and red welts showed where bloody lashes marked his back, over other recent cuts and bruises.

Gilly tore her gaze past the porch scene to where Anna stood motionless on the street in front of the crowd. Lissa was close beside her. The two women held hands.

The sound of the whip striking and Tom's cry brought her gaze swinging back to the closer spectacle on the porch. The one-eyed captain wrapped his dripping weapon like a cord and then grabbed Tom's hair, pulling him up until they were face to face. "Where are they?"

Tom didn't reply.

The Captain released him and snapped his whip. Tom moaned in agony.

Gilly cringed. He was taking this beating for her and Anna. He hadn't even had a chance to properly recover from last night's wounds. Cuts she'd help sew up.

An early morning incident had created the other wounds on Tom's back. Close to sunrise, Jonas, the miller, had discovered Tom in bed with his wife. Apparently, Tom had stumbled, drunken, into his neighbor's house and passed out in the man's bed thinking it was his own.

Jonas' wife, not realizing Tom snuggled up to her and not her husband, had slept on, until her husband returned and found her with another man in his bed. On being shaken awake, she swore she was as shocked as Jonas. Her irate husband didn't believe her.

After the beating, despite Jonas' ire, the compassionate couple had come begging to Gilly to sew up Tom's wounds. Tom had violently protested Gilly seeing him stripped to his waist and bleeding but Jonas had held him down while Gilly worked with needle and thread. The miller had seemed to take inordinate pleasure at Tom's anguish at her hands.

Even Jonas wouldn't wish on Tom the Horsemen's current cruelty. What they all needed was a distraction. Something to focus the Horsemen's attention away from Tom *and* Anna.

She retreated out the back door and into the sheep pen. She undid the gate's latch and the one next door and the one after that. Animals pushed through into the open air.

Chickens, goats, sheep and cows milled at the back of the houses. Her rule about avoiding High Magic no longer applied, for the Horsemen were already here. Since they hadn't found her by the cliff face it stood to reason that they could probably generally sense the region where Light was activated but not be able to pinpoint its particular location. Also explained why they hadn't found her with her baby sister in the woods all those years ago.

Softly, Gilly chanted a song her mother had taught her to draw bees away from the hive with the promise of food. She altered it slightly to focus on animals instead of bees.

White speckled Light immediately hovered in the air and then settled around the animals. The livestock pushed and shoved, slowly at first and then in a frantic fashion, heading toward the village center. People and horses alike were shoved aside in the livestock's attempts to reach a promised bounty.

Pleased with their chaos, Gilly sneaked around front in time to spot One-Eye turn to see what was the commotion, and then bark out orders to his Horsemen.

Gilly made straight for Anna.

Lissa was gone – panic at the Horsemen's brutality must have set her in motion, but the thoughtless girl had left Anna behind. Gilly grabbed her sister's sleeve and pulled her into the closest front door. For once, her sister didn't argue or complain. As the door slammed shut, she realized she'd brought Anna to Vyan's house. Bad choice. Anna was shaking in her hold as she stared fixedly at the dead body.

"What's happening?" Vyan's daughter asked.

"Some animals got loose," Gilly said. "They seem to have upset the Horsemen."

"Good. I hope they trample them to death!" his wife said, raising a vengeful stare. "They killed Vyan, Gilly. They say Tom did it but they must be lying. Why would Tom kill Vyan?"

"What happened?" Anna asked.

"They were talking to my father," his daughter said. "Then I heard a lot of shouting outside. We all rushed to the door to look out. It was just a small fire, easily put out. When we came back, my father had a knife in his chest. The Horsemen stormed out and a short while later a Horseman dragged Tom in here saying they caught him running away. They suspect he threw the knife at my father."

Tom had probably been in the wrong place at the wrong time. She couldn't help another glance at him out the window, still hanging upside down. He was going to die. The idea didn't sit well, but Anna was her top priority. Tugging at her sister's sleeve, Gilly said to the grieving women, "Please don't tell anyone you saw us."

"My husband was stabbed," Vyan's wife said. "Like he was nothing, Gilly. He was the Chief of Nadym. A Chief!"

All that confirmed Tom was definitely doomed. As her heart shrank in grief, a desperate daring idea spawned. Dare she do it? *Yes, she must*. She dragged Anna toward the inside door and earnestly whispered, "You've seen the Horsemen's cruelty, Anna. Is there any doubt about their intentions toward you and your family? Head for the cowshed north of your place. Marton and your children will meet you there. Go. Now."

Anna snagged her elbow as Gilly turned back into the front room. "Where are you going?"

"Just leave." Dislodging her sister's clamp on her arm was made harder as Anna intensified her grip.

"Why aren't you coming with me?"

Her sister was so obstinate. Her reason for not following Anna would just get her insulted again. Considering her crazy plan to rescue Tom, she wondered if she had indeed ale froth for brains. "I'm going to get Tom."

Anna's nails bit into her skin. "He's a drunkard and a murderer. Leave him. They'll kill you if you go out there."

Gilly forcefully pulled loose and was certain she lost skin during separation. "He's taking this punishment for us, Anna. Go to your family. They need you and I can't help him if I have to worry about you, too."

Gilly pushed her sister into the back room and shut the door. Before her courage fled, she headed for the front porch and Tom.

Outside, cows trampled everything in sight. Goats were on the thatched roofs. Chickens flew around the Horsemen, many of whom had been unhorsed. The air vibrated with alarmed moos, clucks, and baas in addition to men shouting and women wailing. A burst of laughter startled her but she couldn't locate where it came from.

One-Eye was further down the street, riding a white stallion and slicing anything or anyone that stumbled into his path. Gilly couldn't look at that needless bloodshed.

She moved to Tom's side and focused instead on untying his rope binding. When the last loop unraveled, he collapsed on the front porch with a heavy thump.

She crouched beside him and whispered, "Stand up."

He didn't move.

With a frustrated cry, she slung his left arm around her shoulders.

"What are you doing?" He slurred the question around a swollen lip and a missing tooth.

"Getting you out of here." She tried to lift him and buckled under his weight. For such a slender man, he was *heavy*. "You need to stand."

"No." His gaze trained on the white stallion, he removed his arm from around her shoulders. "He'll be back. Leave me. Leave Nadym. Not safe here anymore."

"Fine, I'll go. With you."

"No!" His rejection was vehement. "Let me die. I deserve it."

Gilly sat back in shock. "No one deserves to die." She said the words with force and then glanced at the frightened crowd on the street. Had anyone heard? No, the din was too loud, thank the Light. Gilly moved his arm back across her shoulders. "You will not die. I won't let you." She needed to get him off the porch, away from watchful eyes.

"Stop it." His protest was fainter this time and his eyes were closed. Any moment now he would be a dead weight.

She debated stringing together a spell to lighten his weight. It was either that or drag him, which would be slower and louder. Before she came to a satisfactory conclusion, someone lifted Tom's other arm. She gasped in fright before recognizing Anna's scowling face.

Her sister appeared none too pleased to be back out here.

Gilly's emotions rocked from relief to horror. She feared her heart was permanently lodged in her throat. "Why can't you ever listen to me?"

"Do you want help or not?"

"Yes!"

"Then shut up and lift. I don't know why I bothered to help your ungrateful butt. Don't expect a repeat of the gesture. We're done once we leave the village. I only came as a 'thank you' for coming for me. Now and before." She paused to gulp in air, as if admitting to the role Gilly played in both those rescues was tougher than hauling Tom.

Gilly squirreled away her sister's gratitude to cherish later, amazed by its sweetness. For now, what concerned her was Tom's boots scraping so loud the captain might hear it above the screams of his victims and come galloping toward them. At least the sound masked Anna's non-stop whispered rant.

To her astonishment, they made it safely into the house without incident. Anna shut the front door with a final angry muttering of "Idiot woman."

Vyan's wife's gaze was grim but she didn't object to their helping Tom. Obviously she blamed the Horsemen for her husband's death. *Thank the Light.* Gilly and Anna, half dragged, half carried Tom through to the back room and into the animal pen. Once outside, Anna, panting, stopped. Tom slid to the ground between them.

"We'll not make it on foot dragging him," Anna said.

Gilly nodded. She'd come to the same conclusion and had devised a plan. An even more audacious one. Under her breath, she chanted her spell.

An answering whinny came from the street out front. Followed by a protesting shout, several painful sounding thumps and then strident cursing. A white stallion, surrounded by speckled Light, cantered around the corner to the back of the buildings. He halted before Gilly and tossed his head in greeting.

Gilly swallowed a triumphant grin. *That'll teach One-Eye to hurt innocent villagers.* While Anna watched open mouthed, Gilly's next muttered spell had the horse kneeling before them so she could heft Tom to lie across the horse's back. Then she climbed behind him and offered her sister a hand. "Let's go."

Without a word of protest, Anna gripped Gilly's hand and climbed up behind her. Her sister continued to surprise her.

She was wondering if a spell would be needed to ensure the horse could carry them but he rose to his feet with seemingly little effort. As they slowly trotted down the track at the back of houses, she discovered the big stallion was incredibly sturdy. The only spell she had to cast was one to whisk the soil in their wake to hide his hoof prints as they passed.

They reached the outskirts of the village and she risked urging the stallion into a faster trot and hoped he wouldn't collapse before they reached the cowherd's shed. He didn't.

On their arrival at the meeting spot, Marton rushed over. He pulled Anna off the stallion and held her tight in his arms. "I thought for sure you'd get yourself killed."

Skye called from inside the dilapidated structure, "Papa, can we come out?"

"Yes."

The young girl rushed over, and then stopped to smile tentatively at her mother.

Bevan ran straight to the horse. "Ahww!" Reverently, he held out a palm to the magnificent white stallion that stood at least four times his height.

Gilly slid off, landing on both feet without a single twinge. She again wondered if more than the land was affected by High Magic. She would ponder that mystery later.

"Marton," she came around to his side, "would you please help me with Tom. He's hurt and needs care."

Anna nodded to her husband. He reluctantly released her to go to Tom's aid.

Anna opened her arms and Skye ran into them.

"Mama, I was afraid I'd never see you again and never get to say that I don't hate you. I love you."

"I know, baby. I love you, too, though you make me angry enough. This time, you were right. I should have listened."

Marton carried Tom into the tiny one room shack and laid him on the lone cot, face down.

Gilly asked Anna to take the horse into the paddock area and rub him down with straw to dry him out, and then cover him with dust so he wouldn't stand out. Bevan ran along with her.

Skye would have followed but Gilly sent her on an important errand. To heal Tom, she needed herbs – willow bark and a plant with deep-red flowers called Heal-all that grew wild in the grasslands.

Inside the shed, she thanked Marton and knelt to check on Tom. "Please fetch water?"

"There's a stream nearby." Marton headed out.

The welts on Tom's back were truly deep and in need of stitches. With no needle or fire, the rifts would have to heal by themselves.

Marton returned with a canteen.

"Thank you," she said. While he went to help his wife, she ripped strips off her underskirt and set to cleaning and binding Tom's wounds.

His body cringed under her care. Once he woke up and caught her hand. "Stop that," he murmured, eyes half closed.

"You need care."

"Not you..." He lost consciousness still holding her hand.

Gently she pulled free and brushed a lock off his forehead, murmuring, "Who else, Tom?"

Skye came in with the herbs. Clever, resourceful child. "Will he be all right, Gilly?"

"Thanks to these plants, he just might."

"Why doesn't he want you to touch him?"

So, she'd heard that. Gilly shook her head, hiding her hurt. "Probably just fever crazy."

After ensuring Tom's wounds were cleaned, medicine applied and he was no longer in danger of dying on her, she stepped back outside. Anna and her whole family were in the paddock working on disguising the stallion. Her heart squeezed in fear for them. How was she to hide an entire family? It had been hard enough to hide Anna as a baby.

They couldn't stay here. Where to go? Would any plains village be safer than Nadym had been?

She sensed another long discussion loomed. At least, Anna seemed unusually compliant. Maybe the winds of luck were finally at their backs. Not taking that for granted, she went to set warning wards. A short-term measure at best, but better than being caught unaware.

On her return, she called for a conference. "We need to decide about our next move."

"Agreed," Anna said.

A quick check showed the stallion, now dung colored and forgettable, contentedly nibbling grass.

"Let's talk inside the shed," Marton said.

In the cramped space, they sat side-by-side in a circle on the trampled soil. The air was warm and scented with fear. Marton pulled out bread, cheese and pieces of dried meat from his sack. The enticing aroma churned Gilly's stomach with hunger.

"Why does the king want my family dead, Gilly?" Anna asked, sitting to the left of her husband.

Gilly fidgeted with a piece of dark bread. "Your Mam never said. Just that he would stop at nothing to ensure it."

Anna's frustration was clear on her face. "Makes no sense. There must be a reason, some sort of misunderstanding. I say that should be our first move."

"What?" Marton asked around a mouthful of cheese and bread. "What move?"

"We should seek out His Majesty and ask for pardon for whatever crime he thinks my family has done him."

"No!" Gilly and Marton said together.

"It's the only thing we can do," Anna said in earnest. "We can't keep running for the rest of our lives."

"Why not?" Gilly asked, panic returning to drum on her head like a battle call. "I think that's a good plan."

Marton wiped crumbs off his mouth. "Agree. There are lots of villages in the plains. We'll find another one, someplace remote, and start over. Blacksmithing is a useful art anywhere."

"Yes." Gilly could have kissed the sensible man. "Somewhere to blend in and become part of the community."

"No." Arms crossed, lips pouting and brows furrowed, Anna looked like a sulky child. "I liked my life in Nadym. I won't settle in another village only to leave when the Horsemen find us again. I was moved from home to home like second-hand clothing all my life. I'm not doing that ever again."

Gilly opened her mouth to apologize but her sister, eyes glistening, held out her palms in a stop gesture. "That's the past. I don't care why or what good reason there was for it. I promised myself when I married Marton that I was done with that kind of uncertain living. I want a life where people know and respect me...us."

"You can have that." Gilly's guilt churned but she resolutely ignored it. Unlike with her, people always took to Anna. "You'll make new friends."

"I don't want new friends." Anna sliced the air with her right hand, her voice vehement. "I want my old friends. I want to belong and I can't do that if we keep running."

"Anna," her husband said in a reasonable tone, "going to see King Ywen won't make any difference. Also, if we do this, life for us will become difficult."

Thank you, Marton.

He gently rubbed his wife's hand. "We'd be constantly moving through desert and then mountains. Even if we make it to the capital city, why would the king give us an audience?"

"He might hear us out." Anna clasped his hand in return and pulled him closer. "Especially if he's been looking for me for all these years."

Gilly inserted, "He murdered your family." Why couldn't her sister understand the ramifications of that? "He's had Vyan, the chief of Nadym, killed. Ordered Tom beaten. He has no justice in his soul."

"That could be the act of the Horsemen." Anna broke eye contact with her husband to turn to Gilly. "Of that one-eyed captain. This far from the king's power, he might have taken an action that King Ywen wouldn't approve of."

"That's the other problem." Marton put his left arm around his wife and tucked her close. "What if the Horsemen follow us? If the terrain doesn't kill us, they will."

"Then Gilly can take care of them as she did in the village," Anna said.

Gilly shook her head frantically at her sister.

Marton and Skye turned to her.

"How did you get away from them?" the little girl asked in a bright curious voice.

"I, um," Gilly mumbled, her throat suddenly dry and tight, "I released some of the animals into the street and it distracted everyone enough for us to escape."

"If the Horsemen find us in the middle of the desert with no livestock or places to hide," Marton said, "I don't see how that would help us."

Anna remained silent and tight-lipped as she watched Gilly, who returned her gaze steadily. *Please don't speak of the magic.*

Finally, her sister said, "I'm sure we'll think of something. We'll just have to be careful about covering our tracks so they don't find us."

"But Mama," Skye interrupted.

"We'll be fine." Anna patted Skye's knee with confidence. "I'm willing to offer King Ywen my life in exchange for any debt my family owes him. At least then the rest of you will be free." She turned back to her husband with such a pleading look in her pretty blue eyes that even Gilly was tempted to agree. "Marton, if it would mean Skye and Bevan will be free from pursuit, it'll be worth giving up my life. You see that, don't you?"

"Anna, the man's evil." Gilly snapped the words out, hoping to stall Marton's capitulation. "He'll never agree to anything except your entire family's eradication."

"You don't know him, you've never met him. Neither have I." She turned back to her husband, and spoke with a tremble. "Marton, I can't live without hope."

Gilly's fist tightened at that vile word. Hope was for fools. "Anna, if the others' lives weren't enough for that monster, what makes you think yours would do?"

"Courage, Gilly," Anna replied with fervor. Her fighting stance was back and all signs of the weepy, trembling woman vanished as if she had waved a finger and cast a spell. "My mother ran. It didn't do her any good, did it? Why shouldn't I try something different?"

Gilly played her last desperate hand. "Because you'll be risking your husband and children on that perilous gamble."

"They're already in danger. I'm trying to put a stop to that."

Gilly turned to Marton but his heavy sigh signaled his surrender.

"She has a point, Gilly. I don't much care for running." He forestalled her with a raised hand when she would have argued. "I don't agree we should seek out the king. Sorry, Anna, but that sounds dangerous." He waved at his wife when she would have argued. "I'm never going to agree to you giving up your life for any reason. I've been thinking on this problem and it seems to me in a big place like the king's city, with lots of people coming and going all the time, we might be able to hide out better than in a little village, where everyone would know we're newly arrived. We should head for Tibor. There, we might also learn what this family feud with the king is all about and maybe find a way to end it once and for all."

"Thank you," Anna said and kissed his cheek.

He brought her into a hug and gave Gilly a crooked "I'm sorry" smile. "It's said that the best place to hide is sometimes right under the nose of the one looking for you. Besides, if we must run, I'd rather run toward something than away from it."

"You're both wrong," Gilly said.

"This isn't your fight." Anna said in a soft voice, watching her intently from within her husband's embrace. "You don't have to come with us."

Gilly wanted to cry but no tears would come. The fight slipped out of her grasp. Anna going on without her was unthinkable. If her sister was determined to go to the King's city – Gilly shuddered at such a risky move – there was only one thing to do. "Wherever you go, I go."

Considering her sister's aversion to her, Gilly expected Anna to be angry she planned to tag along. Instead, for the merest instant, Anna's lips curved up. However, in a blink, her predictable frown returned.

Had she imagined that unexpected hint of approval? No, she'd *hoped* for it. *Idiot.*

She glanced at her legs – left one stretched awkwardly – and fought the urge to hit something. She used her clenched fist to knead her bad leg and muttered, "Don't worry, I won't slow you down."

A flush painted Anna's cheeks pink. "'Course you won't and you're more than welcome." She shifted to allow Bevan to cuddle on her lap. The boy was on the verge of sleep.

Skye slid an arm around Gilly's waist – a tender lifeline that brought with it the fresh scent of hay and dirt used to disguise the stolen horse. That reminded Gilly of whom and what they fled. An ebony eye patch glinted in her mind's eye as if the Horsemen's captain winked in mockery of their fruitless plans for escape.

"What do we do with Tom?" Marton tipped his head toward the unconscious man.

"He's coming too." Gilly spoke automatically, absently, her mind on evading the Horsemen.

"No, he is not!" Anna said. "He murdered Vyan."

Gilly snapped her head up in time to see contempt obliterate any semblance of softness on Anna's face. She wouldn't insist on leaving Tom behind to die alone and defenseless? Would she?

Chapter 3

"I'll watch Tom," Gilly said. "He's in no condition to hurt anyone."

"He's also in no condition to travel," Marton's tone was gentler than Anna's but dealt as devastating a blow. "You're pretty swift on your own, Gilly, but he will delay us."

"He can ride the stallion with the children until he's well enough to walk."

"He'll be fine in this cowshed," Anna said with finality.

Gilly's fear thundered in her chest as an ominous choice loomed. In the village, she'd returned to save him. What was it about Tom that drew her so strongly to his defense?

With difficulty she spoke with what she hoped was a firm, calm, voice of reason. "I've given him willow bark tea to keep down his fever and to help him sleep, but his cuts and wounds need tending. We can't leave him."

"We don't owe him anything." Her sister sounded frustrated.

Calm gave way to uninhibited panic. "You owe him your life! I'm not saying he killed Vyan, but if Vyan hadn't died, he would surely have told them about you being found as a baby. The Village Chief was not your friend."

Anna looked at the village drunkard, her face a picture of bewilderment. "Why do you keep protecting him? He's nothing to us."

"You can't always judge people by the way they look or act, Anna. Sometimes you need to look deeper, search beneath the surface."

Her words choked in her throat as she realized she spoke as much on her own behalf as Tom's. Over the years, it had hurt that her sister could not see past her labels of hermit, misfit, gimp. "He's a person. Like you or me, he, too, is worthy of our respect and care. Especially during this moment of crisis."

Anna bit her lip, looking taken aback.

"I've always liked Tom," Marton's soft-spoken voice was like water sprayed over flames. "If I had to pick who was more likely to have killed Vyan, I'd pick the Horsemen."

Looking deep in thought, his wife rocked her son.

Gilly's highly-strung tension dispersed and she breathed a sigh of relief.

"We need to decide on our route." Marton moved the food items aside and smoothed the hard packed ground.

Gilly could hardly see the others let alone what he was up to. "We need light."

He immediately grabbed for his pack. Despite having left on short notice, he had come prepared. Anna had picked a good man for her husband.

By the flickering glow of two candles, he roughly outlined the terrain between Nadym and Tibor, marking relevant cities. His methodical work and the calming scent of beeswax soon relieved the nervous energy in the shed. Everyone – except for Bevan, who was fast asleep – leaned forward to study the finished product. Large chunks remained unmarked, unknown.

Marton placed a candle closer on his left, near Anna. "That's Nadym."

He passed the other candle over to Gilly. "Set it in the top middle, for Perm."

Once she positioned it, he said, "To reach Tibor, we must first travel northeast from Nadym to the mountain city of Perm."

That journey alone seemed daunting.

"Once there, we'll have to cross the Makakala range and then due east until we reach Tibor." Bevan's left sandal was confiscated as a marker for that coastal city beside Skye.

"Why can't we cross the mountains in the south?" Anna asked.

"It's impassable down here," Marton explained. "I've also heard that on the other side of the Southern range, the land is covered in bogs that could swallow up horse and man. Even minstrels avoid those swamp lands."

"But if we follow the trade route north, we must go alongside the Kocheya Basin." With her forefinger, Gilly circled the vast desert region in the western center of Ryca. "There's unlikely to be many stopover places once we pass the Steppes and head into the desert. Except for the children and Tom, we'll be traveling for leagues on foot. It's called the badlands for a good reason, Marton. It's scorching hot and little life flourishes there, so replenishing our supplies will be difficult."

"I once heard about a place in the basin called Erov, where there's reputed to be plenty of food, ale and friendly folk," Marton said in a whimsical tone. "Trouble is, it's rumored to never be in the same place twice; vanishing and reappearing at will."

"Oh." Skye's eyes lit up. "Can we go there?"

"That's just a children's tale," Anna scoffed, drowning that foolish dream.

Gilly gently rubbed Skye's back in consolation. "If we go too far into the badlands looking for a capricious, mythical city, we might run out of food and water and never make it out. If we must go to Tibor, I say we go east first, until we reach the base of the southern mountain range. Then we can gather supplies and, skirting the desert, head north to Perm."

"I like that idea," Marton said. "Our pursuers will be looking for us either on the western trade routes or heading south, toward other plains' villages. This route is longer but safer."

"When do we leave?" Anna asked.

"Not in the dark," Marton said. "I'll keep watch overnight. We should make sure we're packed up first though. If I hear anything remotely like hoofbeats, we'll run for it. You should all rest while you can. Even if the Horsemen don't find us, we have a long trek ahead."

"I'll take watch turns with you," Gilly said. "I'll need to check on Tom."

"Good." Marton sounded relieved. Poor man looked as weary as the rest of them.

Gilly picked up a candle to check on Tom.

"Skye, go wash up by the stream before bed," Anna said. "Watch your step in the dark." Shutting the door behind her daughter, she came over to where Tom lay. "May I see his wounds?"

Gilly moved aside and held up the candle.

Anna leaned over, intently studying Tom's back. The bandages were already blood-soaked and beginning to smell. "He needs stitches. He's never going to live otherwise."

The judgment was harsh but mirrored Gilly's private fears. If those wounds were left untended, by morning, their argument about taking Tom along would be moot. "In my rush to leave, I forgot to pack my needles and threads."

"Tom will need new bandages at least," Anna said. "The bag Skye packed is outside. See if my sewing kit and the spare clothes are in it. I'll watch him while you choose what you need. The bag is by a birch to the left of the shed. Take the other candle."

"Thank you." Gilly handed her light over to Anna and hurried outside with the spare one, feeling a warm glow at her sister's unexpectedly kind gesture.

It had grown dark. Gilly had a hard time locating the birch. When she finally did, there was no sign of a bag.

Skye found her still searching. "What are you doing, Gilly?"

"Where's the bag of clothes you packed?"

"It's on the other side of the shed. I'll get it."

As the child raced off, Gilly's her heart pounded with suspicion. Praying to the Light to keep Tom safe, she raced back to the shed. *Please don't let Anna have sent me on a goose chase so she could harm him.*

At the shed, she softly opened the door. Anna's candle was on the floor. It shone an eerie light upward, highlighting her sister's intent face. Anna skimmed her hands over Tom's back. Then Gilly realized why she could see her sister's hands in the dark. Her sister's palms glowed.

Suspicion transformed into stunned wonder. Anna drew on Light. The result looked different than when Gilly practiced the craft. It almost seemed as if the Light had become a part of Anna. Could this use of Light, done so intimately, be less traceable than when Gilly used it? She prayed it was so.

"Here you go." Skye came up behind her with the bag of clothes.

Anna jerked backward, hiding her arms behind her back.

Gilly took the bag, her gaze trained on Anna.

Her sister wore a guilty expression. "You're back. Good. I'm tired, so I'm turning in." Avoiding Gilly's searching gaze, she picked up her candle and walked over to where Bevan lay.

"Tom's breathing isn't as loud," Skye whispered.

"You'd best turn in, too." Gilly shooed her toward her mother. Slowly, holding up her candle, Gilly peeled back the bandages on Tom's back. Every single one of his gaping wounds was in the process of closing. There were still a few slim, angry breaks but nothing like it had been earlier.

So, that's why her sister hadn't run away when Gilly used magic. She, too, could work Light. *My Anna is a healer.* How long had her sister known about her ability? Had she confessed to anyone? Knowing how the villagers felt about magic, she suspected Anna would have rarely used her talent, and then not told anyone, perhaps not even Marton.

She was doubly glad of her wards now. If Anna drew the Horsemen to them tonight, Gilly would be warned. Would it be in time to escape?

After tending to Tom, she, too, lay down beside her family and hugged herself. Somehow, despite the danger, finding out about Anna's ability made her feel less lonely.

After two breaks to take her turn at watch, Gilly awoke at daybreak bleary eyed and anxious to leave. The quicker they sped from this cowherd's shed, the happier she'd be.

Bevan rode the white stallion while Marton gently laid Tom behind him. Belly down and secured in place, he wouldn't fall off. Everyone else took to the track on foot.

Skye, who'd never gone past the fields where Gilly grazed her goats, repeatedly brought over an unusual colored flower or a long-tailed scaly thing her mother refused to stroke no matter how hard Skye begged.

Gilly, used to solitude, was tempted to go on ahead, but she needed to warn her sister about the danger of arbitrarily using magic, even for as good a cause as helping Tom. As it was, her neck ached from continuously checking behind to see if that illegal draw on Light last night had set the Horsemen on their trail.

So far, the answer to that concern was a comforting, *No*. She had to warn Anna to be more careful though. Raising the taboo subject with her entire family within earshot was a problem.

The family traveled clustered together for several miles, fear acting like a corral. After a few hours, with no sign of active pursuit, Skye began to wander farther ahead, only to run back to report on her findings. When she dragged Marton to show him her latest discovery, Bevan slid off the horse to follow and the stallion took that moment of inattention to munch on grass.

Anna, too, stopped and bent to stretch her legs.

Gilly seized on her only opportunity since they left to be alone with her sister. "Anna, we must talk."

"About what?"

"Magic."

Anna met her gaze. "What about it?"

"While I appreciate what you did for Tom, never do it again."

Anna met her gaze with wariness. "Because magic is evil?"

"Magic is not evil."

"Then what is it?"

Other than the basics, Mam had said little about the forbidden art; probably afraid her little ones might be tempted to practice and thus draw the Horsemen to them. Most of what Gilly understood about magic, she had learned from watching what happened after she cast a spell.

"Few people can work Light, which is the source of all life," Gilly said, starting at the basics. "There are two types of Light practice. High Magic draws power directly from the Light. The other is Hearth Magic, which is made up of minor spells. Anyone who has a bit of inherent talent, strong belief and after much practice can set warning wards. I do that often to alert me to intruders. Or to heal wounds or find water. Hearth Magic merely tweaks what's already present in the natural world, it doesn't transform it like High Magic,."

"High Magic affects the world?"

"Yes, whenever I've cast a High Magic spell, everything around me changes."

"How?"

"The land grows lush. Dead plants come back to life."

"That doesn't happen when I heal."

"What you do is Hearth Magic, but on a grander scale than any I've witnessed. You didn't just nudge a body's healing process along; you healed Tom's wounds. Also, for all that they decry use of magic, I believe the Horsemen, too, cast spells. Their enchantment scorches and burns the earth." Gilly's fists clenched. "Their magic doesn't enhance the world, it destroys it."

"That's what caused the destruction around Nadym?" At Gilly's nod, she came closer. "When have you used High Magic, Gilly? Was it when you made those pigs, sheep and chickens scatter?"

"Yes." There was a better example. Gilly's stomach trembled at mentioning how Skye had almost died while in her care. It had to be done, though. Whatever the fallout with her sister, Anna must understand the consequences of using High Magic. "Yesterday, Skye tumbled off a cliff."

"What?" Hands on her chest, Anna checked on Skye squatting on the ground examining something with Bevan and her father. The murderous light in her little sister's eyes when she turned had Gilly stumbling backwards as she blurted out her story. "Skye was chasing a goat on the cliffs. Then she fell over and the branch of a dead tree she clung to cracked."

Anna sucked in her breath and grabbed Gilly's forearms. "What happened then?"

Gilly ignored the nails digging into her skin. "I cast a spell to stop her fall. Leaves gathered to cushion her, and bring her back up into my arms. Shortly after, the dead tree looked lush and alive. There is a terrible consequence to using High Magic, Anna. The Horsemen can trace its use. That's why they arrived in Nadym moments after."

Anna released her, leaving behind curved white dents along Gilly's arms where nails had dug in.

Oddly, Anna now seemed more thoughtful than furious. "So, the Horsemen can trace a High Magic user with speed, but not precision? And they can't detect Hearth Magic at all?"

Gilly blinked in surprise at her sister's quick and accurate assessment. This abrupt turn in conversation, however, brought them to the very point she wanted to make. "Thank you for what you did with Tom, but I'm unsure which category of magic it falls under, so you should avoid doing it again, just in case."

"There weren't any changes to the land around the cowherd's shed. What I do might be as harmless as your wards."

"With children nearby, can we take that chance?" Gilly asked.

Anna nodded. "You're right. I've only ever healed little cuts and scratches before this. Tom's wounds were severe and healing them left me exhausted. Afterwards, even though I was worried about the Horsemen, I slept like a baby. It's possible the Horsemen sensed what I did but didn't find us before we left. It's too risky to heal again. I won't do it. I promise. Let's hope I won't need to."

Skye ran over then to show her mother a long-legged spider. "Mama, isn't it pretty?"

Not daunted by the crawly insect, Anna pulled Skye into a tight hug. "It's beautiful."

The stallion's clip clop drew Gilly's gaze backward. Tom, draped over the horse, had been close enough to overhear her confession. His body was motionless though, suggesting he was asleep, or unconscious. She breathed a sigh of relief and rubbed her sore arms before facing her sister. There were tears in Anna's eyes as she hugged Skye. For all their fighting, Anna adored her daughter.

Wanting to give mother and child privacy, Gilly pressed on. She had said her piece and, hard to believe, Anna had agreed with her concerns.

Before her third step, her sister called out. "Gilly!"

Should have known that agreement came too easily. Shoulders stiff and ready for the next blow, she turned back. "Yes?"

"Thank you." Two words never sounded so heartfelt.

Gilly's eyes stung and a glow warmed her chest as she nodded and left. She passed Marton and Bevan who were waiting for Anna and Skye. She avoided Marton's curious gaze, and winked at Bevan. The boy gave a shy grin and ducked behind his father.

Once alone, Gilly hugged herself to contain her joy. It was happening. *Anna is starting to like me.*

• • • •

THREE DAYS LATER, THEY camped by the foothills bordering the Kocheya Basin. Gilly took turn at watch. After a circuit to ensure her wards were active, she found a suitable log to rest on and stared at the third sister riding high over the desert in her half-moon form.

Although they planned to skirt this barren land, not delve into it, being this close to dunes raised goose bumps on Gilly's arms. Having lived most of her life in rich pasturelands within walking distance to lakes and rivers, the idea of entering this vast wasteland terrified her as much as encountering King's Horsemen. Surely not even the mythical, magical Erovians that Marton spoke of could survive deep in this parched landscape.

She was pondering the wisdom of their continued trek in the morning, when the hairs on the back of her neck tingled. Someone had triggered a ward. She jumped up and her left leg protested. High Magic might have strengthened her leg for awhile but the positive effect obviously didn't last long. In a rush to warn the others, she ignored that sharp stab of pain and limped through the brush.

She'd placed her wards about a hundred feet from the campsite, far enough she'd thought at the time, but now this intruder might be closer than that. She should have spread those warning charms farther out to give her family more time to flee.

She woke Marton first. He shook his wife awake and while Anna hid the children behind a large boulder, Gilly accompanied Marton to investigate the "noise" she had heard.

They left Tom lying on his stomach with a wool blanket covering him head to toe. If he were lucky, he would be taken for dead and left unharmed.

Up ahead, a horse nickered. A soft voice promised the animal a treat. Gilly and Marton crouched behind a wide bush. A few feet away, a man was brushing his horse. His cloak was black, not Horsemen green, though it was hard to be certain of in the semi-dark. The absence of sword was reassuring. He was also apparently alone.

"A scout?" Marton whispered.

"The doublet, hose and boots speak of a guild."

He nodded. "Likely a traveling merchant."

"Our luck he chose to camp so close to us."

"I'll approach and speak with him," Marton said. "Best we know who he is."

She placed a hand on his forearm. "Be careful. Anna will never forgive me if you are hurt."

He nodded acknowledgement, gave a reassuring pat on her back and strode toward the stranger.

The two men spoke and Marton gestured toward their camp. He then waved Gilly over.

She stayed put. Had he lost his mind?

"Gilly," he said. "Come. This is Cullen, a minstrel. He's familiar with the territory we're heading into."

She leaned back on her heels, mouth agape. Had he told this intruder where they were going?

"Come," he said again.

Now they'd done it. Their trip was surely cursed. First they were forced to go on the run, then they chose in all familial wisdom to go directly toward the very man they should be running from, and, now, Marton had taken a perfect stranger, who could very well be in King Ywen's employ, as a bosom friend. They might as well turn themselves over to the Horsemen now and save the agony of the hunt.

"Marton," Anna said from behind her.

Her sister waved and sprinted toward them, all smiles, golden hair streaming behind her in waves. "Is he a friend?"

Of course, why bother to hide when it's so much easier to get caught out in the open?

Skye crouched beside Gilly, Bevan a shadow in the darkness of his sister's skirts. "I tried to stop her but she wouldn't listen," the young girl said. "She never listens."

Gilly gave the children a comforting hug. "We'd best see what we can salvage from this. Keep your wits about you in case we need to save your parents from themselves."

The children nodded and the trio slowly approached the stranger. He was a thin man of medium build, with what was left of his gray hair receding toward the crown. His clean narrow face had close-set eyes, which looked guarded under the moonlight. His hooked nose, like a vulture's beak, shadowed thin lips that appeared a stranger to smiles. Hardly worthy of such trust at first meeting.

When she drew close enough, he switched his attention from saluting Anna to greeting Gilly.

"These are my children, Skye and Bevan," her sister said, "and this is our servant, Gilly."

Anna poked her in the ribs and gestured for her to take care of Cullen's horse. Gilly gritted her teeth at that instruction but had no one to blame but herself. She was the one who shied from admitting they were sisters. The day for that talk would come soon enough.

Cullen took out a brush from his saddle and gave it to Gilly with a courtly bow. He believed her a servant but still treated her with respect. Her estimation of this stranger improved as he accompanied Anna to camp.

Skye pulled at Gilly's sleeve.

Gilly was intent on Cullen's retreat.

Skye tugged insistently at her sleeve.

Gilly pushed her away. "What, Skye? What's so important it can't wait for two breaths?"

"You sound like Mama," Skye said. "I thought you were different. That you liked me."

Gilly blinked in surprise. *I snapped at Skye. Why?* Absently, she corrected her niece. "Your Mam loves you." She gave the girl a hug. "Come, help me brush this mount."

The child nodded agreement.

The mare was hot and lathered as if from hard riding. Cullen must have been in a hurry. "Skye."

"Yes, Gilly?"

"What do you think of this stranger?"

"He smiles only with his mouth," her niece said. "His eyes are strange."

"Angry," Bevan said.

How strange. Even odder was that the quiet child had spoken. "He didn't look angry to me, Bevan. Are you sure?"

The little boy gave a solemn nod.

Gilly finished with the mare and then sat on the ground, calling the children to her. She ripped a thread from the bottom of her skirt and tearing it in two, she tied one around each of the children's ankles, moving their hose out of the way until the thread touched skin. She mumbled a chant under her breath as she worked. Her fingers tingled when they smoothed the thread down.

"It feels warm," Skye said, touching it tentatively.

"Hot," Bevan affirmed, pulling a face.

"It'll cool in time. Don't take it off unless you tell me first. It's there to protect you against harmful magic."

"Lissa says all magic is evil," Skye said.

"Magic is like a hunter's knife, Skye," Gilly said. "Treated with the right heat it can help heal an infected wound, or slice open a deeper one. It depends on who wields it, and for what purpose. Now, return to camp. If you notice anything else odd about Cullen, come find me. Fast."

With trepidation, she watched them leave. A dangerous task to set for little ones. She set off to strengthen her wards and spread them further out on the off chance their next visitors wore green capes and carried swords.

Chapter 4

Once Marton took over Gilly's watch, she returned to camp to rest. Anna whispered to her that they explained away Tom's silent restfulness as an injured companion recovering from a fall from a horse. Cullen was a lone figure on the smoldering fire's far side. Wisely, none in her family strayed closer to him.

Marton tapped her shoulder. Her turn again. He cuddled next to his wife and slipped an arm over Anna's waist. Gilly checked on Tom lying between her and the children, his head moving side to side as if restless dreams bothered him.

Positioning her body so Cullen wouldn't see what she did, Gilly slipped a primed ward into Tom's hand and closed his fingers around it. Before she could withdraw, he tightened his hold on her, trapping her to his side. Her pulse jumped, half startled, half delighted. A quick check, however, showed his eyes were shut. In moments, his fingers relaxed, releasing her.

Her stroll around the perimeter this time was in an oddly happier frame of mind. Her fingers tingled where Tom had clutched them.

Within moments, the soft pad of two sets of small footsteps suggested that Skye and Bevan had slept as restlessly as she. The three of them had circuited halfway around the camp when the clatter of hooves had them crouching in fear.

"Another visitor?" Skye whispered.

"Shhh." Had they picked a trade route intersection for their campsite? More travelers seemed to pass by here than in the entire village of Nadym.

This stranger stopped twenty paces from where Cullen's mare rested near a tree. "Ho there. I come in peace and ask for traveler's courtesy."

The man's deep voice and clank of chainmaille sent fear shooting up Gilly's back. He'd made a perfectly legitimate claim so she had to reply. The only reason not to respond would be if she were a thief or fugitive. Both were true.

She finally said, "Who are you?"

Her question was greeted by silence. Well, she'd taken long enough to answer, so he had a right to think before responding.

"My name is Talus." His voice held a note of amusement. "And who be you, missus?"

"I be armed," Gilly said, "and not shy of using my weapon. Please step away from your mount and come forward, arms raised, if indeed you come in peace."

A loud burst of laughter greeted that request. "If you are a robber," Talus said, "you have polite manners. My experience tells me those two characteristics within one female are unlikely. I'll assume you are merely cautious. A wise act in these troubled times."

He slid off his horse and strode forward, arms extended to the moonlight. He wore a shirt of interlocking black rings over a leather tunic. A black metal helmet shaped like a dolphin sat snugly on his head. Over leggings, hard leather greaves protected shins from harm.

As Talus came closer, Bevan breathed, "Oohh."

This man was indeed impressive, even more than the white stallion the boy had last "*oohed*" and "*aahed*" over.

Talus removed his helmet and bowed respectfully to the bush they hid behind. Above a full mustache, the prominent bridge of his nose separated wide set, twinkling blue eyes. Thick eyebrows and blond hair flattened by his helmet bordered a smooth wide forehead. A handsome face.

Gilly tried to fit Talus into a familiar mold she could hang a label on but he was nothing like Marton or any other hardworking Nadym villager of her acquaintance. Nor did he resemble a needlessly cruel King's Horseman.

If anything, this man came closest to Tom, whose touch could make Gilly's heart thump erratically. Except Talus was unhurt, supremely fit and didn't appear to be haunted by demons that drove Tom to drink.

Stuck for a marker, she said the only thing that soothed her worries. "You're not a King's Horseman."

He laughed. "No, missus. A King's Warrior you see before you, returned from the wars in the Makakala Range."

"In the mountain region?" Alarm rose again. "Between here and the King's city?"

"The very same. You know the area?"

"No, not at all. Is the fighting over?" Say, *Yes*. Her family was headed to the Makakala range.

"Waning, missus. We near victory over the mountain people. The rabble are severely wounded, their numbers reduced. Soon the rebellion will be quelled and they will be unable to attempt another organized assault against the king."

Gilly detected an incongruous note of regret in his tone. As a King's Warrior, he should be proud of his efforts to protect his king's sovereignty, however foul a member of humankind the monarch might be. How odd.

"Bevan," she whispered. "Are this man's eyes angry?"

Her nephew shook his head. "Sad."

Ah, so I'm right. This warrior is sympathetic to the rebels' cause. "Do you pity these rebels, sir?"

Talus's eyes narrowed and he stood taller. She had displeased him. Gilly clutched the children's hands, a spell of protection on her tongue. Then his shoulders lowered.

He released a sigh that seemed to come from deep in his soul. "They claim to fight for a noble cause. That is politics, and hardly a fit subject to discuss on such a lovely night with someone I've yet to meet." Humor had crept back into his voice. "May I have the pleasure of knowing the name of the bush I speak with?"

His manner disarmed her. With a nod to the children, she stood and limped forward, right arm extended. "I am Gilly."

His gloved fingers entirely circled her forearm, but his grip was gentle.

She smiled a genuine welcome. "This is Skye and Bevan. The rest of our party is camped on that hill. You may break your fast with us. The children will show you the way."

"You're not coming?"

"It's my watch until we depart. You may leave your horse if you like. I'll rub him down."

"You are most kind, Missus Gilly, but I can care for my mount. If you will allow it, I will keep watch with you."

"I prefer to watch alone. Good day."

Gilly bent to whisper to Bevan. "Go warn your parents about Talus."

The young boy took off at a run and she nodded to Skye, indicating that she could lead Talus and his mount to their camp.

Two strangers in one night. That doubled the chance they'd invited a scorpion into their midst. Still, how could she turn Talus off after Anna and Marton had invited Cullen? Seemed unfair.

If Talus was the problem, then they were doomed, because none of them were capable of fighting off a King's Warrior whose sword was bigger than Bevan.

First she tested each of her wards, *little help they'd been*. Next she ensured there wasn't a camp of King's Warriors waiting nearby for everyone to fall asleep before attacking. Satisfied that her family was as safe as she could make them, she returned to the stump where she'd rested when Cullen triggered her ward. The sand dunes rising up on the horizon only a few hundred feet away looked imposing.

Tomorrow, they would set out into that unfamiliar terrain. She sat and buried her face in her hands. *Oh, Mam, how am I going to keep our family safe?*

A hand settled on her shoulder.

Gilly squealed, jumped up and swung around, arms extended, her fingertips tingling with the flare of a protection spell. Then she recognized the man who had touched her. It was neither Cullen nor Talus, but Tom. Under moonlight, his skin looked pasty and beads of sweat dotted his forehead. He dropped to his knees.

"Tom!" she said in alarm and ran to his side.

"Strangers at camp," he breathed out, head dipping forward. Any moment he would fall forward and smack his face on her stump.

"You shouldn't have followed me. I know about the strangers. We invited them to camp. You were safe there."

Lie. As safe as the rest of her family, then. Safer than stumbling around in Tom's fever-ridden state.

"King's Warrior."

"I know." Kneeling beside him, Gilly tipped him toward her – so little effort – until he slumped, his forehead coming to rest on her shoulder. "One of the strangers is a King's Warrior called Talus. The other is Cullen, a minstrel."

"Don't like him."

"Bevan agrees with you."

"Know him."

From where? Tom had lived in Nadym all of his life. Had the minstrel come there to entertain? "Tom, are you sure?"

His forehead was burning hot against her neck. In his current state, she was surprised he knew her.

His breath was a warm breeze of lemony herbs as he said, "Be careful."

Gilly's alarm spiked. *Careful about what?* Cullen or Talus, who were both near her sleeping family?

Tom had fallen asleep so she couldn't ask him. She wasn't strong enough to carry him back to camp so she laid him on the ground. Just as well. If Tom did know Cullen, and his *be careful* had sounded like it had been an unhappy acquaintance, then she didn't want Cullen recognizing Tom while he was in this vulnerable state.

Better to let him sleep here in safety. She fetched some fallen brush to hide Tom and hurried back to check on her family. At the campsite, Gilly found everyone asleep. Her thundering pulse quieted and a shiver of relief washed over her. They were all safe and the two strangers looked asleep.

Tired as she was, Gilly didn't wake Marton for his watch, preferring to let him rest. That decision also allowed her to keep a closer eye on Tom.

Still an hour before dawn. She might as well put it to good use and replenish her herb supplies before tomorrow's trek into the desert. The better prepared they were, the quicker they could all leave this place that no longer seemed so safe.

After dropping her sack full of medicinal plants and edible berries by her bedroll, Gilly returned several times to refill her family's canteens with fresh water. That she managed to do so without waking anyone showed how tired everyone was.

On her final trip with Skye's canteen filled, Talus turned over. Gilly froze. He muttered something unrecognizable. He sounded angry. His right arm swung, fist clenched as if wielding a sword.

Five heartbeats later, he stilled, his arm dropped to his side and he began to snore. She breathed a sigh and glanced at Cullen. He still lay unmoving. Creepy fellow.

She tiptoed away as the sky lightened, signaling the start of a new day.

If all remained quiet and peaceful today, after they sent their two unexpected guests on their merry way to wherever they were headed, then she would get Marton's help to load Tom onto their horse.

Time to check on her patient. She didn't want Tom stumbling back to camp before Cullen and Talus had left.

A few yards from her stump, her ears started to ring. She shook her head but the annoying peal persisted like a warning bell. Soon her head began to pound. She was probably overtired. Should have woken Marton.

By the time she reached Tom, her head was throbbing and sleep beckoned like a strong undertow. She checked under the branches and found Tom fast asleep, with a smile on his face. She'd never seen him so peaceful and happy but the air thrumming with unease obliterated her enjoyment.

Someone else was coming.

No, not someone. *Something*.

Must stand. Warn Marton. Her limbs wouldn't move and her head grew so heavy it dipped toward the ground. Then darkness descended over her thoughts like a heavy blanket.

• • • •

A STEADY MELODIOUS chanting pulled Gilly away from her dreams. She stretched lazily. That was the best sleep she'd had in days. Her stomach grumbled in hunger. How long had she been asleep? Marton said they were supposed to leave at sun up. She blinked open her crusty eyes to find the sun riding high, blinding her. She shaded her face. *It couldn't be noon, surely? Why hadn't Anna woken her?*

"Lord Aton!" a strange voice called out. Others echoed the name, the sounds moving further away with each shout.

Gilly sat up. At first, she couldn't make out where she was. Not near her stump, where she'd fallen asleep. Tom was next to her, but so was her family. A glance around confirmed this wasn't their campsite. All around them were large colorful tents and when she clenched a hand, her fingers sank into sand.

There were people everywhere. Not King's Horsemen. Nor King's Warriors. These people had dark skin and eyes as colorful as their tents. They were dressed in flowing robes of dark brown, amber or gold. They stared at her with shy smiles.

Skye sat up on the other side of Tom and gasped.

Not a dream then.

Bevan sat up beside his sister, and then, with a cry, ducked under his sheet.

Gilly crawled past Tom toward Anna and poked her. "Wake up."

Her sister rolled over and said, "Shush."

"Anna," Gilly said, hysteria a note away, "Wake up!"

Anna groaned. "Head hurts, Gilly, shut up."

"More than your head's going to hurt," Gilly replied, "if you don't wake up. Now."

Anna sat up and rubbed her eyes. "These feel like all the dust in the Kocheya has become wedged into them overnight." She yawned wide and stretched.

"Gods of horse manure," muttered a dry voice from the other side of Bevan. "I swear I'll never sip another drop."

Tom! He was sitting up and looking around.

"Swearing!" Anna said. "What else can you expect from a drunkard?" Then she focused beyond him, and her mouth dropped open.

Marton scrambled to his feet.

Cullen stood as well.

Talus was crouched in a fighter's stance, sword drawn.

Gilly leapt to her feet and then groaned as pain shot from her left foot to her hip. Her leg was apparently as reluctant as her sister to wake up.

Movement stirred among the watching crowd.

A man in a white robe came forward. His skin was as dark as his people, his eyes a brilliant sky blue. Not a wrinkle indicated his age and his black hair fell in ringlets to his shoulders, glinting like moonlight at midnight. Arms akimbo, he wore a pleased smile. "Strangers, indeed."

He spoke Rycan in an accent that tickled Gilly's eardrums. He studied each of them in turn, appearing to grow more amused, until finally his gaze touched Gilly. His smile faltered, then turned brilliant. "No, not strangers at all, but long awaited guests." He gestured expansively toward his people. "Welcome to Erov."

The crowd echoed his words like an intonation. *"Welcome to Erov."*

"Erov?" Cullen said. "That's a myth. It's not real."

Gilly blushed at his rudeness. Obviously Erov was no mythical city. They were in it. *Brought* into it in a manner that was surely no minor magical sleight of hand. That conclusion both thrilled and terrified her because it implied High Magic must be at work.

Cullen flicked his hand with contempt. "Erov is the stuff of children's dreams and nightmares."

"Dreams of children are the future of the world," the white-robed stranger answered, "their nightmares a chance to change that future." Then he focused on Gilly and his features softened. He swept her a deep bow, a flamboyant gesture that involved elaborate movement of both arms. "My people name me Aton. You honor us with your visit to our paltry encampment, my lady."

Stunned, Gilly didn't know what to say and then gave a hasty curtsy. Her game leg buckled. She barely caught herself before she fell. Face flushed, she straightened and said, "I am Saira." *I didn't say that out loud, did I?* "I mean Gilly, my name is Gilly."

"As Chief Councilor of Erov, I bid you welcome, Lady Saira-Gilly." Lord Aton's twinkling eyes were infectious.

Her sister pushed her aside. "Please don't mind her, our servant gets confused around strangers."

Gilly bit her lip on the words, *I'm your sister, not your servant*! This lie between them had to end soon. She had stomached Anna's ill treatment when her sister thought her a stranger. Now Anna knew Gilly had saved her as a baby, her slights stung deeper. The blade sharpened with a personal edge.

"I am Anna and this is my husband. Marton." Her sister gestured Marton forward. "He is in charge."

Marton tried to emulate Lord Aton's gesture and his right arm swung dangerously close to cuffing Anna.

Her sister ducked, and Gilly hid her grin.

"We didn't realize we had camped in your village," he said.

Understatement, since they'd been sleeping on dirt-packed ground and now there was sand squishing between their toes.

"We didn't mean to intrude," Marton continued, as steadfast as only a practical blacksmith could be, when faced with the impossible. "We were on our way to Perm, sir. Are you able to tell us how to get there from here?"

"We know of many cities and many people," Lord Aton said. "We can speak of those later. First, I insist that all of you enter my home and accept my humble hospitality." He stepped around Anna and offered Gilly his hand, palm up. "You and your friends are welcome, Lady Saira-Gilly."

Gilly stared at him dumbfounded.

He took her hand and wound it around his arm so she had no choice but to follow. He matched his tread to her halting steps.

"Lady!" Anna's shocked voice faded into the crowd's excited chatter.

Lord Aton's people beamed their smiles of curiosity and welcome at her. Having hid from attention all her life, blending into the background and avoiding confrontations, Gilly found being their focus overwhelming. In her heart though, if she were truthful, like Anna, she had really longed to belong, to be accepted, to be loved.

Now, amidst such unequivocal acceptance by all these strangers, she was excited and terrified. She tightened her grip on Lord Aton's arm, and his strength flowed into her.

There was something else odd going on. That buzz she'd been hearing was not just these Erovians' chatter, but also their thoughts and emotions being broadcast at a more intimate, subconscious level. Her mind reeled as pictures flitted by of desert flowers, cool night winds, clear blue skies, and hot healing sunlight. The flashing of a hundred images and the emotions they evoked made her giddy.

Lord Aton led Gilly into a lavish marquee of overlapping tents. He invited her party to change out of their traveling clothes and bathe in the soothing waters of Erov before they sat for their meal.

Erov has water? Perhaps a side effect of all this magic. The air thrummed with power. How is it that the Horsemen didn't detect this place? It surely gleamed like a sunbeam.

Within the large tent, men and women led them to separate quarters. Anna insisted on remaining with her children and husband.

Several females followed Gilly into her room and insisted on helping her change. They chattered constantly in a language she didn't understand. Try as she might, she couldn't convince them she was capable of taking care of herself.

She was taken to a secluded pool and unclothed. She sank gratefully into the warm waters and her muscles began to unwind. Her whole body relaxed in the gloriously scented bubbling water. Her leg stopped aching and she rested, leaning back against the pool's stonewall. One of the girls massaged her scalp with soap and Gilly enjoyed the soothing sensations.

She must have dozed off because the next moment she awoke to find a tall young woman standing beside the pool. Skin black as ink, smooth and shining with life like the rest of the girls, she bowed displaying a gentle smile. "Lord Aton awaits you."

I'm late! Gilly hurried to get out of the pool. In one swift move, her new attendant pulled her up and onto the landing and handed her a thick towel.

"Thank you." Gilly dried and covered herself, acutely aware of each of her scars and her ungainly posture beneath this woman's curious gaze.

This time, when she said she was capable of dressing herself, the young woman graciously nodded assent. She placed an evening robe and a beautiful pair of sandals on the bed and left Gilly to fend for herself.

Once dressed, Gilly followed the lure of mouth-watering aromas to a room taken up by a low three-sided supper table. Her family was among the twenty or so guests, all of whom were seated on cushions placed on the floor. She was indeed late.

Lord Aton was seated at the table's center. The tall young woman who'd helped Gilly from the pool sat to his left. Gilly's family and friends were on the right hand limb of the table. Even Tom was there, looking pale but not as sickly.

Guilt stung that she had not checked on him before seeing to her needs. She hurried to his side. Before she could sit, Lord Aton was beside her.

His delighted smile brought a matching one to her lips. "I've saved you a seat by me."

His singular attention was inexplicable. She glanced with unease at her family to see how they took his behavior.

Anna seemed utterly astonished, her eyes appearing twice their normal size. The children and Marton didn't notice at all, as they gleefully tasted from the variety of dishes placed before them.

While Talus only had eyes for the pretty women serving him, Tom and Cullen didn't look pleased as Lord Aton led her away to the head of the table.

"Lord Aton," Gilly began, wanting to return to her family.

"Please, call me Aton." He urged her to sit at his right side.

"Then you must call me, Gilly," she replied checking on the pillows placed on the ground beside the table with concern. The simple act of sitting would prove embarrassingly awkward. It did. She had to stick her left leg straight out since it refused to bend to allow her to position herself cross-legged as the others sat around the table.

"A pity my son Jarrod could not join us," Aton said once he took his place. He passed her a dish of pitted dates. "But we are blessed to have his betrothed, Mayla, here with us." He nodded to the young woman on his other side. From beneath long lashes, she gave Gilly a gracious nod.

She'd been asked to sit at Aton's side, as his son's wife-to-be had been? *Why?* Gilly did some quick counting. Aton could be anywhere from forty summers old or more. If he had a son, he might have a wife. Where would she sit?

"Is your wife here?" She looked around the table.

"My wife died many years ago. It was a sad time for our people. She was well loved."

Gilly received a picture of a beautiful woman in green flowing skirts and matching top. The image was accompanied with such love and loss, her heart squeezed in sympathy. "Your son must miss her."

"Jarrod was but a boy when she departed our world, but you are correct. Every day, his eyes reflect the same sorrow I see in your gaze."

"Whatever do you mean?" Anna asked from down the table.

Gilly hadn't realized her sister was following their conversation.

"Have you never wondered about your Gilly's past?" he asked her sister.

"Of course not," her sister said, not batting an eye at his phrasing of, "your Gilly."

Gilly's pulse, however, shot up. Was Aton aware of her connection to Anna? Seemed the most likely reason for saying her name like that. These people could share thoughts. Had he read hers? If so, she didn't want him spilling her secrets, not in front of everyone. Especially not in front of Talus, who was a King's Warrior. Besides, she wanted to be the one to tell Anna that she was her sister.

Desperate to change the subject, Gilly said, "Where is your son?"

"Jarrod is researching a recent event in the Makakala Range. Erovians are the historians of Ryca. We record all major events. As my successor, my son is training in all aspects of the art."

"How do you manage that?" Cullen asked, seated beside Talus. "Why have I never heard of your people's travels? As a minstrel, reciting history is also my pastime."

"You have an inquisitive mind, Cullen. I have your name correct, I hope?" Aton's tone put grave doubt about Cullen's name. Seeing the minstrel squirm caused her doubts to firm into certainty. The children were correct, something about Cullen was not right.

The minstrel offered one of his spectacular smiles, which immediately made her wonder why she'd doubted him.

"What you do, Cullen," Aton's lips twisted as if the minstrel's name left a bad taste in his mouth, "is tell stories. What we do is record the truth. Is it any wonder our paths never crossed?"

Gilly held her breath. Aton had just accused the minstrel of being a liar.

Cullen chuckled. "What is truth but a fabrication from different minds?"

"Truth is love," Aton said. "Separate the two and you lose the integrity of both."

"Then you must be a dreamer," Cullen said. "You would make a good minstrel."

The discussion wandered off onto a definition of love and truth and Gilly's breath began to go in and out of her chest with fewer impediments. She was relieved to hear genuine laughter among her companions.

Then Cullen spoke. "I hope you don't mind my asking, but how is it that your city of tents was surrounding us when we awoke this morning?"

A question obviously on everyone's mind, except for Gilly's. In the excitement of meeting Aton and his fascinating people, she'd completely forgotten the amazing manner in which they'd been transported here. This city had not merely landed on them; they had been removed from their sleeping places and brought into the middle of the desert.

"The experience stinks of magic," Cullen added.

The room grew silent.

Chapter 5

Marton's arm went around Anna protectively. If trouble broke out, Anna would be looked out for. Gilly loved Marton's protective instincts. Anna couldn't have chosen a better husband.

"We deeply appreciate the hospitality you've shown us," Marton said. "I'm sure there is a reasonable explanation for what happened."

Yes, High Magic. Gilly's first thought on this topic mirrored Cullen's recent declaration. She had simply been too polite and weary to speak up.

"This far from Tibor," Talus finally tore his gaze from his voluptuous server with what appeared to be great difficulty, "you might not be aware that there is a ban against magical arts. King Ywen views such practices with grave distrust."

"We are aware of Ywen's views, Sir Talus," Aton said. "But I appreciate the reminder."

Gilly was surprised to hear him refer to the king as simply "Ywen." It seemed such a familiar way of speaking about their king. She'd assumed the Erovians were conscious of titles, since he referred to her as "Lady" and addressed Talus as "Sir."

"Does that mean you disregard the king's injunction?" Cullen asked with dogged determination.

The minstrel was intent on getting a confession of wrongdoing from Aton. So far from the king's power, why would he be set on this course? And toward his host? Perhaps Aton's earlier hint about Cullen being a liar had stung.

"Erov is a wandering city," Aton said. "We shift with the change in weather and seasons. Our animals need water and fresh fodder. There is precious little within the desert. The Kocheya basin can be a harsh mistress but bountiful to those who support and respect her ways."

He looked around the table until he held everyone's attention. "We are a people who are accustomed to moving quietly and quickly when the need arises. Our labors have become so habitual that we did not notice your presence until this morning. Why you did not notice our coming, is up to you to discover within yourselves."

As an explanation, it left much unsaid. Cullen, too, seemed dissatisfied with this answer.

Aton didn't wait for his response. He turned to Gilly. "How long will you grace us with your presence, my lady?"

"We have to leave come morning," Anna said before Gilly could answer. She gave Gilly a stern look as if to warn her to behave herself. "We're on our way to Perm. A long distance to travel, so, not much time to socialize."

"That is a pity," Aton said. "There is much I must speak about with Lady Saira-Gilly."

"Such as?" Cullen asked, then laughed out loud. "Unless it is of a private nature. In which case, I sincerely apologize for the intrusion."

"It could hardly be private, Cullen," Gilly said, the tips of her ears burning. "We've all just met."

First her sister insinuated she was about to misbehave and now Cullen suggested that Aton had designs on her person? All because he treated her with respect? It was probably Aton's normal manner toward women in general.

"While you remain here, you are all welcome to wander about the city at will," Aton said. "My people will answer your questions and assist you in any way they can."

Sensing a dismissal, everyone rose.

Gilly, too, tried to rise but Aton laid a restraining hand on her arm, holding her in place. "I would be honored to show you a little of my city, Lady Saira-Gilly."

The offer was touching. She agreed and reminded him to call her Gilly. Let the others think what they would. She was curious about Erov. Like Cullen, she did not quite believe Aton's explanation of Erov's wandering capabilities without the use of magic. It was rare indeed to come across a whole city enshrouded by High Magic.

Down the table, Tom stood and swayed.

"I must see to my friend first, Aton," she said and stood. "To ensure his needs are met. He is still recovering."

"You are a caring child," he said, also getting to his feet. "But have no fear. One of our healers already has him in his sights."

Indeed, a man intercepted Tom and gently guided him out of the supper tent. Still, she wanted to see to Tom herself. "I'd like to check his progress. I won't be long."

"I will await your presence in the alcove by the entrance."

She smiled at his courtly words and followed Tom from the room as quick as she could.

The healer was laying Tom on a cot when Gilly entered. Tom's weary brown gaze flicked in her direction and then closed.

"I am Nader," the healer said. "You have taken good care of your friend. His wounds have sealed. You have a healer's touch, my lady."

"Please, call me Gilly," she replied, unable to correct him that it was Anna who was the real healer in the family.

They spent a few minutes quietly discussing various medicines that Gilly knew and others she'd never heard of. She watched over his shoulder as he gently explored each of Tom's wounds and discussed the next stage in the healing process.

"Hate to interrupt," Tom said, his voice gruff and eyes angry. "I realize that Lord Aton is waiting for you. Don't let us keep you from that enjoyment."

"I want to know that you're going to be well, Tom." She touched his forehead to see if his fever had returned. His skin was cool and smooth and...

He caught her hand. "You don't want to keep your new beau waiting."

She snatched her hand back, her cheeks heating as Nader's speculative gaze flicked between her and Tom. She hadn't blushed so much in all her life.

"Best let him rest, my lady," Nader said, in a compassionate voice.

As the curtains slid closed behind her, tears of frustration stung. In the space of a few hours, the whole world had turned upside down. When had she gone from being Gimpy-Gilly, the Madwoman of Nadym whom everyone liked to avoid into Lady Saira-Gilly, the center of everyone's attention? She didn't belong in this world.

She hurried away looking for the alcove Aton mentioned to let him know that she had changed her mind about the walk. He was mistaken in whom he took her to be. Time she let him know that.

Within a few steps, a hand grabbed her arm and pulled her sideways. Gilly found herself in a secluded alcove, but not with Aton. Anna's angry face was the last one she wanted to see right now, but it was the one that was presented.

"We have things to discuss," her sister whispered.

Behind a tent flap at her sister's back, children's laughter erupted. "Have Skye and Bevan settled down?"

"Never mind my children. What are you doing?"

"What do you mean?" *She meant Aton, of course. Everyone meant Aton.*

"I'm speaking about your relationship with the ruler of this city."

"Chief Councilor," Gilly said. *Someone far above my reach.* Not that she'd ever contemplated reaching. If she had, it would have been for Tom. Except now he seemed to be disappointed with her. Her heart ached at the thought, even more than Anna despising her. At least the latter emotional pit was a familiar one.

"You're fooling yourself and making the rest of us look bad with your flirting," Anna said. "What must these people think to see you throwing yourself at him?"

Gilly shut her eyes at the unfairness of that accusation. She counted goats, a trick her mother taught her to help control her temper. It didn't work now, any more than it had when she was ten. "See to your family, Anna, and let me see to myself."

"I'm only trying to help."

"You're interfering. This is unusual since I never thought I mattered enough for you to care."

"Fine." Anna folded her arms. "Don't say I haven't warned you. You are supposed to be our servant."

Gilly hesitated, seeing the hurt in her sister's gaze behind the brash words. How could she have forgotten that even if she had never dreamed of being a noble lady, Anna probably had. She'd seen her act out the role in every village play, in every attempt to outdo her friends, in every slight she'd thrown at Gilly to make herself seem superior.

Anna isn't embarrassed by my behavior, she's envious of the attention Aton is lavishing on me.

Her heart softened for this abandoned child who had never felt truly loved. "Why don't you, Marton and the children come with me?"

The excited light in Anna's gaze was answer enough. About to warn her sister to hurry, a shout drowned her out.

That sounded like Tom. It came again and Gilly left Anna behind as she raced toward him.

It was Tom, and he was staggering backwards when she reached him.

"Tom!" Gilly said, rubbing her aching left leg, "what are you doing out of bed?"

"Where did you get that bloody dagger?" Anna asked, breathless from her sprint to catch up.

Gilly's heart lurched at the sight of the blood-streaked blade in Tom's hand. He looked confused, shocked, devastated. The same emotions raged through her. *Oh Tom! I should never have left you.*

Time crawled as the three of them stood before the alcove, none willing to push the curtain aside and look in. To see whose blood was still dripping off the dagger Tom clenched.

Behind that curtain was where she had agreed to meet Aton.

Suppressing dread that rose like a serpent about to strike, Gilly stepped around Tom and toward the partition. She lifted the flap. Aton lay sprawled on the ground, motionless.

There was a scream. Hers? Anna's?

Gilly's knees buckled and she dropped to the floor beside the body. She braced herself with one hand and warm blood wet her fingertips, soaked into her sleeve and dampened her skirts. The sight caused a wave of nausea. *Mustn't faint.* He could be alive.

Aton's gentle brown eyes were open and glazed, his expression one of shock. Her heart ached for the man who named her Lady Saira-Gilly. *Be alive!* His chest was motionless. Still, she had to hold her fingers beneath his nose. No hint of breath caressed her skin. "He's gone."

"I didn't do it," Tom said in a shaky voice from behind her. "I was looking for you to apologize for my bad manners. Instead, I found him. The blade was in his chest. I pulled it out and tried to stop the bleeding. He was already dead."

Anna grabbed Gilly's hand and tugged. "We have to leave. That scream would have raised the alarm. People will come."

"We can't leave," Gilly said. "We have to tell them what we saw."

"Which is what?" Anna asked. "That one of our party killed their Village Chief?"

"Chief Councilor," Gilly replied automatically. "And Tom said he didn't do it."

"Yes, of course," Anna said. "He looks perfectly innocent standing here with that bloody knife."

Too late to argue. People approached, whispering. *What's happened? Did he stab someone? Who? Why?*

Then Mayla was there. White as a sheet.

Tom dropped the weapon.

It thumped beside Gilly.

In a cold hard voice, Mayla ordered Tom be taken to his quarters and guarded, while Gilly's party remain in their tents, under guard. Then she picked up the dagger and set to arranging for the removal of Aton's body.

Gilly insisted on accompanying Tom to ensure no one harmed him. One Erovian escorted Anna to her family's quarters while three others went with Gilly and Tom. Once at Tom's room, two men stood guard outside while the third followed them inside.

Gilly helped Tom lay back on his cot. In his ear, she whispered, "Don't worry."

He caught her forearm. "I swear I didn't do it."

"I believe you and I promise I won't let them hurt you."

She pulled away and he tugged her back. "No! You can't keep saving me. It's too dangerous for you to stay in this magical tent city. Their spell casting is sure to draw the Horsemen here. You must leave. That's what I wanted to warn you about before. I'll deal with this and then follow you."

This time he released her and shut his eyes. He was letting her go, not just from here, but also sending her away from him.

As she left, his vow lingered. *I'll follow you.*

Did he mean it? There was certainly no love lost between him and Anna. So, to want to follow her party meant that he must care for her. His declaration was more comforting than he might realize. Cherishing that tiny spark in her cold heart, Gilly sought out Anna. She must convince her sister that, no matter how it looked, Tom couldn't have committed this murder. Else her sister's loose tongue might cause him irreparable harm.

• • • •

GILLY REQUESTED HER guards remain outside before she entered Anna and Marton's tent. Skye ran up to hug her. The child was shaking.

"We're going to be fine, Skye," she said in a firm, reassuring tone to her niece.

The child's grip did not slacken. Bevan was nowhere in sight. If Skye was frightened, he was probably terrified. Gilly wanted to squat and search under all the beds and cubby-holes for the boy but Anna's glare said that her sister was already furious. Best not antagonize her further until after she talked Anna out of publicly accusing Tom of murder.

Holding Anna's gaze, Gilly pointed outside and put a finger to her lips in warning that they could be overheard.

"You can save your words," Anna said, thankfully in a whisper. "He murdered Vyan at Nadym and he's done it again here. He'll probably try to kill King Ywen when we get to Tibor, if we ever do."

"Anna, that's enough," Marton said.

"No, it's not," his wife said. "I told her it was a bad idea to bring him but she wouldn't listen. We should have left him at the cowherd's shack. Better yet, we should never have rescued him. Then your precious Lord Aton might still be alive. Also, why did he call you a lady? That makes no sense. I told him you were our servant."

It was a question that confused Gilly as well, so she had no answer.

"This isn't helping," Marton said. "First of all, Gilly isn't our servant, she's a friend, and Lord Aton probably guessed that. These Erovians seem very good at reading people. Second, I viewed Lord Aton's courtesy toward her as good manners."

Gilly was impressed by Marton's insight into the Erovians. Her sister, however, seemed to take her husband's censure to heart for her lips trembled. Gilly's heart squeezed in sympathy. Anna might talk harsh but underneath that hard exterior, she was vulnerable to criticism. She wanted to hug her but Marton was there first.

He pulled his wife close and tenderly kissed her forehead. "I know this has been difficult for you, Anna, but it doesn't help to tear into the people who have been trying to help us. What we must do instead is decide on our next step."

"That's easy enough," Anna said. "We simply allow Erov's justice to deal with Tom."

"He didn't do this," Gilly said.

Her sister raised her arms in frustration and pulled away from her husband.

"But mama says you found him with the knife, Gilly," Skye said, the only one who still remembered to whisper, bless her. "That he could have killed any of us."

"He said he didn't do this," Gilly insisted quietly.

"That's all it takes?" Her sister stared at her as if she *were* the Madwoman of Nadym. "The word of a drunkard convinces you he's innocent despite the evidence of your eyes? Skye, come here. Now do you believe me when I say she's a bale short?"

"Anna!" Marton said

"Mama," Skye said, "please don't say that about Gilly."

Gilly raised her shoulders and let them drop, shaking off her hurt. Fear had brought out the old Anna. This wasn't her sister who was beginning to like her. Who hadn't told Marton that Gilly could do magic. Who, at first sight of that bloody dagger, hadn't run away, but had instead taken Gilly's hand and tried to tug her from the site of danger. She had come to learn that with Anna, her actions often spoke truer than words.

"I agree that we should let Erov's justice take its course, Anna," Gilly said, seeking to reach the new, more approachable Anna. "all I ask is that you not convict Tom before he's had a chance to speak on his own behalf."

Her sister bit her lip, her gaze narrowed.

Gilly left her sister to think that request over.

The rest of the day dragged on. Confined to her room, Gilly had nothing to do but think and her thoughts were not pleasant. A girl brought her food but refused to be coaxed into staying to talk. Two silent Erovians stood guard outside her door. She tried lifting the material at the back of her room but couldn't budge it from the floor. Finally, exhausted by all that had taken place, Gilly fell asleep on a bed of soft pillows.

She awoke the next morning to several girls scurrying about her room. The previous days' welcome smiles were replaced by shared nostalgic images of Aton that brought tears to Gilly's eyes.

As she dressed, like viewing a flurry of wild flower petals drifting in the breeze, scenes of him going about his daily life flitted by her. In one, he taught young children to read, in another, he tenderly helped an elderly man rise, or spent lonely hours recording the events of Ryca. Then she experienced his joy at first sight of his baby boy.

The girls' sorrow at Aton's death enveloped Gilly's heart with anguish until her chest was as thick and heavy with grief as when, at ten years of age, she finally accepted she would never again be with her mother, brother and sister.

"Lord Jarrod awaits you," one girl said.

"Lord Aton's son?" Gilly asked, anxiety fluttering in her tight chest. "I thought he was in the Makakala Range. How did he get here so fast?"

"Hurry."

They refused to listen to her assurance that she was perfectly capable of dressing herself. Gilly gave up the struggle and allowed them to care for her. The dress was slipped on, shoe ribbons tied up her calves, while a girl brushed out her long red locks with gentle strokes.

She still couldn't understand why it was necessary for so many to assist her. After yesterday's events, she was surprised they still wanted to dote on her. At least Mayla wasn't among this group. She wasn't ready to deal with Aton's daughter-in-law-to-be yet. Nor his son.

Once she was dressed, the women escorted Gilly from the room, constantly whispering to each other in their musical tongue. Their presence was strangely comforting as if she were once again held safe within her mother's arms.

She arrived at the room where her party had dined the day before. A younger version of Aton sat at the head position. Lord Jarrod. She put him as barely having passed twenty summers. So young to have lost his father. Her breath caught in her throat as her worried glance flew toward Tom. He sat beside her family and was not clapped in chains. A good sign surely.

Her party had taken their previous seated positions on pillows placed around the three-sided table. This time the room was packed with Erovians standing around the inside edge of the tent.

Anna gave an annoyed glance at the bevy of women who had accompanied Gilly as she stepped into the room. Had these girls not helped her sister dress, too? Of course they had. Her sister was probably irked that Gilly warranted the same attention. She lifted her chin in defiance and approached the empty place beside Tom.

"Lady Saira-Gilly." Lord Jarrod stood.

She was beginning to hate that name.

He motioned beside him, at the head of the table.

What was it with this family that they continually treated her as if she were some important personage? Or did he merely want to question her about Tom? Well, she couldn't remain frozen to the spot.

Feeling every eye on her clumsy movements, Gilly approached Lord Jarrod and allowed him to assist her. Her blush was back as she tried to position her left leg comfortably. One of the girls hurried forward to lay a pillow beneath Gilly's extended foot and heat rose up to Gilly's hairline.

A gesture from Lord Jarrod, and Tom stood and approached the center of the room until he stood directly across from the new Chief Councilor.

"Tell me your truth," Lord Jarrod said.

Tom spoke slowly, relaying the events of the day before. He'd come in search of Gilly. A young woman sitting beside her was diligently recording everything spoken. Tom finished by saying he had tried to save Lord Aton's life but he had arrived too late and the wound had been too severe.

Lord Jarrod gestured to Anna.

Her sister stood, took Tom's place and related the events as she experienced them. She refrained from making any judgments about Tom. Neither did she mention the other murder Tom had been accused of in Nadym. Gilly wanted to hug her.

Lord Jarrod then turned to his betrothed. His expression softened. Their connection could prove deadly for poor Tom. "Tell me your truth, Mayla."

The girl spoke in Rycan. "The strangers were by Lord Aton's body. That man Tom carried a dagger and there was blood on his clothing. The woman

Gilly spent much time close to your beloved father, doing what unspeakable things I cannot speculate."

Really? Unspeakable? That was her truth? Something else about Mayla's account bothered her. It was how she addressed her. She'd called her *Gilly*, not Lady Saira-Gilly as everyone else from this city did. Even Lord Jarrod, who had just arrived. Why the change? Unless the murder had unnerved her and she blamed Gilly as well as Tom?

"The woman Anna said to the other two that they should flee."

Gilly winced. She did not just blame her and Tom, but apparently their entire party.

Next, it was Gilly's turn. She would have stood but Lord Jarrod bid her to remain seated while she gave her testimony. She thanked him and began her version of events.

"Tom did not kill your father." Gilly put as much heart and certainty into that statement as she could muster. "He said he found Lord Aton's body and tried to revive him. When Anna and I arrived, we checked as well to see if he might still be alive." She glared at Mayla. "I did not do anything unspeakable to him!"

Releasing her tension with a sigh, she continued. "Unfortunately, Lord Aton had already passed through the gates of this world. In this life, for the short time I had known him, he was the kindest and most gentle man I had ever met. I wished him well. No one in my party wished him harm. Certainly not Tom. He did not kill Lord Aton."

"Your faith in your friend is a testament to your character," Lord Jarrod said. "But you have no proof, my lady. You may speak of your true heart, but it is never wise to gauge the purity of another, nor expect it to reflect your own."

"What are you going to do?" she asked, trembling.

"Erovian law requires that the punishment reflect the crime. The penalty for murder is execution."

Tom's face blanched.

"No!" Gilly cried out. "You cannot."

"It is our way," Lord Jarrod said. "That is how we honor our dead."

"But he is innocent," Gilly said. "Please, give me time to prove it. You have no proof that he is guilty, either."

"What more proof do we need than the blade in his bloody hands?" Mayla asked. "Merely because they are strangers does not mean they are exempt from our laws."

"Lord Aton said last night that truth and love are one and the same," Gilly said. "Well, I...I love Tom."

Anna snorted.

Tom's eyes widened.

"As a brother, or a friend," she added.

"Me, too." Skye shot to her feet. Her mother shushed her and grabbed for her hand but she squirmed away. "I love Gilly and if she says Tom is innocent, then he is."

"Thank you, Skye." Gilly's heart warmed toward the generous, loving child. She faced Lord Jarrod. "If what Lord Aton said was true, then our caring for Tom should prove his innocence. Please, give me a little time. In honor of your father."

Mayla jumped up. "You have no right to use Lord Aton's words against him. She is like the rest, no respect for our authority or for your father."

Shame writhed inside Gilly. She had used poor Aton's words in a bid to rescue Tom. What choice did she have?

There was a moment of silence.

"Lady Saira-Gilly," Lord Jarrod said, "you may have one day. After which, Tom's fate will be decided and your party must leave our land. You, however, may visit with us longer, if it pleases you. We have much to speak about once this sad business is finished."

Gilly blinked in surprise. His words were almost an echo of Aton's from the night before. What could either of them possibly have to say to her that was so personal and important?

A quick look around the table showed the same surprise on her family's faces as well as on Cullen and Talus. They, too, were all wondering what could possibly be her connection to Erov?

She didn't have time to ponder the newest mystery among so many others in this strange city. What was important was that she had one day to prove Tom's innocence. With that decided, she had something else to say that was long overdue.

She laid a hand on Lord Jarrod's forearm. "I offer my deepest sympathy on the loss of your father."

Tears flooded into his gray-green eyes and he squeezed her hand. "You are everything my father said you were," he said quietly. "It was his honor to have met you before his death."

How could Aton have spoken to Jarrod about her when his son had been away on his trip? Could those in Erov somehow communicate across vast distances? The girls had been able to send her impressions of Aton's life. Could Aton have contacted his son in the same manner, even when the two were not in the same room? The other thing that bothered her about Lord Jarrod's words was his statement that it was a special honor for Aton to meet her. How could that be, when she was but a simple goat herder from a strange land?

Everything about this place was confusing, from Erov's mysterious appearance overnight, to their recording of Ryca's history, to this uncanny ability to communicate without speech. Cullen would say somewhere at the heart of all this was the stink of magic.

To compound matters, before all this ended, she might need to cast a spell or two in order to save Tom. It would have to be a last resort. First, she would question the people who worked in this gigantic tent with its multitude of rooms, and in the surrounding tents.

One of these Erovians might have been near the alcove before Aton was murdered and unwittingly seen something of importance. Something they might not even realize was pertinent to his murder. She bid Jarrod goodbye and hurried off in search of the girls who had helped her dress.

Chapter 6

True to Lord Jarrod's word, Gilly was given freedom to roam within his city and speak to anyone she pleased in order to seek out proof of Tom's innocence. He even suspended the guards around her family and travel companions' rooms but he strengthened those around Tom's quarters. There would be no running away from Erov with the supposedly guilty party.

While moving about this amazing city, she gained an impression of vastness. Each tent she entered felt bigger on the inside than it seemed on the outside. She could not explain it any other way than magic. Her growing concern for Tom, however, kept her curiosity from straying to explore that intriguing notion. For with every Erovian Gilly questioned, his or her answer was alarmingly similar.

"I did not see anything suspicious, my lady."

"I know of no arguments."

"The day was peaceful. Until that heart-wrenching cry."

The only new information she uncovered was about the initial scream at the discovery of Aton's body. It hadn't come from Gilly's throat. Or Anna's. It had been Mayla's shout that brought people racing to the bloody corpse.

By sunset, Gilly was out of time. She had no choice now but to tap her most dangerous option. Magic. Her questioning had failed to uncover the real killer so she crafted a spell to lead her inner sight to the murderer.

She returned to her room to scrounge for ingredients, from candles to herbs to touch stones. Finally, heart hammering, she lay on her bed of pillows and rehearsed the words of her spell.

Shortly after midnight, she crept into Anna's room. She needed someone to watch her physically while her mind traced the killer. Her sister was aware she could cast High Magic spells and had not told on her. Convincing her to help, however, would require a bit of manipulation.

Anna was fast asleep snuggled beside her husband. Marton was snoring.

Gilly laid her candle on the floor and gently shook Anna's arm.

Her sister groaned and pushed her away.

"Wake up," Gilly whispered. "I need your help."

Her sister opened one eye. "Have you regained your senses and admitted to Tom's guilt?"

"You were right," Gilly said, with a sorrowful face.

Both her sister's eyes were now open but her gaze was drenched with suspicion. "You're just saying that."

"Being wrong means I now need your help."

"With what?" Anna's whisper was supremely wary.

"I'm afraid I'll make a fool of myself tomorrow when I tell Lord Jarrod I was mistaken about Tom."

"You should have thought of that before you started defending the drunk."

"Please, Anna. Help me word what I must say."

"Oh, is that all? Fine." She turned over and cuddled into her husband's side. "Come see me in the morning."

Marton shifted his arm, wrapping it around his wife's waist and pulling her tight. Then his soft snore came again.

Gilly breathed a sigh of relief and tugged at Anna's sleeve. "I must do it now."

"It's late."

Gilly grabbed a pair of sandals from beside the bed and put them in her sister's hand. "I can't sleep. You always know the right things to say."

Flattery worked where pleading failed and her sister reluctantly sat up and gave a heavy huff. "All right, all right." She looked half asleep as she put on her sandals.

"Thank you." Gilly picked up her candle, took her sister's hand and led the way. Anna, probably still half asleep, didn't realize where she was being taken until they arrived at the alcove near the tent's entrance where Aton had died. Once she did, she came to an abrupt halt and pulled her hand free.

Now completely awake, she wrapped her robe tighter and looked around with fear. "I thought you were taking me to your room."

"The fresh air will help me think," Gilly said.

"Then let's go outside."

Gilly hurried her into the alcove. Inside, Aton's body was gone and the floor cleaned of his bloodstain. If what they'd seen wasn't so ingrained, she might never know that terrifying deed had taken place here.

"I don't like it in here." Anna's voice shook as she followed Gilly inside.

"It's private and I don't want anyone staring at us. We're on everyone's thoughts as it is."

"But everyone's asleep," her sister said.

"How should I start my speech?" The switch in topic seemed to help. Her sister turned her back to where Aton had been found and suggested one phrasing after another.

Gilly walked in a circle around the alcove and dropped her herbs while mouthing the chant.

"What are you doing?" Anna asked as Gilly reached the end of her circular route.

"Setting a protective circle so no one will disturb us." Chant completed, Gilly sat on the floor and pulled five candles from her satchel. She lit them before placing them in a smaller circle in front of her.

"You lied to me!" Anna pointed at the lighted circle. "You're casting a spell. You told me never to do magic again. Have you lost your mind?"

Gilly was shocked at how fast her spell worked. Light balls floated upward from the candles and in their midst Aton appeared, and then another person. *It wasn't Tom!* She grabbed Anna's skirts. "A woman was with Aton that night in this alcove. I see them talking. Aton looks upset."

Anna glanced around. "Gilly, you're frightening me. All I see is the candlelight."

"The woman's face keeps shifting. It's as if there's something inside her, pushing outward. It's hard to tell who she is but she resembles..."

The evil shade inside the woman broke free and, like a blazing dark star, swooped toward them.

"Anna!" Gilly said in warning.

Between one breath and the next, that demonic light struck Gilly full across her face. Her cry was choked and heat speared her eyes. She covered her face but it was too late.

"Gilly, what's wrong?"

"My eyes burn."

Skirts rustled and she guessed Anna approached closer. Her sister grabbed her wrists and tugged. "Move your hands so I can see. You probably got dirt in them."

Gilly blinked rapidly but couldn't see anything. *Had the candles gone out?* Her eyes were aflame.

"Oh, Gilly," Anna said.

"What? Do you see anything? Why is it so dark?"

"Wait, I'm moving a candle closer to see better."

"Anna? Where are you?"

"Hold still and keep silent." Her sister hissed the command. "Do you want all of Erov to witness our folly?"

Gilly clamped her mouth shut as Anna's cool hands passed over her face. Soothing ice invaded her painful eye sockets, easing the burning sensation. Her skin tingled and sparked wherever Anna touched her. Gilly relaxed her shoulders and neck so she could lie back to allow Anna's hands to work the pain out of her eyes and face.

Slowly, she began to see shapes again. Shadows flickered in the candlelight. Anna was staring at her with concern. She moved her sister's hands aside and found them covered in blood and soot. Her breath caught. Had all that come from her face? She tentatively touched her cheeks and found them wet and sticky. "What happened, Anna?"

Her sister slumped back onto the ground, wearing a dazed expression. Her fingers were trembling.

"Anna, what did you do?"

"Your eyes, and the skin around them, were so black," she said softly. "As if they had been burned through."

Gilly shook at what her sister described. "I can see. My eyes don't hurt anymore. Did you heal me?"

Anna looked at her shaky hands in wonder. "I must have, but it wasn't any kind of healing I've done before."

"Anna, tell me exactly what you did."

"I...I couldn't stand to look at your eyes. They seemed so painful. I covered them with my hands and wished your eyes back as they were. Oh, you're right. They couldn't have been burnt or you wouldn't be able to see now. I probably wiped away the dirt covering your face."

"That wasn't dirt. It felt like hot coals sinking into my head through my eyes."

"I don't care what it was." Anna rubbed her hands on her dress as if to wipe away evidence of whatever had happened. The red streaks her hands left on her dress only emphasized that something extraordinary had taken place.

Gilly hugged her sister close and held her until their shuddering subsided.

Anna finally pulled away and stood. "I hate this place. Tom can rot in the sands of this blighted city for all I care. We're leaving Erov tomorrow, with or without you."

Gilly tried to stand and fell back. Her good leg was as weak as a day-old puppy and her clumsy one was useless.

Anna helped her up, muttering how mad Gilly had been to bring them here, at this time of night, with a murderer on the loose. Did that mean her sister no longer thought Tom was the murderer? Because Tom was under guard, not running free to terrorize people.

"Anna."

"What?"

"The attack on me tonight suggests this murderer can defend himself, or herself, with magic."

"I thought you said it was a woman with Aton?"

"A woman was with him shortly before he was killed but I didn't see her actually stab him. He was upset with her."

"Did you recognize her? You've spoken to lots of Erovians today. Could it have been one of them?"

"It could have been Mayla but it was hard to tell. I think someone was controlling her. Her features kept wavering. I need to talk to her. Ask her some questions." She tugged free of her sister, wanting to go to that Erovian woman now, but she didn't know where her quarters were. "Did you know that, after us, Mayla was the first to arrive at the murder scene? She was the one who screamed."

"Talk to her tomorrow," Anna said. "Right this moment, one look at you would send anyone off screaming. We don't need that happening two nights in a row."

Gilly accepted that advice and allowed Anna to support her to her room. Considering how shaky she felt, she wasn't surprised that she looked terrible.

She was still reeling at her sister's extraordinary healing ability. *She wished my eyes back to the way as they were, and it just happened?*

Once they reached Gilly's room, instead of leaving, Anna stayed to wash away the blood from Gilly's face and helped her to bed, all the while scolding her.

Despite her gruff words, Anna's voice was as comforting as her touch. Gilly lay awake among her silken pillows, more troubled by what she'd seen in that circle of candlelight than by the attack on her sight, or even Anna's healing. Even if she had no proof of Tom's innocence, she now had a viable suspect besides him.

It had been hard to tell in the dark but the one facing Aton had looked a lot like Mayla. Yet not Mayla. If she had killed Aton, the girl had not acted under her own auspices. Also, Gilly still had no proof of Tom's innocence.

If she accused Mayla without proof, she would incur the wrath of Lord Jarrod and all of Erov, and probably on her family, too. Where did that leave Tom? At death's door, that's where. By morning, he would be executed and there was nothing she could do to stop it.

Warm tears soothed the lingering ache in her eyes, but the sorrow in her heart grew deeper.

Anna's footsteps retreated. Her sister was returning to her husband. Gilly owed Anna a heartfelt thank you for not abandoning her at that alcove, for healing her, for taking care of her afterwards. She wanted to at least say good night. The words that slipped out were, "Please don't leave me."

Anna's steps halted, hesitated for all of three slow heartbeats, and then, remarkably, she returned to Gilly's side. Her sister pushed the covers aside and crawled in beside her and wrapped her arm around Gilly's waist and pulled her close.

"Thank you," Gilly whispered, relishing the comfort of having her sister hold her.

"You can't save him," Anna said.

At that flat but accurate statement, she shuddered and shut her eyes. "I know."

"No one ever expected that you could save everyone."

Her sister's matter-of-fact words burst open the floodgates of grief that Gilly had kept boarded up for twenty years at her utter failure to save Mam and Tamara and Garren. Her shoulders shook, her sobs refused to stay silent, and her tears fell free. Mortified by her breakdown, she pulled away but Anna held her tight, refusing to allow her to grieve alone. Finally exhausted, but also strangely comforted, Gilly drifted off to asleep.

She wasn't sure how long she slept but a sense of extreme unease brought her suddenly wide-awake. It was still dark inside the tent. All was silent outside. Beside her, Anna slept curled up with her arms tucked in. In lieu of light to show her what had awoken her, Gilly sent her inner sight scouting. Her wards had dissipated overnight like a fire dying; she hadn't had the energy to strengthen them before turning in. A foolish mistake.

Close to the tent flap that led out to the corridor, her mind brushed a shadow so foul her pulse leaped in alarm. She scrambled up, kicking the blankets aside. She tangled with a long pillow and tumbled to the floor, jarring her ankle with a painful thud.

Anna gave a startled cry and sat up. "What's happening?"

"Stay down." Before she finished speaking, the intruder was beside her and sent a vicious kick that struck Gilly's lame leg above her knee.

Excruciating pain stabbed her thigh and Gilly scrambled away from her attacker and closer to the bed.

A second kick came but swiped empty air, missing Gilly.

Voices sounded outside Gilly's curtained room and lantern lights flared. Help was coming, *thank the Light*.

Gilly could now see and recognized Mayla. The woman's eyes were glowing unnaturally, her wild hair flared behind her like a dark curtain as she raised a dagger.

Anna, the foolish woman, lunged at Mayla's midriff, and sent both of them rolling. The dagger skittered across the floor.

Ignoring her pain, Gilly grabbed for the weapon as Mayla lunged at her.

Anna scrambled off the floor and jumped onto the intruder's back. Gilly rolled out of the way and then joined her sister in subduing Mayla. Between them, they sat over the struggling, cursing, Erovian girl until help finally rushed in.

• • • •

LORD JARROD CALLED another meeting to ascertain what had taken place in Gilly's room that night. His long curly black hair looked rumpled and knotted and several sleep lines marred his smooth dark cheeks giving a terrifying cast to his frown.

Gilly barely had time to run her fingers through her hair before she was summoned to the tent where they'd all last discussed the events of Aton's murder. She avoided Lord Jarrod's "why aren't you sitting beside me" gaze and planted herself beside Tom. Her leg still throbbed from being struck. Anna had offered to help with the pain, but Gilly refused.

She wasn't ready to let anyone near her game leg yet. Maybe soon, though. Anna's concern was hard to resist. After years of being scorned by her sister, their new close relationship was both warm and wonderful.

Tom's hand slipped over hers and he squeezed her fingers in appreciation of her support.

Anna was on Gilly's other side and beside her sat Marton and the children. Cullen and Talus were across the room on the other arm of the three-sided table. The room was again filled with Erovians, most standing at the rear. Mayla stood in the center of the room. Although she had recently fought the woman, Gilly was disturbed by her bound hands and head bowed in defeat.

Lord Jarrod called the meeting to order. His gaze was filled with confusion and sorrow as he gazed at his betrothed. "What have you to say, Mayla?"

She did not respond.

"You must have an explanation for your actions tonight." He sounded imploring.

Gilly's heart squeezed with sympathy. He'd lost his father and now the woman he was to marry had attacked a guest.

Mayla turned to Gilly and there was such hatred on her face, Gilly's stomach clenched.

"I had to avenge Lord Aton's death."

"But it is the man Tom who is accused of my father's killing, Mayla," Lord Jarrod said, "not Lady Saira-Gilly."

She pointed at Gilly. "She killed him. I know she did. If we don't stop her, she'll kill us all."

Gilly shivered at the menace in her eyes.

"I speak the truth." Mayla sent Lord Jarrod a defiant look. "Would you believe an outsider over one of your own? One whom you promised to love?"

Lord Jarrod leaned back, shock on his face.

Gilly was floored by that artful plea. No matter how formally and politely Lord Jarrod treated her, surely he wouldn't accept her word over his betrothed's? Except, this wasn't the real Mayla speaking. Of that she was certain.

"Truth," Lord Jarrod said in a deep somber voice, "is Erov's sacred trust. We are the truth sayers of Ryca."

As he spoke, Gilly's ears rang with an ominous clang. She released Tom to cover her ears.

Anna, too, looked uncomfortable, shaking her head and swiping her hands over her ears as if a fly were buzzing nearby. Even Bevan and Skye were crouching as if in pain.

"See!" Mayla said. "The evil ones are affected by your sacred words. That proves what I say is true."

With a guilty start, Gilly dropped her hands to her side.

"We are an ancient people," Lord Jarrod said, "with old laws and ways of assaying the truth of matters."

He gestured to his aide. A tall man ran to retrieve an overflowing tome from a nearby table and brought it over.

The tome's pages stuck out at odd angles. Jarrod straightened them, but for all his efforts, the book looked as jumbled as before he started. With a sigh, he gave up his efforts to organize the book and looked up.

"Here," he tapped the cover, "lies a record of Ryca's history. Falcon's Tome is named after our ancestor who was first charged with keeping the records of this land's passage. It recounts many truths, and most recently, it had been my father's honor to trace the tale of Ywen the Blind."

"How dare you insult our king?" Cullen's voice, dagger sharp, sliced toward Lord Jarrod.

Talus, too, looked startled, his concerned gaze trained on Lord Jarrod. As a King's Warrior, he must feel bound to challenge over that name slight. Though he didn't say a word, his grip on his sword tightened, his knuckles showing white.

"I but name the king as it is recorded," Jarrod said, in an unruffled tone. "These pages may only contain truth."

"You take much liberty, my lord." Cullen jumped to his feet. "Noting a term as 'truth' doesn't make it so."

A collective gasp erupted from the Erovians.

Lord Jarrod's cold stare sent a shiver up Gilly's spine. She was grateful to not be the one under that censure. Nor Tom. She reflexively squeezed his fingers. He returned the pressure.

"You are forgiven your outburst, sir," Lord Jarrod said in his calm tone, "since you are unfamiliar with Erov's customs and traditions. Allow me to enlighten you. Only the truth can be recorded in Falcon's Tome,"

"That stinks of magic." Cullen crossed his arms. "Talus, as a King's Warrior, are you not responsible for upholding the king's laws?"

Talus stood, hand on his sword hilt. He looked irritated at being drawn into this drama but wasn't shying away. "What you say does suggest a banned practice, Lord Jarrod."

Gilly held her breath, her chest tight as Lord Jarrod and Talus stared at each other. The fingertips on her free hand began to tingle. She glanced down and discovered dots of Light dancing on that palm. Her gaze flew to Cullen and Talus but both were focused on Lord Jarrod. The young Chief Councilor of Erov, on the other hand, was looking at her with a tiny smile curling his lips upward.

Heart hammering, she clenched her left fist to quench the magic. What had she planned? To fling a spell at Cullen or Talus? The image that immediately came to mind was of both men being hurled far across the Erovian desert.

The shuffle of feet and knees bumping against her back had Gilly checking behind her. The Erovians had moved closer to her, leaving Cullen and Talus standing alone on one side of the room. Had one or more of them put that idea of hurling Cullen away into her mind? If so, they'd done it strongly enough for her to reach for her magic without even being aware of it.

Lord Jarrod's focus turned to Talus and he shrugged nonchalantly. "What ancient custom of one people is not like magic to another? We travel from place to place recording the history of life while the people of

Perm have homes tunneled into the ground, as if to root them in place. The merchants of Tibor sail to far off places returning with amazing items that turn wheels as if by magic. The farmers of Nadym rely on the passing of the sun and seasons, which cannot be explained but by the magical whimsy of life itself."

"He has a point," Talus said to Cullen.

"No, he doesn't," Cullen said, stubborn to the end.

"Above all," Lord Jarrod continued as if the minstrel had not spoken, "we prize truth, and our records reflect that belief. Is that so magical, a King's Warrior must intervene?

"No, it is not." Talus sat down.

Gilly released a relieved sigh. A slight breeze at her back suggested many Erovians did likewise.

Cullen's mouth was a flat line of anger but he returned to his seated position.

"Good," Lord Jarrod said. "Then let us resume our discussion. We have gathered here to discover the truth of what happened to Lord Aton. The question raised is whether to believe Mayla, a woman of our culture, and one who, over the years, has shown herself to be an honest aide to my father and a true friend to me."

He opened his tome and the pages fluttered of their own accord for far longer than one could comfortably term, *natural*. Finally, as Gilly was bracing herself for another outburst from Cullen, the pages fell open at about two thirds of the way into the book.

Cullen grunted, but otherwise kept silent.

Perhaps because Talus was so busy tending to his fingernails, he couldn't be accused of noticing that over-long fluttering of pages.

Anna rolled her eyes at Gilly.

Lord Jarrod placed his finger on a notation. "The accused is Tomas." He looked at Tom. "He is not from Nadym as he claims."

"You're mistaken in that," Anna said with a frown. "He is from my village. We are not close, but I've known Tom all of my life and I'm from Nadym."

"These proceedings would go faster if each statement I make is not questioned." Lord Jarrod gave her a cross look. "Falcon's Tome has a record of all births, of all Rycan people. Tomas the Brave is not from Nadym."

"The Brave?" Anna gave a laugh. "How can you expect us to believe what you say, when it so clearly contradicts what we know?"

"She is correct," Tom said. "I'm not brave. Tomas the Coward would be more accurate."

"Tomas the Brave," Lord Jarrod continued, "Apprentice to King's Warrior and Child of Tibor, is accused of the murder of my father, Lord Aton, the late Chief Councilor of Erov."

Everyone stared at Tom. The weak and slender man didn't look as if he knew what a sword looked like never mind how to wield one. His gaze met and tangled with Lord Jarrod's. Tom was the first to look away.

Gilly, frowning, gazed from Tom to Talus, comparing that King's Warrior's broad frame to Tom's slender form.

As if he'd noticed her evaluation, Tom pulled his hand out of her grasp. Gilly clenched her empty fist with remorse.

"Defending Tomas, is Lady Saira-Gilly." Lord Jarrod nodded to her. "Child of Ryca and Defender of the Light."

Anna's peal of laughter rang through the room. Her husband poked her ribs and she covered her mouth to hold in her humor. Her gaze remained filled with mirth.

Gilly was more curious than amused. Was that really how she was referred to in that tome? Had Aton seen her in that absurd manner? That might explain why he, and Lord Jarrod, treated her so royally. What strange people these Erovians were. This was the truth that would determine if Tom had murdered Aton?

"One of you knows what happened to my father," Lord Jarrod said. "One of you is lying. It would be easy for me to say that Mayla speaks the truth and the stranger Tom is the liar and murderer, as Mayla has accused him. Since Lady Saira-Gilly insists on Tom's innocence, the matter is more complicated."

"How so?" Cullen asked. "Isn't she just as much a stranger to you as Tom?"

Gilly could have kicked him.

"Lady Saira-Gilly is the Defender of the Light," Lord Jarrod said, as if that answered the question. It didn't to Gilly's mind, nor by their confused looks did it satisfy her family and their companions. However, all the Erovians, except for Mayla, nodded as if in perfect agreement.

"Before this day is ended," Lord Jarrod said, "I will know which of you speaks the truth. To determine this, we will utilize an ancient Erovian custom called the Telling Ceremony, which will guide us toward the one who can be trusted, and the one who must be executed for my father's murder. Each of you, in the order of Mayla, Tomas and Lady Saira-Gilly, will recite a portion of the history of Ryca that you have experienced in your life. The recitation will be checked against Falcon's Tome for veracity."

At his gesture, a few Erovian women stepped closer and led Mayla, Tom, and Gilly to the center of the room. The tables were removed and everyone gathered around them, until Lord Jarrod and the crowd stood facing the accused, his defender and the accuser.

Chapter 7

"Let the Telling Ceremony begin," Lord Jarrod said.

A young woman clicked a small golden cymbal between her thumb and forefinger. Its note rang clear in the silent room. Flames flared in unison from sconces scattered about the room.

Cullen's eyes narrowed and Gilly's pulse sped up.

"Mayla, you will speak first," Lord Jarrod said.

With eyes as blank as a trout out of water too long, the dark-skinned Erovian woman took two steps closer to him, her long black curly hair swinging about her shoulders. She looked different from earlier. Less aware of her surroundings, as if instead of merely influencing her actions and words, someone had reached out and snatched full control.

"Are you well enough to speak?" he asked.

She raised her head and replied in a monotone. "I am well, my lord."

Lord Jarrod looked as unconvinced as Gilly but he continued. "My father loved you as a daughter, and encouraged us to join as one to chronicle the passing of time. We played as children, learned lessons together, and believe the same history. Yet, custom dictates that I ask you to repeat a piece of history. Mayla, how was Prince Keegan the Blessed rent from our world?"

Mayla spoke with a soft, mesmerizing voice. "The prince lay sleeping innocently in his bed when his wife, overtaken by evil, used glamour to seduce him. In a maddened frenzy, she then stabbed him with a charmed weapon that tore through the prince's magical defenses and pierced his heart."

The Erovians gasped. Gilly wasn't shocked because she had heard this story many times and knew it by rote.

"Prince Ywen heard his brother's screams," Mayla continued, "and came running to his aid, but it was too late. His beloved brother was dead."

The muttering in the room increased until Jarrod stilled the sounds with a swipe of his hand.

"The murderess tried to escape with her evil spawn and they all ran into the balcony corridor," Mayla carried on, as if unaware of her audience's growing unease. "She encountered Tamarisk The Charmer."

Gilly's left leg muscles stiffened, as if they instinctively sensed what would come next.

"The magician attempted to restrain the princess," Mayla said in her dead voice, "but she threw one of her children at him and fled. The wild child attacked his face and in defense, he threw her over the railing to the ground floor."

Gilly curled and uncurled her toes to relieve her leg cramps that sent little shock waves shooting up to her hip.

"The child hit the ground, her bones cracking. She should have died but her mother cast a spell that kept her soul from departing on its final journey. With the undead child in her arms, she and the rest of her evil offspring fled into hiding."

Gilly pictured that poor child falling, heard her screams, felt those bones crack as if they were her own. No matter how crazed the child had been, there was no call for the sorcerer to react that way. She had never been fond of King Ywen, but she held his sorcerer in deep contempt. If he was as powerful as everyone proclaimed, he could have defended himself without tossing a child over that railing.

Her fists were scrunched so tight, her nails bit into her palms. Slowly, she released the pressure, but her anger against the sorcerer still simmered.

Shocked silence settled around the room in wake of Mayla's tale. The dark skinned men and women of Erov whispered to each other, shaking their heads. They acted as if the tale was false. As if Mayla had not spoken the truth. How could that be when this was a familiar story told all across Ryca?

Lord Jarrod sighed heavily. "Mayla, tell me you jest? You and I have read and heard Prince Keegan's story many times. How could you speak such falsehood?"

"She speaks the truth," Talus said. "Every word she said is as it happened. That is how Prince Keegan died."

The Erovians shook their heads, their murmurs growing frantic and Gilly was bombarded by a series of clear pictures where classes of young Erovians were taught another version. It would be interesting to hear their fanciful account of that terrible night.

For now, the fact that Mayla spoke a different tale than expected by her people showed she was being controlled. The trouble was how to point that out without bringing up the topic of magic? Gilly was tempted to check with her second sight to see if a spell was cast on Mayla. The idea of casting that seeker spell again was terrifying since last time the backlash had blinded her. She was aware of the danger now and might be able to protect herself better, but that wasn't a guarantee.

Under Lord Jarrod's orders, Mayla was led away. With sadness in his eyes, he turned to the remaining two people awaiting his judgment. "Tomas the Brave, tell us what happened the night Prince Keegan the Blessed was killed." He held up his hand before Tom could speak. "I do not want a retelling of what we just heard. Instead, tell us what you personally saw and experienced that night."

That sounded as if Lord Jarrod believed Tom had not only come from Tibor, but had also been present at the time of Prince Keegan's murder. Was that even possible? Tom would have been no more than eleven or twelve summers. *Old enough to be an apprentice to a King's Warrior.*

She turned to Tom with new eyes. He was leaning sideways, as if standing for so long had drained him. Gilly wanted to put her arms around him but held back. If he had once been a warrior's apprentice, he wouldn't appreciate her pointing out his weakness. Explained why he hated her tending to his wounds.

"The night seemed no different than any other," Tom said quietly. "A son begged his father for a chance to guard the prince's rooms. The father hesitated, but then agreed, saying he would go fetch their supper. All was quiet as the proud boy stood watch in the corridor outside the prince's chamber. Then he heard footsteps. Tamarisk The Charmer, approached. Once the prince's advisor, this man was now barred from the castle. The boy's grip on his sword tightened as his anxious gaze shifted from the intruder to the stairs his father had taken. The man gestured to the boy to approach him."

Tom looked at the floor, seemingly lost in time.

"Go on," Lord Jarrod said.

"The boy stood his ground. The man gestured again. Fear exploded in the boy's heart. His pulse beat rapidly and something heavy but invisible slammed against his chest, pushing him against the door. With a cry, he shoved it back. As the boy fought, a sibilant voice whispered, *"Leave or you will die. Run!"*

Tom's pale cheeks were flushed as he stood beside Gilly, his gaze trained on the floor, as if he couldn't bring himself to meet anyone's gaze. "The boy bolted."

Gilly's heart went out to that young Tomas, King's Warrior Apprentice. She wanted to hug Tom and say, *It wasn't your fault. Tamarisk put a fear spell on you.*

She bit her lips for now, but once this crisis was over, she planned to have a talk with the grown up Tom about magic, and spells, and how effective they could be when used on someone, even if the person was protected as she'd been in that alcove doing her seeker spell. Never mind a young lad all on his own with no magical defenses.

"The coward that he was," Tom said, "he ran to find his father rather than stand and face the enemy. When he returned with his father, it was to encounter the pregnant princess escaping with her children. She screamed, *He's murdered my beloved. He's murdered Keegan.*

"The boy's father drew his sword and shouted, *Who? Who killed Keegan?*

"The princess screamed and pointed over the warrior's shoulder. Boy and father turned. Before either could react, Tamarisk stabbed the boy's father through the chest. His father grabbed the sorcerer's sword hilt and sword hand, and hung on. He shouted to the princess, *Run!*

"The boy jumped toward Tamarisk but his father released the sword and flung his boy back. The boy hit his head on the banister and fell, losing consciousness."

Tom went quiet.

Talus was the first to speak. "I'd heard the prince's bodyguard was killed that night, but I didn't know he had a son. I've lived in the castle for years and never heard of a boy who witnessed those events."

Cullen waved in dismissal. "Because there was no witness."

"On the contrary," Lord Jarrod said. "Tom has spoken the truth as it is written in Falcon's Tome."

Tom's head jerked up. "That's recorded in your book?" he whispered. "How? No one knew of this except Tamarisk, and the fleeing princess."

"We are the historians of Ryca," Jarrod reminded Tom kindly. "It would never do to have an incomplete version of events. We have not seen the Royal Princess since she fled the castle. She and her children would have been welcomed here, but she chose to go elsewhere for protection."

"The princess is wanted for murder," Talus said.

"Exactly," Cullen said, and patted him on the shoulder.

"At Prince Keegan's death, and that of his father, the children became the true heirs to Ryca." Lord Jarrod pointed out. "Whether or not their mother committed murder is questionable, but the fact that her children are heirs to the throne is not."

"King Ywen renounced them all as tainted by the magic that killed his brother," Cullen argued.

Her attention trained on Tom, Gilly only half listened. Had he truly been at the castle during Prince Keegan's murder? Had the horror of that night and his role in the murder induced Tom to drink? Her heart softened to the devastated apprentice warrior.

"Tainted or innocent," Lord Jarrod said, "Prince Keegan's offspring are more the rulers of Ryca than Ywen the Blind, who could not see past the hatred in his heart to the good in his brother or the power of magic to do good."

"As King's Warrior," Talus said, "I am also the protector of King Ywen's family and those children are his nieces and nephews. I, too, would like to know where they are."

"We come now to the third party called to speak the truth." Lord Jarrod nodded to Gilly. "You have stoutly defended your Tom and he has shown us that he is indeed innocent. I do not for a moment believe you would have hurt my father, Lady Saira-Gilly, but custom dictates that once a Telling Ceremony has begun, it must continue to its inevitable conclusion."

"I understand," Gilly said. "However, I wasn't present at Prince Keegan's murder and my knowledge of events of that night is from hearsay, and the same as Mayla's version."

"What I ask of you, my lady, is for you to recall events from your past. Those, too, are recorded in Falcon's Tome. Tell us what happened the night you hurt your leg."

Heat stole up her cheeks as everyone's attention swung toward her ugliness. Her left leg twitched. Of all the things she'd expected Jarrod to ask her to recite, she never imagined he'd pick on this.

"I have no memory of that event." People usually avoided looking at her injured limb, or pretended she did not limp, or talked about her presence slowing their progress but never come right out and ask for details about her gimpy leg.

Now he wanted her to talk about what caused her deformity? In front of everyone? Standing in the middle of the room, with all gazes aimed at her left leg, the silly thing began to shake. She self-consciously rubbed that hip, and then cringed as every gaze seemed drawn to the area.

"I have limped since I was a small child," she said, hating the tremor in her voice, left hand clenched.

"Tell us more." His tone was implacable.

A hand covered hers and small fingers broke into Gilly's tight fist to link with hers. Skye's smile was drenched with sympathy. Bevan butted in between them and covered their hands with his in silent support.

Gilly's throat clogged with grateful tears. She nodded to the children, took a deep breath and with its release, her resistance to this unpleasant chore dissipated. Closing her eyes, Gilly willed her mind to play back her past. She wove her way through her memories of pastoral life at Nadym. She had arrived there in the dark, terrified of being found by the Horsemen.

Further backward was the cottage in the woods where Mam brought her children in hopes of finding a safe haven. Except the Horsemen came there anyway. The time before the cottage was unclear. She recalled snatches. A picture of Mam insisting that her children call two strangers *Uncle* and *Auntie*. When Uncle threatened to turn them over to the Village Chief, Mam had taken them and run away.

Before that was hidden by wisps of danger and hints of betrayal. She did recall a dream of dancing with a man who laughed and hugged her and said she was his little princess. Too far back, that was *before* the fall.

Gilly snapped open her eyes as her memory flooded back and her body shook with the shock of that knowledge. Her injury was not the result of a careless accident. A terrible wrong had been done to her. To a child. A child no older than Skye. She gripped her niece and nephew's hands, determined to never allow these children to be so violated.

"Someone threw me down a dry well." She spoke with a fury that masked the terror of that moment. "Mam found me," she said, her voice trembling, "and kept me from dying, but my hip and leg had shattered when I hit the bottom." A fiery twinge raced up her leg and she cringed with remembered pain. "There was no time to fix me properly. Mam did enough to get me moving and then we fled."

The end of her tale brought a cold sweat that cooled her temper and solidified her resolve to protect her family at all costs. She hugged the children closer.

"Do you remember who threw you?" Lord Jarrod asked, his voice infinitely gentle now.

Gilly shook her head, and then suddenly, she did know. "He loved my mam and wanted her to love him back. When she said she never would, he held me out of her reach."

She recalled being lifted off her feet by hard ruthless hands, held up for a terrifying moment as Mam cried for mercy. Then the release. She was falling. Gilly shut her eyes at the horror of that memory. Arms circled and held her close in comfort while her body heaved with sobs for the cruelty of a man she'd once trusted.

When her tears subsided, Gilly realized it was Anna who rocked her and whispered soothing sounds.

"I'm all right, Anna." She wiped at her tears and knelt to hug Bevan tight and soothe the boy who was keening in distress. "I'm safe now." Leaning into his ear, she whispered, "Nothing like that will ever happen to you or your sister, I swear."

He quieted and leaned back to look at her. His bottom lip jutted out and he said, "Me, too!"

Gilly nodded with pride for the brave boy and then stood to face her sister. "I'm sorry I upset you and your children, Anna."

"Nothing for any of us to be sorry about," Anna said in a hard voice. "The only one who will be sorry, once I find out who did that to you, is the perpetrator."

Anna's powerful reaction was a surprise. She had witnessed her sister furious before, but her anger was usually directed at Gilly, never on her behalf. Anna's hand came to reverently rest on her Gilly's injured hip and warmth infused into her, spreading a glow of happiness and suddenly, surprisingly, her left leg no longer ached. She removed Anna's hand, afraid her sister was unconsciously using her healing magic.

"A most touching tale," Cullen said and faced Lord Jarrod, "but what do any of these stories have to do with Lord Aton's death?"

"It tells us neither Tomas the Brave, nor Lady Saira-Gilly, murdered my father, for they have spoken the truth." Jarrod sent Gilly a curiously intense glance and softly added, "The truth as they remember it." He then continued in a sad tone, "While Mayla has knowingly lied."

"Then by your logic, Lord Jarrod," Cullen said, "Mayla is the one who murdered your father. Since your ceremony has cleared our party of wrongdoing, are we free to leave Erov?" Cullen did a flip with his hands as if to signal this distasteful matter was finished.

Gilly's chest tightened in sympathy for poor Mayla, whom she was now convinced was as innocent as Tom. "We cannot leave yet. If Mayla killed Lord Aton, I'm certain she must have done it at another's instigation."

"What makes you say that?" Talus asked.

Cullen wore a long-suffering expression. "Why say such a preposterous thing?"

"Mayla had no reason to kill Lord Aton," Gilly said. "She had a wonderful future to look forward to. Lord Aton loved her like a daughter. Why would she harm him?"

"She was a raving madwoman earlier," Anna said. "Maybe she's lost her mind."

Gilly shook off Anna's support. Her sister could choose the most unhelpful moments to be brutally logical. "We should speak with her. Find out who forced her to act against her better judgment."

A scream rang out. Gilly shuddered. With that painful cry, the victim broadcast her anguish in the most amazing fashion. In her head, she clearly saw Mayla glance down at her chest where a dagger protruded. Everyone around Gilly rushed past but she remained transfixed by that haunting vision.

With a gasp, she picked up her skirts and limped out as fast as her halting gait would take her.

Chatter of concerned voices led her to Mayla's crowded chamber. At her insistence, people shifted aside until she could stand beside the girl sprawled on the floor. A dagger hilt stuck out of her midriff. Beside the still body, a pool of red seeped into the rug. Mayla's face was ashen and her eyes half open. In her stillness, she looked peaceful.

Gilly's heart shuddered with pity for this beautiful young woman whose life had been used and then discarded as if she did not matter.

"She appears to have stabbed herself," Talus said.

"She must have," Lord Jarrod said, shaking his head in disbelief. "The guards outside say no one else entered or left."

"Well, this ends the mystery," Cullen said, standing directly behind Gilly.

She was unconvinced. Just as they were about to question Mayla, she took her own life? Too easy.

Lord Jarrod ushered everyone out of the tent. "Let us leave Mayla's remains in peace, she has suffered enough." Some protested while others openly cried. Lord Jarrod was insistent and urged everyone to return to his or her quarters and pray for Mayla's safe journey into the Light.

Gilly's family and travel companions left for their quarters and the other Erovians departed the premises, their sorrow hovering like a cloud heavy with rain.

Gilly laid a gentle hand on Lord Jarrod's shoulder. "I'm so sorry. You have lost two people you loved in a short time and in such a violent manner. I have no adequate words of comfort."

"My father will always be with me in spirit. As for Mayla," he shook his head, "I do not understand her actions. My people are taught to value life, so her taking her own is more inexplicable than my father's murder. Why did she not come to me for help?"

"Are you sure she took her life?" Gilly glanced through the open tent flap at Mayla's still body.

"How do you mean?" Lord Jarrod asked.

His confusion made no sense to Gilly. "Do not all Erovians mind-speak? Share their thoughts? Before she died, she showed me the dagger used to stab her, but not how it got there. I hoped you might have seen more."

"You read her thoughts at her moment of death?" He glanced into the room and then at Gilly with a stunned expression.

"Didn't you?" she asked, confused. "It was so clear."

"My lady, Erovians can only share our thoughts when we pray and focus. The ceremony is long and takes a great deal of concentration. More significantly, that ability only works between Erovians. Are you saying you are able to see into our thoughts? Can you tell what I am thinking now?"

"No!" Gilly's cheeks flushed hot, as if she had been caught spying on someone's bedchamber.

"Are you able to see your family's thoughts, too? Your friends? Even strangers?"

She shook her head. "No, just Erovians, and only when you are thinking of me. Oh, that means Mayla must have been thinking of me the moment she died. Why? I was as far from her as you."

"Perhaps she was calling to you for help," Lord Jarrod said in a sorrowful tone. "Lady Saira-Gilly," he took her hands, "perhaps she was trying to warn you that danger stalks you, too. I understand your stay here has been unpleasant but I wish you would remain with us a little longer. You are safer inside Erov than outside it."

"I wish that, too, but convincing Anna to end her journey here will not be easy. I will ask her, Lord Jarrod."

"Call me Jarrod." He lightly squeezed her fingers. "I am not your lord. I hope I am your friend."

"Then I am Gilly," she said with a smile.

"Calling you Gilly, my lady," he said with a slight smile, "will be harder for me, than for you to call me Jarrod."

"I cannot imagine why. You, sir, are the Chief Councilor of Erov, while I am a goat herder who is terribly missing her goats."

"You, my lady, were born to save our world, while I was born merely to record your inspiring quest. I am more certain of that now than ever."

She shook her head at his fanciful words. "Jarrod, with expectations as unrealistic as that, I fear you may have been born merely to be disappointed."

His smile was indulgent as he released her.

She felt bereft of his touch. He had a comforting feel for such a young man. "I cannot believe your faith in me remains unshaken after the tragedy I brought to your father and Mayla."

"They have moved to another plane of Light." He glanced toward where Mayla lay and a shadow of grief passed over his face. When he again met her gaze, his sorrow was contained, replaced by resolve. "None of this is your fault."

Gilly was not so sure. Death seemed to stalk her and her family from Nadym to Erov. First Vyan had been murdered, then Aton, and now Mayla. Anna would be quick to point out that Tom had been with them the whole time. Staying in Erov with him would be akin to inviting the wolf into the fold. The idea of sending Tom away brought a pain to Gilly's chest, one as hurtful as the thought of saying goodbye to her family.

She firmly took a step away from Jarrod. "I suspect we shall leave at dawn. Though I fear the Horsemen will not be far behind us. They are likely to have caught up to us by now."

Jarrod's eyes lit with mischief. "I have a surprise."

"What is it?"

"Speak to your sister first and if she insists on leaving, then I shall tell you all on the morrow. Promise you will not go without seeing me first?"

"Of course, Jarrod."

"Good. Well, if this is to be your last day, I have preparations to make. While I am busy, will you do my people the honor of meeting with them?"

Gilly covered her hot cheeks with her cool palms. She simply didn't understand Jarrod or his people. After the trouble she'd brought them, however, the least she could do was grant his wish. "It would be my pleasure, Jarrod. May I bring Anna and her family along?"

"Please do, and the pleasure will be ours." Jarrod offered her an expansive bow before he bid her goodbye.

With a nod, Gilly hurried away. As she turned the corner, she gasped as sorrow as deep as a well overwhelmed her. She halted and slowly peeked back around to where she had left Jarrod.

He was staring into the tent where his bride-to-be lay. Finally, now everyone had left him, his tears flowed and his young shoulders shook with his silent cries. He took a step inside and the room's curtain closed behind him.

Gilly stood there in shock. *I can read an Erovian's emotions even when he is not thinking of me.*

Chapter 8

As Gilly and her family set out on their promised tour of Erov, she viewed the vast tent city and its inhabitants as a panorama of colors. The enclosures were constructed of bright blue, green and purple material. People wore clothing in shades of mainly gold or amber. Once they met a man dressed all in white. When questioned, their guide said that he was a city elder approaching ascension to merge with the Light.

Gilly took that to mean he was near death. For Light was not only the source of all magic, but where souls returned after death, to replenish the Light.

Every dark skinned Erovian they met was astonishingly friendly. The men shook arms with Marton and bowed to Anna, Gilly and the children. One young woman asked about Nadym's progress and details of its inhabitants as if she were intimately familiar with the village, yet Gilly who had lived in Nadym all of her adult life, had never met her. Wares were proudly displayed, from books and scrolls to fanciful writing implements and even toys. One vendor offered a curly, black-haired doll as a gift to Skye and a hand puppet for Bevan.

Most disconcerting of all, however, was their behavior toward Gilly. In whichever direction she turned, a path would open. People flung colorful scarves before her feet. Everyone, it seemed, wanted a chance to touch her. With each gentle brush, came a shower of emotions. A sense of joy, deep sadness, shudder of fear or a breathtaking burst of happiness. Most often, however, she sensed hope.

As if they expect me to save them from catastrophe. What could I possibly do, that Jarrod could not do better?

• • • •

AT SUNRISE THE NEXT day, with enough food packed in their bags to last a week, and all the herbal medicine Gilly could have wished for, a guide escorted her party to the outskirts of Erov. The desert stretched ahead as far as the eye could see. On their right rose the Makakala range. The tall tents behind them likely hid the copse of trees where they had camped when they first encountered Erov. A large crowd had come to see them off.

Marton adjusted Bevan and Skye on the white stallion's back while Talus and Cullen were beside their horses, checking equipment.

"Why have we not left yet?" Anna asked Gilly. "Marton says you asked him to delay our departure."

"We're waiting for Lord Jarrod." Gilly looked for the Chief Councilor's tall figure in the crowd.

Tom stood a little to her left, looking off in the opposite direction, toward the desert. He seemed worried. Probably wondering if he was strong enough to keep up on foot. The question bothered her as well but he was so proud, she dared not suggest he ride with the children.

Then she spotted Jarrod hurrying toward her carrying several objects. Happy to see him, she waved both her arms.

"He cannot miss you," Tom said in a quiet voice.

Gilly self-consciously dropped her arms.

"Thank the Light, you are still here." Jarrod arrived at her side and immediately dropped all but one book and a fancy quill. A scroll rolled over until it bumped against Tom's boots.

Gilly hid her grin as she and Tom bent to retrieve the Chief Councilor's fallen items. Their hands touched and a shiver ran up Gilly's arm. She dropped the scroll she had picked up and Tom scooped it up.

"I was looking everywhere for a map of Perm's streets and alleyways and another with some little used routes from Perm to Tibor," Jarrod said, and took a deep breath. "Then I couldn't find the record book I wanted to give you. I'm glad you didn't leave without saying goodbye, my lady. I mean Gilly."

"On friendlier terms now, are you?" Tom whispered in her ear before they stood.

"Thank you for going to so much trouble for us, Jarrod," Gilly said, with a bright smile that hid her confusion. *Is Tom jealous?* "The maps especially will be useful. What is this about a record book?"

Jarrod gave her the leather bound book and quill and taking the scrolls from Tom, he led her aside. The quill was brown with gray markings. From a desert bird?

"Do you write, Gilly?" Jarrod asked once out of earshot.

"Mam taught me. She felt it was an important lesson for all her children to master." Her elder sister and young brother had not lived long enough to put that talent to good use. The reminder dropped a dollop of sorrow into this bright new day.

"Your mam was a wise woman. I would like you to use this book to record all that passes on your upcoming journey."

"I will diligently record our adventure to Tibor, Jarrod. I promise."

"Thank you. I give you these gifts for another reason. If at any time you need my aid, write my name in the book with that quill and I will know."

Gilly stared at him in silence. This was his first solid admission that he practiced magic.

The Chief Councilor of Erov returned her unspoken question with a bland look.

"I am honored that you trust me," she said.

"You are the Defender of the Light. Who else would I trust in these dangerous times?"

Gilly's attention perked. He had called her that once before, at the start of the Truth Telling Ceremony. Pieces of a puzzle began to fit into place. Could he and his people believe she was the defender of magic in Ryca?

Jarrod tucked one of the scrolls under his arms and unrolled the other. He indicated where Erov was now located and Gilly caught her breath in shock. This city was leagues north of where they had last camped. This must be his surprise. If so, Erov truly was a magical wandering city!

By whisking them leagues from where the Horsemen might be searching for them, he had literally saved their lives. "Thank you, Jarrod."

He nodded and then accompanied her back to her friends and spread the map on the floor for them to study.

Cullen was the first to speak. "We should travel down this pathway," he said, pointing with confidence to the southern border of the desert. "Then if we go due north, in a day shy of a sennight, we will be at Perm's gates."

Gilly and Jarrod shared a private glance and she shivered at what they must now reveal. Swallowing past a throat swollen, with trepidation she pointed a forefinger far to the north of where Cullen said was their starting point. "We are currently here, at the northern edge of the Kocheya basin. So this route will take us to Perm in two days."

"That's correct," Jarrod said.

"That's impossible," Cullen said.

Gilly insisted he must be mistaken about how far he'd traveled before joining them. Surprisingly, Anna backed her up. Marton gave Anna a worried look but receiving her firm nod, he sided with his wife.

Talus shrugged. "I had not been keeping careful track of my movements." A slight twitch of his lips suggested the astute King's Warrior was well aware magic might be at play here but chose to give it a pass. Why?

Whatever his motivation, Gilly breathed a sigh of relief at that monumental favor. She was starting to like Talus more every day. Tom had been unconscious during their trip to Erov, so he could offer no corroboration to Cullen.

Alone in his dissension, Cullen finally gave in. Talus offered to ride ahead to find a camping spot for them for the coming night. He asked Cullen along, saying, "Two heads are obviously better than one at gauging distances."

The minstrel seemed reluctant to split off, but finally agreed and the two men rode off.

Gilly breathed a sigh of relief to be left alone with her family and Tom. They waved goodbye to the observing Erovians and set off to cheers of well wishes.

Before they left, Jarrod held Gilly back and then as Tom reluctantly left her side to follow her family, the Chief Councilor of Erov gave her an unexpected goodbye hug. "Stay safe, Gilly."

Touched by his concern, she tentatively hugged him back and received a strange sensation, as if she were embracing a hot desert wind. Light whirled about her, a whirlwind of magical energy that enveloped her as if welcoming home an old friend. Then he was solid again in her arms. She blinked in surprise. Had the ethereal moment been real?

Then she became lost in an entirely different sensation of being held tight by someone who genuinely cared about her. For a goat herder who had lived alone most of her life, having lost all but one family member, and then having her sister despise her, this physical closeness was an extraordinary experience.

Tears sprang to Gilly's eyes as memories returned of a time when hugs were an everyday occurrence. Hugs from her father and mother, from her brother and sister, and even from friends and servants. *I had servants?* Her cheeks flushed hot with remembered joy, followed by a sense of profound loss.

"Thank you," she whispered and gently pulled away. Wiping away her tears, she turned and ran to catch up with her party. In no time, she was huffing, and her left leg was protesting. When she reached Tom, she stopped. At least her run gave her an excuse for her flushed cheeks. Marton and Anna were a few steps further ahead with the stallion carrying the children.

Tom did not acknowledge her arrival. His coldness was back, restoring her racing thoughts and emotions to a calm normalcy. This estrangement with Tom, from everyone, she understood. This was her life. Her pulse slowed and she glanced down with saddened resignation.

"Maybe you should have stayed with Lord Jarrod," Tom said, in a hard tone. "Since leaving him makes you sad."

Gilly did not know how to answer so she let silence intrude like a wall between them. Though words were lost to her, her emotions refused to be still. A gaping hole grew inside her with each step she took away from Erov and Jarrod. She quietly acknowledged that leaving the kind, funny and gentle Chief Councilor of Erov was indeed hard, but staying in Erov would not assist her goal to keep Anna and her family safe. She glanced sideways at Tom and admitted that harder still was the idea of leaving Tom, despite his bad mood since his recovery.

She took a deep breath and released it slowly as a new startling realization settled. As much as she wanted to protect her family, Gilly also did not wish to be parted from Tom.

How long had she had this attachment for this man? She had known him most of her life but they had hardly conversed. Yet, when he was in danger in Nadym, she refused to leave without rescuing him. At every turn, she had acted to protect him as fiercely as she would Anna and the children and Marton. It was as if her fondness for Tom had snuck up on her, unaware. Did she truly know him?

The Truth Telling Ceremony had revealed that he was not the village drunkard Anna labeled him, or even the beaten up dairy farmer Gilly stitched up in Nadym. Tom had been present when Prince Keegan was killed.

Most astonishing of all, in all likelihood he was the son of a King's Warrior, one groomed to become a King's Bodyguard.

Talus, too, must have noted that possibility, for before he left, he had looked Tom eye-to-eye and seemed to stand a little taller, as if he were in the presence of an equal or better.

Tom had looked away first, and Gilly had spotted shame. She wanted to tell him the prince's death was not his fault. Young Tomas the Brave had been prey to a spell. How could she do that without admitting to knowing how spells worked? After hiding her true self for decades, words to explain who she was clogged her throat.

The material around her neck was suddenly tight and she absently adjusted it. On advice from their Erovian guide, they all wore thin see-through cloths about their necks for use when the wind picked up. Even the stallion had a see-through cloth wrapped around his head to protect eyes and nose. An hour into their journey, she was grateful for that forethought as sand swirled, stirring a fine layer of dust.

Marton ordered the children to make use of their neck cloths. Gilly's eyes were a little sore from the attack two nights ago, so she, too, slipped on her mask.

Two hours into their trek, Gilly's left hip was aching and each lift of her foot off the shifting sands took more effort than the previous. Thoughts of rubbing a soothing ointment on her aching limb come nightfall kept her trudging onward.

If she were having this much trouble, Tom must be in agony. "Do you need me to attend to any of your wounds?" she asked, finally finding her voice. "Has any sand worked its way under a dressing?"

"I'm fine." He slowed his pace so that within three strides, he was behind her, a lone sentinel at her back.

Gilly's heart squeezed with pain at that rejection. She quickened her steps until she was beside Anna.

Marton pointed to a lone bush where two branches were bent side by side. "Talus's mark."

A comforting sight that signaled they were on the right path in this vast barren landscape.

Once the wind died, Marton lowered his mask and entertained his children with stories about their destination, Perm.

Situated at a crossroads and nestled into a mountain, Perm was located at the northwestern edge of the Makakala Range and noted for being a hive of activity during the summer trading season. On any given day, hundreds of mud-splattered merchants' tents flanked the city's walls. Perm was also reputed to be the home of the Rycan Warriors.

"Are they like King's Warriors, Papa?" Bevan asked.

"Like Talus?" Skye asked. "Do they wear chainmaille and carry swords, too?"

Marton gave his children a fond smile. "Rycan Warriors are nothing like King's Warriors. In fact, if we cross their path, Talus is likely to lop off their heads."

"Marton," Anna said in a warning tone.

"Oooh," Bevan said. "I want to do that, too."

"That's barbaric," Skye said. "And wrong. Isn't it, Mama?"

"Yes, it is, Skye," Anna said, with an approving nod.

"It would be better to put a spell on them," the young girl said, "so they're so weak they can't lift their swords to strike."

"Skye." Anna gave Gilly a worried glance. "Where did you learn about magic?"

Gilly glanced down, thinking about that string she had tied around the children's ankles.

Bevan made a face at Skye and then swung his right arm in an arc. "Better to lop off their heads."

"No heads need fall," Marton broke in. "These Rycan Warriors aren't looking for a fight, they're searching for the true rulers of Ryca."

"The princess and her children that Lord Jarrod spoke about?" Skye asked.

"Yes," her father said. "They've ridden the range from one end to the other searching for Prince Keegan's offspring."

"How will they recognize them, Papa?" Skye asked.

"Legend says a child marked by her father's death will carry on her person the secret of the true rulers of Ryca."

"What mark?" Bevan dropped his arm and stared at his father with wide fascinated eyes.

"No one knows. The Rycan Warriors have no fondness for the King's Warriors, whom they insist betray the royal line they are sworn to protect by safeguarding King Ywen."

"Will Talus be in trouble in Perm?" Skye asked with a concerned frown.

"Talus can take care of himself," her papa said with assurance.

That quieted the children.

As the day wore on, the barren landscape gave way to low shrubs and grasses and the ground grew firmer. Plants blooming in rich summer shades and releasing enticing scents became more frequent.

At the hottest part of the day, they stopped for a light meal, to feed and water the horse and take a much needed rest. Two hours later, they were back on the trail.

Close to sunset, Marton waved to two approaching men. Talus and Cullen greeted them outside a copse of trees forming an oasis. Talus took hold of the stallion and went with the children to rub him down while Cullen brought Marton and Tom up to date on what he and Talus had discovered on their scouting trip. Anna and Gilly went to investigate the campsite.

Two rabbits and a wood pigeon were roasting on a spit over a blazing campfire attesting to the fact their scouts had arrived here in time to do some hunting. Gilly and Anna soon had a pot of boiled cabbage started to accompany the meat. Gilly seasoned the food with salt, sorrel leaves, mint and rosemary. Marton joined them and unpacked Erovian dark bread and a large leather flask of ale.

They set to their meal with gusto, discussing what to expect come morning. Talus estimated they should reach the outskirts of Perm by nightfall the next day. He advised them it would be best to keep going until they reached the city wall.

After eating her fill, Gilly inched closer to the fire and took out the book Jarrod had given her. Since the Chief Counselor hadn't supplied her with ink, she suspected the quill was likely to work all by itself. Such work, however, would prove too damning in front of Cullen.

As it was, the man's keen interest in her activity matched Tom's glare at her book. She ignored everyone and made a show of mixing ash and water to use in place of ink.

"I didn't realize you could write, Gilly," Cullen said. "My pardon. Should I call you Lady Saira-Gilly?"

A shiver of dread crept up Gilly's neck. "They had some strange customs in Erov, didn't they?" she said. "You may call me anything you like, Cullen."

"Names are important. They define who we are."

She looked directly at him. "Is your name truly Cullen?"

At her question, the air wavered about his face. He suddenly seemed familiar. From where? Then the feeling slipped away and the same old Cullen displayed his charming smile. Her eyes were smarting as if another desert wind had been stirred up. She blinked as tears formed to soothe her irritated eyes. She cleaned her quill and put it away.

"Cullen, you didn't answer Gilly," Anna said.

She hadn't realized that her sister was following their conversation. Anna was leaning against Marton. Bevan was fast asleep on her lap, with Skye nearby, eyes droopy. Her sister was right, though, Cullen hadn't answered her. Strange that she hadn't noticed.

"Of course my name is Cullen. If you're looking to place a more fanciful appellation on me, we should have checked with the good Lord Jarrod and his Falcon's Tome."

Marton stood then with his son in his arms and extended a hand to his wife. Once on their feet, her family said their good nights. Tom said he needed to stretch his legs and went for a walk. Gilly was watching his retreating figure when Talus offered to take first watch.

She nodded absently and then realized she was about to be left alone in the campsite with only Cullen for company. She put her book and quill away and excused herself. Something about the minstrel unnerved her. Must be his dislike of magic.

She made her way toward the stream. Time for that leg rub before she lay down for the night, else her limb would be stiff as a board by morning.

With moonlight to guide her pathway, she aimed for the sound of trickling water. The stream ended up being far enough from their camp to offer privacy, so she dropped her sack on the bank, tied her skirts up and waded in until she was knee-deep. After the scorching heat of the day, the water was blessedly cool.

Once invigoratingly clean, she sloshed back to shore, well pleased with her day. Her eyes were still sore, so she rummaged in her sack for her packet of sage. Then she mixed in a pinch of dried sage with a handful of water and after straining the leaves out, used the sage-infused water to dab at her sore eyelids. That vastly eased the ache and with a heartfelt sigh, she leaned against a tree to tend to her leg.

A quick check confirmed she was alone by the stream, so she hiked up her skirt and rubbed ointment the Erovian healer had given her on her left leg. Working the salve into her skin loosened her tight muscles at her left hip and thigh. The burning sensation she'd lived with all day eased out of her limb.

"Must feel good," a voice said from beside her.

Gilly jumped in fright. Pulling her skirts down, she twisted to see who had crept up. She had an alarming suspicion that it might be Cullen.

It wasn't.

Under the moonlight, the serious eyes that briefly met her startled gaze were the dark delightful brown of Perm's mountainside. She swallowed as an entirely different kind of alarm jangled her nerves. "Tom, I didn't realize you were nearby." *How long were you watching me?*

"You seemed lost in your enjoyment, I didn't want to disturb you." He looked off into the distance.

Had he seen her deformed leg? Gilly focused on the twinkling stream. If he didn't leave soon, she would embarrass herself and cry.

"You didn't finish." His glance met hers again.

She looked away. "Finished enough."

"We have a long steep climb ahead of us tomorrow to reach Perm, which is situated halfway up a mountain. Your legs will need to be at their best to keep up."

"I'll be fine."

He came around in front of her and squatting, he picked up the pouch of ointment. He smelled it and then made a face at its stringent medicinal odor.

She grinned, her tense shoulders relaxing. When she reached for the ointment, he held it away and smeared some onto his fingers.

"What are you doing?" she asked, alarm bells ringing again.

"Seems only fair." He sat cross-legged three feet before her and moved her left foot onto his lap. "You took care of me when I was ill. Time I returned the favor."

She slapped his hand when he pushed her skirts upward. "That's unnecessary. I'm not ill. Let go of my foot."

"You'll hurt yourself if you twist like that. Sit back and relax. Will you trust me?"

The question sounded heartfelt but the mischievous look on his face made her think he'd be the last man on Ryca she should trust right at this moment. Other than tussling with him, what choice did she have when he refused to release his hold? She leaned against the tree and folded her arms across her tight throbbing chest.

If he felt the need to return a favor, she could allow him to rub her foot. It wasn't as if she disliked people touching her. Just this morning she had allowed Jarrod to hold her.

At the first caress of his strong, callused fingers sliding under her foot, pleasure raced up her nerves like a bolt of lightning. While Jarrod's touch had been comforting, Tom's was electrifying. Then he moved onto her ankle and she was ready to bolt for the campsite. His free hand on her right knee held her firmly in place.

"I never had a chance to say," Tom said in his soft seductive voice, "how much I appreciated you tending me at my every waking moment."

His tone suggested that thanking her wasn't on his mind. Gilly's heartbeat sped up like a salmon racing upstream. His touch on her flesh evoked feelings she couldn't place as fear, discomfort or excitement.

He began to massage her calf with both hands now, as he continued his litany of her apparent misdemeanors. "You changed my clothes, dressed my wounds. You tenderly massaged ointment into my back. You washed me from head to foot, not missing a single part." His gaze locked on hers and her cheeks blushed hot and suddenly she was unclear if her touch had been all that innocent. She had enjoyed taking care of him. Had she slowed her movement more than she should have? Relished caressing him instead of impersonally cleaning him?

His eyes were drenched with purpose and was that desire? *For me?* His longing, if that's what that intense look was, at once enticed and confused. Then his fingers gently skimmed the underside of her knee and heat shot up to her hip. Shocked by the wildly inappropriate sensations churning in her body, she instinctively kicked out with her good leg and sent Tom sprawling to the ground.

She jumped up, mortified and upset. "Oh, I'm so sorry! Did I hurt you?"

She knelt beside him and turned him over. At the smile on his face, she scrambled backward. He was fine! *The fiend!*

She gathered her belongings, dropping them as often as she kept items in her flimsy grip. "Thank you. I'm done now. Anna is probably looking for me. I'll see you in the morning."

He lay on the ground with arms outstretched, a slight smile on his face, watching her.

Having finally gathered all her bits and pieces, she hurried away toward the campsite.

"Good night," Tom called out.

"Good night," she replied not turning around, but with every lopsided step, she was acutely aware of him following her cowardly retreat. All the while, an oddly pleasurable tingle played along her leg where he had caressed her. As well, an alarming yet titillating thought kept pace with her. Could it be that while she tended Tom, as he lay injured, despite the pain he was in, she had churned this conflagration of pleasurable emotions in him?

Surprisingly, the idea made her want to grin and added a cheerful spring to her step.

Chapter 9

The next morning's trek took Gilly's party closer to the foothills of the Makakala Range. Each new hour brought dramatic changes to the terrain. The undergrowth became denser. The trickling stream they had camped beside now gushed past, flowing down from the mountains ahead.

In the distance, those white-tipped summits loomed like the folds of a giant rumpled carpet. Perm was built halfway up one of those tough rocky ridges. As if to herald their approach to that popular trading city, more and more travelers converged onto the road from various side paths.

With each step, Gilly's stomach knotted tighter at getting closer to a city where the King's Horsemen would be prevalent. This time, instead of riding off ahead, Talus and Cullen walked their horses in front of Gilly's party. Then rhythmic pounding of horses' hooves sent her pulse careening as a battalion of green-cloaked King's Horsemen trotted toward them, with helmets glinting in the sunlight. Her worst nightmare had come to life.

"Ho!" Talus called out.

The captain of the guard raised a hand and drew his men to a halt. "Welcome, Warrior." The captain's gaze slid from one member of her party to the next, as if he were memorizing their faces and demeanor.

He wasn't the one-eyed captain from Nadym, but her relief was short-lived. One-Eye could have sent word that a family wanted for questioning was traveling this way. Was that the reason for his scrutiny? Was he on the lookout for a stolen white horse?

Bevan leaned forward on the back of his dung-colored mount and held out his hand for the captain's horse to snuffle.

Gilly watched with mounting horror, and then Skye pulled Bevan back and hugged him. Profound relief flooded through her.

"These people are under your protection, sir?" the Captain asked.

Talus nodded. "We're heading for Perm, on our way to Tibor. Trouble ahead?"

"Had a few skirmishes with the Rycan Warriors, but their numbers are down. Were you at the Makakala War, sir?"

Talus nodded and gave his name. "I'm taking a lazy route home, now the war's broken. You're on patrol?"

"We are ever vigilant, sir. Our garrison is inside the city. You can report anything suspicious to us there." The captain raised his palm in a sign of peace before riding off with his men. Their hoofbeats faded into the distance, and Gilly realized that her every muscle had seized in fright. She relaxed her fists and almost collapsed when her weak leg buckled.

Tom steadied her. Until then, Gilly hadn't noticed that he'd moved closer, shielding her from the Horsemen.

"Thank you," she whispered, touched by his protective stance. On impulse, she brushed his hand in appreciation.

He gave her a startled glance, as if she had signaled an important change between them. Had she?

Embarrassed, she withdrew, but he wove his fingers through hers. A possessive gesture that left her breathless with wanting. "I will never allow any harm to come to you again, Saira," he said. "You have my word."

She shuddered with shock at that solemn vow. At his use of her given name, *Saira*.

She played back their rare conversations and realized that Tom had never called her Gilly. Not once. As if he had always known that "Gilly" was not her real name. How? He didn't know her secret. Did he?

Fear scurried up her back and she attempted to pull away but his grip tightened. After a moment of nervous contemplation, she accepted his hold but remained deeply unsettled.

How much does he know about me? In all these years, while I watched Anna so carefully, was someone watching me?

Those uneasy questions kept her company for the rest of the morning as wagons rumbled by on wooden wheels rimmed with iron stakes. For extra support while going up the mountain? She wanted a bit of support herself, but while Tom's hold was comforting, it was now also a little alarming.

By mid-day, road congestion grew heavy, and Marton called a halt. They rested on a patch of open ground to eat their meal and watch the traffic. Compared to the desert's silence, this was like being in an echo chamber as people chattered, donkeys brayed, cows mooed and chickens clucked.

Anna asked, "How long will we stay in Perm?"

"Half a day should be enough to replenish our dwindling supplies," Gilly said. As far as she was concerned, the sooner they departed this King's Horsemen stronghold, the better.

"I hoped to see a bit of this fabled city," Anna said.

"There's also coin to be made at such a plump purse." Cullen rubbed two fingers and thumb. "Won't need long. A week should suffice."

"A week?" Gilly's voice came out high-pitched with panic but she didn't care. In a week, that one-eyed captain who whipped Tom could catch up to them.

Marton gave her a cautious glance that said he understood her concern. "We can spare two days."

Gilly did a quick calculation on the lead Erov's magical travel had given them. She wasn't happy with the result, but nodded. Two days was better than a week.

"That also suits me," Talus said. "It's adequate time to visit with the King's Warrior encampment in Perm."

Once Tom agreed, Cullen, likely sensing his companions might go on without him, shrugged his reluctant consent. "I'll come, too. Safer traveling long distances in a group than alone."

They returned to their trek toward Perm.

"I'll keep an eye on Anna and the children while we're in the city." Tom's rusty brown gaze was steady on Gilly's, as if inviting her to rely on him.

Wanting to show that she did believe in him, she boldly wove her fingers through his.

His smile grew so bright it rivaled the white-tipped Makakala range. He stood a little taller, and a warm flush of happiness infused her, pushing her worries into forgotten crevices.

The rest of the afternoon was uneventful, which gave Gilly time to think of her future. Something she had not done in a long while. Since her escape from the cottage with baby Anna in her arms, Gilly's sole purpose had been to keep her sister safe, and then to watch over Anna's children, too. Now she contemplated a future in which Tom might play a prominent role.

Her previous worry immediately surfaced. How had he guessed at her real name? The only rational explanation was that he had taken it out of what Aton and Jarrod called her, Lady Saira-Gilly. Since Erovians claimed to be

Perm's record keepers, perhaps Tom placed credence on how they addressed Gilly. Before she could confirm his accurate guess, she must first tell her sister. Anna deserved the truth. Her sister would rage at such a disclosure, and her fury would be justified.

Surely, facing her sister's anger wouldn't be any harder to bear than what she had already suffered? For decades Anna had scoffed at Gilly, ridiculed her, and worst of all, ignored her. The result? Gilly had lived in a state of never-ending loneliness.

Until this past week.

After years of being disregarded, Anna's recent thaw felt precious. Losing their new closeness was unthinkable. Gilly hugged her midriff with her free arm and blinked away her tears.

Yet, this had to be done, and not only so she could grow closer to Tom. For, while Anna repeatedly refused to heed advice about the king's evil intentions from a woman she considered no more than a cowardly servant, there was a slim chance she might heed her sister's warning.

That breath of optimism kept Gilly company until they arrived in Perm. As it was twilight, the gates were locked. Gilly glanced up at the tall gray stone wall. High above, crossbow-armed men patrolled, while below, layers of dull colored tents surrounded the fortress like a many-layered skirt.

"Why is everyone living out here?" Skye asked.

"Space inside is reserved for Perm's permanent populace," Talus said. "Marton, will you guard the women and children while Tom, Cullen and I scout for a suitable place to set up Lord Jarrod's tent?" He hefted the sealed bag over his shoulder. "We might be awhile."

Marton nodded.

Gilly watched the men leave, her worries returning in a rush now Tom no longer held her hand.

While Marton tied the horses to a post and checked on his children, Anna pointed to a bench. "Let's sit over there. My feet are killing me, so yours must be sore, too."

Gilly nodded, glad for a chance to rest.

"Are you excited to see the city?" Anna asked, adjusting her skirt.

"Yes," Gilly rubbed her throbbing left thigh, "but I don't like being this close to a King's Horseman's garrison."

"They won't notice us if we act like every other stranger who has come to visit Perm's markets. We'll be safer inside this city than in Tibor."

Anna held up her hand before Gilly could plunge into her opinion about the daft plan to go to the king's city. "Yes, we're still going, Gilly. Our feud has to end. Which won't happen until we show His Majesty my family and I are no longer a threat. I'm more certain of that now than ever. Also, we cannot keep hiding from the Horsemen for the rest of our lives. They're a part of Ryca and we must find a way to make peace with them, too."

Gilly's chest tightened with each word. *Tell her!* "Anna, I need to confess something."

At the same moment, Anna said, "What I'd rather discuss is why you were holding Tom's hand all day?"

Gilly was horrified that Anna had noticed that gesture, while Anna frowned at her as if with concern.

"It meant nothing," Gilly said, her cheeks warm.

"It's none of my business, of course," Anna began and then gave her a cautious glance, "but since we've been on the run, you've become almost a part of my family."

The admission was hauntingly touching, and vastly shocking.

"Marton commented on it, too," Anna continued. "He's happy because he likes Tom, but Tom's not right for you."

That set Gilly back, and instead of hotly denying there was anything for Marton to be happy about, what came out instead was, "Why not?"

"He's not good enough."

Gilly's racing thoughts screeched to a halt. "He was training to be a King's Bodyguard!"

"Whatever he was training to be, he's now a drunkard."

"He hasn't touched a drop since we left Nadym."

"Only because he hasn't had access. Now we're in Perm, let's see how long he stays away from an alehouse. Also, even if he was proven innocent in Erov, he could still be responsible for killing Vyan in Nadym."

"He is not!" Gilly said in a fierce whisper. She could not picture Tom killing anyone.

Skye ran over then. "Mama, Papa says I'm not to disturb you and Gilly, but I want to know what you're talking about." She squeezed herself between Gilly and her mother.

Marton strolled over with Bevan asleep on his shoulder. "Sorry, Anna, tried to keep her away."

"But she's willful," Anna finished in mock anger and tucked a lock of her daughter's hair behind her ear. However, she looked as relieved as Gilly felt about the interruption, for they had been on the verge of another fight. Her sister could be so trying. If she didn't know better, she'd almost think Anna was jealous of her growing closeness with Tom.

Which was ridiculous. Or was it? Anna was territorial. Evidence, her objection to Skye becoming fond of Gilly. *For Anna to feel possessive of me, she would have to really mean what she said earlier, about considering me part of her family.*

"Mama," Skye snuggled closer to Gilly, wrapping a slim arm around her midriff, "now you know her better, do you love her, too?"

Gilly held her breath as her gaze locked with Anna's. Her sister's answer meant more than she would ever realize.

Finally, Anna said, "I'm working on it, Skye."

Gilly's breath eased out of her tight chest and she broke eye contact before Anna noticed her mist up. She hugged Skye to hide her distraught face.

Cullen returned then. "We've found an open spot. Talus and Tom are setting up." He fetched his horse. "This way."

Anna stood. "We can finish this conversation later."

"Tomorrow." Gilly planned to discuss something more personal than Tom's innocence.

They arrived at their camping spot to find it surrounded by a crowd commenting about their tent. No wonder. Even at dusk, the bright sky-blue tent was unmistakable beside its darker muddier companions. Gilly's cheeks grew hot with mortification.

"Better than getting rained on, I suppose." Talus tied the last string in place and grinned at Tom as he stood up. He playfully shoved his new friend's shoulder. "We'll have to buy our neighbors a few ales to quiet their laughter, eh Tom."

Anna sent Gilly a knowing glance that she ignored and stepped into the tent, fingers crossed it wouldn't be bigger insider than out. It was a perfectly ordinary tent, if bright colored. She released a big sigh of relief. That would have been truly hard to explain away to Cullen's inquisitive mind.

After a light meal, she went outside to place a few discreet spells but Cullen was at her heels. "After that climb, I'll sleep soundly tonight," he said, stretching his arms wide.

With her spell stones biting at her skin within her tightly clenched fists, Gilly nodded without replying.

"Erov was a strange place, huh?" he said. "Did you get the feeling they practiced magic?"

"Magic is forbidden." Gilly's rising tension matched her spell's rhythmic vibration.

"Indeed, it is," Cullen said, "but it doesn't seem to stop foolish people from playing with fire."

Gilly gave up on her plan to place a few protection spells around the tent. If the minstrel followed her every step, using magic was out of the question. "I think you're right."

He gave her a startled look. "About what?"

"I'm tired, too. Good night."

She stepped inside. Unfortunately, Cullen followed her in there, too, tracking her progress to her pack laid beside Anna. Unease crawled up her back. Her fingers tingled as the unspent magical energy of her stones sparked.

She settled down and laid her head on her pack, discreetly tucking her stones out of sight. Where her spells were absent, the men in their company would have to guard them. That worry, however, did not keep her eyelids from closing. Bone tired, she lost track of murmurs around her as darkness swept in.

She awoke with a gasp from a terrifying dream, her heart thudding against her chest. Dawn had barely broken and the tent was still fairly dark. Everyone was asleep. She took her pack and tiptoed outside and then started at finding Marton there. He nodded to her. She breathed in relief. She must still be jumpy from her dream. "I can take over after I wash up."

"Not necessary. I just took watch from Tom."

She nodded and made her way toward a nearby stream flowing down the mountainside. The water was blessedly cool on her hot cheeks. While her dream had begun joyfully, with her walking around Perm hand-in-hand with Tom, it soon turned nasty with people pointing and laughing at her lopsided gait. Then green-cloaked Horsemen careened around a corner shouting for Tom, accusing him of Vyan's murder. She had woken up as they tore him from her embrace.

As the morning rays lightened the day, she realized her dream had been a mishmash of recent events and conversations. The part that was most difficult to shake off was her limp, for it was very real and mirrored a fear she had lived with since she was old enough to crave a man's touch.

In Nadym, she had not minded her deformity. *Much.* After all, everyone in the village knew her and had seen her irregular walk most of her life. In Erov, they had treated her like royalty. Even if she didn't deserve such attention, she had felt cherished and honored.

The visit to Erov, however, had also revealed another fact. Tom belonged in Tibor, at the palace, among men like Talus. Not with a lame goat herder who was too afraid to use her real name. She now viewed their growing closeness with unkind shameful eyes.

She could picture Tom in Tibor, being strong enough in body and mind to reclaim his role as King's Bodyguard. Perhaps even pick a courtier as his wife. While the only place she saw herself belonging was in a village like Nadym, with her goats. She had been perfectly content with that lonely life once. She could be again after she convinced Anna to forget about Tibor. As long as she was with her sister, she could be happy anywhere but in Tibor.

Bells began ringing as she left the stream. A clarion call to announce the opening of the city gates.

Determined to stay put this day, Gilly had thought up a more reasonable excuse to avoid going into Perm with Tom. She arrived at their tent in time to see Talus wave goodbye. Tom smiled a warm welcome from the fire where their breakfast was cooking and offered her a spot beside him.

Gilly, mindful of her intention to keep her distance from him, sat beside Anna.

Her sister gave her a nod of approval while Tom's shoulders stiffened and his bright smile dimmed.

"Where are the children?" Gilly leaned past Anna to look inside the pinned-up blue tent flap.

"Off making friends," Anna said.

"Cullen's offered to escort us to the marketplace," Marton said. "He says they have all manner of entertainment."

"I'm going to stay here," Gilly said in a firm tone. "To guard our belongings."

Tom looked crestfallen and Gilly died a little inside.

Anna's approval vanished, replaced by a thunderous frown that said an argument was imminent. Luckily, just then, Skye and Bevan ran over with a crowd of children.

"Mama," Skye said, "this boy says I lied and I didn't."

Anna turned to the group. A boy about her daughter's age looked belligerent. His fists resting on his hips dared her to contradict him.

"What do you believe she lied about?" Anna asked.

"She said she came from Erov," the boy replied. "That's a lie. Erov is a legend. It doesn't exist. My ma said so."

Before anyone could respond, Cullen spoke up. "That's exactly where we've been. You can tell your mother Cullen the Minstrel said so."

The boy's jaw dropped and his eyes lit up. "You're a minstrel? A real one? Will you tell us a story, sir?"

"I might." Cullen was at his best, all smiles and gracious gentleman. "If you're good and your parents wish to pay for the pleasure. I'll be in the market, come find me."

The boy turned to Skye with more respect in his eyes. Belonging to the party of a minstrel had raised her status. "I'm going to ask my ma if we can go for a telling." He was off at a run, and the other children scattered, suggesting Cullen's corner of the marketplace was about to become popular.

Anna took a hold of Skye and Bevan before they ran off.

"Do you think that was wise?" Gilly asked Cullen. "Admitting we were at Erov?"

"Why not?" Cullen said with a smirk. "We have nothing to hide, do we, *Lady Saira-Gilly*?"

"What Gilly probably meant," Marton said, "is that we want to go to Tibor, not be the center of attraction at Perm."

Bless the Light for sensible Marton.

"Our tent's color destroyed any hope of being inconspicuous," Cullen said. "Besides, sharing this kind of delicious news is part of how I make my living. Right now, it's the best story in my arsenal."

Anna bent to speak with her children. "Your papa will take you into the market. You are to stay with him no matter how tempting anything seems. No straying. Understood?"

"Yes, Mama." Skye took her brother's hand as if she never meant to let go.

"You're not coming with us, Anna?" Now Marton appeared as despondent as Tom.

"I'll meet you there soon." Anna kissed him goodbye. "I want to speak with Gilly first."

Tom came around the fire and knelt on one knee beside Gilly. "Are you sure you won't come with us?"

"I'm looking forward to resting a little this morning, Tom. It was a long hike to get here."

"Would you like me to stay with you?"

"That won't be necessary," Anna said. "Because Gilly will be coming with me."

"No, she won't. I mean I won't. I don't need company either. I had a restless night so I'll probably sleep most of the time." She added in an undertone to Tom, "You promised me you would keep an eye on Anna and the children."

He gave her a reproachful glance, but then relented and joined Cullen, Marton and the children.

Gilly watched them walk away with bittersweet relief.

Her sister's threat of a talk boded ill so Gilly went inside their tent and took out the journal and quill Jarrod had given her. The excuse of recording recent events would be a great way to look busy.

Anna spoke to someone outside before she followed Gilly. "I've been asked to speak about Erov."

That brought Gilly's nose out of her book in short order. "Anna, despite what Cullen said, we should hide our knowledge of Erov. Especially with Horsemen nearby."

Her sister's face took on its customary stubborn cast. "You're a great one for hiding, aren't you?" Anna's narrow-eyed glare said they were no longer talking about Erov.

Gilly had been waiting for this moment. Lying was no longer an option. *Tell her who you are.*

Her throat constricted, her pulse sped up and her breath became trapped in her chest. The silence stretched like a vibrating cord. *Anna, I'm your sister.* So clear in her head but not a whisper slipped passed her lips.

Gilly looked away first, her defeated gaze falling to the words she had written. They were lines without meaning, a hazy scribble, as silent as her confession.

"One day, you'll have to give up your secrets," Anna said.

Ashamed of her cowardice but unable to do anything about it, Gilly did not reply.

"Unlike you, I'm not ashamed of who I am, or what I look like, or how I walk." With a swish of her skirt, her sister swung around and left.

Gilly glanced up at her scraping movement, and with astonishment observed her sister's left hip rise unnaturally high and then fall in a circular motion as Anna limped outside. It was a fine imitation. Anna had done this before, in Nadym, when she made fun of Gilly. Then, her unkindness had hurt enormously.

Today, a smile spread Gilly's lips at her sister's antics, for Anna was provoking her into facing up to her insecurities. Her heart swelled with love for her little sister.

A tear of pure joy slid down her cheek and splashed across a blank space on her open journal and beaded. If she tried to wipe it away, she would make a worse mess. With a defeated sigh, she waited for the wetness to spread and smudge nearby letters. To her surprise, the teardrop lay on top, and then sank into the page in a sparkling of blue-white Light.

With a trembling finger, she touched the spot and found the paper was tinder dry, no stain in sight. Beneath her finger, a new line of text appeared. She moved her hand aside and written on the page were the words, "Anna, I'm your sister." Then that scribble, too, winked out of existence.

A titter of laughter outside broke through her stunned concentration. About twenty feet from the opened tent flap, Anna sat on a stump. Women were crowding closer. Her sister's face was aglow in the morning sunshine as she basked at being the center of attention.

Gilly had forgotten how much Anna craved belonging, being respected and listened to. Finally, she had something important to talk about, not merely to repeat idle gossip, but to share knowledge about a place right inside Ryca that few knew.

She was describing the tour they'd been given in Erov. The colorful tents, their manner of dress and the quills and scrolls on display in the Erovian marketplace. From the rapt attention of her listeners, Gilly suspected there would soon be a surge in the sale of writing implements in Perm, whether or not the buyers could read or write.

It was a while before Anna ended her tale, answered a myriad of questions and then returned to the tent. Her relaxed face wore a smile that curved her lips up and lit her eyes with happiness. A rare state for her sister, and it brought a warm glow to Gilly's chest. "Been having fun?"

Anna stopped and raised an eyebrow, as if in surprise. "Yes. I never realized all that I missed while living in Nadym. There is a whole wonderful world out here."

Gilly nodded. "I've been thinking the same thing."

Anna gave her a thoughtful stare and then came closer. "We're a lot alike, aren't we?"

Gilly had to laugh at that. "In Nadym, you would have sworn we had not a thing in common."

Anna restlessly paced back to the tent opening. "I was a fool in Nadym," she said in an angry tone to the world at large. "I knew nothing and pretended to know everything."

Gilly frowned at her sister's stiff back. What had her so upset? "Don't be hard on yourself. Only by traveling and seeing different places do we open our minds to other possibilities."

Anna swung around and glared at her "You know all about that, don't you, Gilly? You've traveled to many different places with my mother, brother and sister, and later, with me. You've been all over Ryca, while I only ever knew Nadym."

Her sister's envy and loneliness was heartbreaking. Anna had never known her family, only the one she built for herself. "You, too, have traveled much of late."

"Yes, I have, and I'm learning more and understanding others better every day for it. I liked meeting the people of Erov and now these tenters." She rushed closer and dropped to her knees before Gilly, her bad mood forgotten. "What do you say we find Marton and the children and explore Perm? It feels like forever since breakfast and I could use one of those spicy meat pies I've heard they sell at the marketplace."

Gilly shook her head. "You go."

"What are you going to do here by yourself?"

Cast a protection spell, wash out my clothing, rub ointment on my leg without Tom watching. The choices were endless, if lonely. Gilly pointed to the book with her quill. "I want to finish this."

Perhaps I will take a lesson from that teardrop and write to you, what I can't seem to say out loud.

"You've been at this long enough. How much is there to say? And don't give me any foolish talk about protecting the tent. I heard outside that our possession will be perfectly safe. It's a code among tenters that while neighbors are inside Perm, their things are not to be violated."

Anna's entreating glance made Gilly squirm with guilt but she stood her ground. Safer for all if she stayed out of sight, and out of Tom's way.

Now that he was well, he might be ready to find a woman to entertain him in Perm. He could have already. One who wouldn't kick him when he touched her. Each new realization bore a deeper hole into her heart. She bit her lip. "You should go now. Marton will worry if you stay away any longer."

"It's not safe for me to walk alone in a strange place," Anna said in a stubborn voice. "Until I find him, I could use your swishing." She emphasized her words with a wiggle of her fingers, "In case there's trouble."

Gilly chuckled. "I told you, it's not safe to use High Magic, especially so close to a Horsemen garrison. We'd get caught."

Anna shook her head. "Some of the women out there let slip that in Perm they still revere magic, though no one practices it. I don't think anyone would tell on us. Let's go."

"Anna..."

"Just until I find Marton. Then you can scurry back here and hide in the tent."

"I'm not hiding!" Gilly said, annoyed in part because her sister was right. She was hiding from the future Tom promised. It would be so different from what she had lived with in the past. Accepting Tom meant inviting another person into her solitary world. *Am I so content to be alone?*

One look at her sister and the answer was clear. *No!* "All right, I'll come."

She barely packed her sack with her books and quill before a crowing Anna shooed her outside.

Chapter 10

Gilly and Anna made their way to the city entrance and discovered a long line of people ahead of them. Their walk to the back of the line to get into Perm was disheartening. When they finally reached the gate, there was a toll to pay. Without a wagon of merchandise, however, it was a small fee. By the time they walked through, Gilly was starving, having missed her breakfast and midday meal.

It had been so noisy among the tenters that Gilly had assumed it would be even more so inside Perm, but there was hardly anyone about. On this side of the city's immense wall, a cobblestone road stretched far into the horizon on either side of them. Across the road, about a hundred paces away, houses were carved right into the rock, making this city appear nestled within the mountain.

The people who had come through the gates ahead of them walked briskly toward various doorways and vanished within. The only one loitering nearby was a man adjusting a strap on a heavily laden donkey.

Gilly's stomach growled in complaint and she lost interest in the man. "First thing I'm going to do once we're at the marketplace is eat."

"I'm hungry, too, but which of those doors leads to the main market?" Anna sounded both awed and anxious.

Before she could make a guess, the man pulling the overloaded donkey walked by and pointed to a doorway to their right. "Layabouts don't get the early worms, you know, and if you two don't hurry up, all the best goods will be gone." He sounded appalled by their late arrival. "The market closes an hour before sunset!"

Gilly gave him a curious glance at that unlooked-for advice, but he hurried away up the road. She shrugged off his bad temper and studied the door he pointed out. On its lintel, was a colorful carving of people gathered around a booth. "Think that's a marketplace sign?"

"Could be," Anna said.

They were about to cross the road when a pair of King's Horsemen in green capes rode by, horses' hooves clip-clopping on the cobbles. That terrifying sight instantly decided Gilly's course and she hurried Anna forward.

The doorkeeper confirmed this was indeed Perm's market and held his hand out for an entry payment. Gilly cringed at the exorbitant charge he quoted but Anna handed over the two bronze coins without complaint.

The moment they stepped inside, the mystery of the missing people was solved. The noisy hallway had several open doors but the loudest chatter came from the far end, which had a wider opening flanked by marble columns. With shared smiles, they hurried through that opulent entrance only to find two green-cloaked Horsemen on foot who stood guard at the opening.

The one closest to her nodded a narrow-eyed greeting and Gilly nodded back before looking away. She took Anna's hand and within two steps, they were engulfed in a stream of people. The experience was akin to having a cloak of invisibility swept over them. Gilly, never one to like crowds, now thanked the Light for this one.

Her ears were reverberating from the noise inside this gigantic room.

Anna squeezed her hand and shouted, "Can you . . . believe . . . this place?"

Her sister was unlikely to hear her any more than she could understand her, so Gilly simply squeezed her hand.

Every guild imaginable appeared to have a stand – dyers, masons, bakers, shoemakers, and rope makers. Gilly's mind reeled at the number of trades showcasing their talents. She trembled at the wondrous sights. Being among so many people was overwhelming. The crowd flowed around them like a gushing river.

What did stand out among this crowd were many green-caped Horsemen positioned along the far walls, each standing about twenty paces apart.

Behind them, the tall gray stonewall was smoothed to a brilliant shine that reflected the lights of hundreds of lanterns and torches hung high above. On the ceiling, vast colorful murals depicted Ryca's history, from its origins as an isolated coastal fortress built by a few hardy souls to a violent bloody scene of Prince Keegan's murder at the hands of his queen.

Gilly frowned, feeling that scene was unreal after the revelations in Erov about the night the prince died. She blinked and Prince Keegan's killer shifted. The murderous queen transformed into a stooped, twisted man with a jeweled dagger. In a blink, the earlier version returned and Gilly sensed the mask of a spell rippling over that mural.

The people of Perm played with fire by displaying such a magical artifact publicly, right in the midst of this Horseman-controlled city. She shivered, afraid for everyone in the room.

The vision of reoccurring green capes beside the gray walls was a stark reminder this was a dangerous city for her and those she loved. Though she was glad she had acquiesced to come with Anna, she was no longer certain she wanted to leave her sister and the children, not even in Marton's protection. In fact, finding him in this crowd might prove a problem.

Together, they toured the chamber for a sign of a familiar face. Lost was her trepidation she was not good enough for Tom as she anxiously searched for his dear angular features and dark brown hair.

At the heavenly scent of meat pies, Gilly halted, her hunger overtaking her worries. "This is too good to pass up, Anna."

"Tasty pies. Best in all of Perm." The vendor's gaze skimmed over Gilly, lingering on her lame leg before swinging up to meet her gaze with intensity. "Better than even a palace cook could produce, eh, missus?"

Gilly sniffed a crusty top that was wafting amazing flavors of rosemary and thyme. "I'll take two, please."

"Just one for me," Anna said, with a chuckle.

They lingered beside the meat cart, eating and watching the crowd.

"Move along!" a King's Horseman said.

Gilly started at the barked order. She'd not noticed the Horseman so close. After exchanging a worried glance with Anna, Gilly licked salty meat juices off her fingers, wiped her hand clean and took hold of Anna again. They returned to their search.

Once out of earshot of the Horseman, Gilly said, "I'm unhappy with leaving you here."

"That makes two of us," Anna said. "The sooner we find Marton and the children and leave this marketplace, the happier I'll be too."

"Good." Relief washed over Gilly as they passed a man tossing flaming torches in the air as if they were no more dangerous than a half dozen sticks. Gilly stopped to watch him in fascination.

"Bevan would love this." Anna's grip on her loosened. "Stay here, while I fetch him."

"No, I'll come with you." Gilly clenched her sister's withdrawing fingertips but a large lout barged between them, forcefully breaking their hold.

She tumbled backwards and into the juggler. Her cry of, "Anna!" was lost in the juggler's loud curses and the spectators' alarmed exclamation as flaming torches plunged to the ground. Metallic rims struck a ringing clang against the stone floor and sparks flew in all directions. Spectators surged away to avoid getting singed.

Gilly regained her feet and covered her hot cheeks with her cool hands. She had ruined his act. "I'm so sorry!"

As the torch flames died, people broke into laughter and pointed at her, a chilling echo of her dream. By the time she helped the juggler retrieve his fallen equipment, Anna was nowhere in sight.

Frantically, she scanned for a sign of her sister's distinctive blond head among so many brunette and black haired people. How hard could she be to spot? Anna should stand out like a blazing light in this sea of darkness.

Fear holding her fist clenched, she circuited the gigantic room. The children were not by the acrobats. She was sure that act should have drawn Bevan's attention, if not Skye's. At this point, even running into Tom in the arms of another woman would have been a profound relief.

As she searched and failed to spot anyone from her party, her heart began to pound with true panic. Could Anna have found Marton and the children and returned to the tent? *Would she have forgotten about me?* Seemed unlikely considering how hard her sister had gripped her hand since they spotted the first Horsemen at the entrance.

She could have panicked, wanting to get her children out of this chamber. The sensible thing would be to return to the tent to check if anyone had gone back there. Gilly was reluctant to leave without Anna in hand. Just one more quick circuit about the room, and then she'd go back to the tent. When she returned to the hallway, she went into every open doorway. Nowhere did she spot a recognizable face.

Exhausted, and having lost track of time in the underground rooms, she made her way back to the columned entryway and stared blindly into the large chamber, her mind numb.

"Move along," a nearby Horseman said. "You're blocking the entryway."

Afraid he might chase her out, Gilly hurried inside. Also, the crowd felt thinner. The mule driver had said the market closed an hour before sunset. Surely it wasn't so late already?

Cullen! He had come to set up a booth here. People were sure to remember him. He might have seen Anna, Marton and the children or know where they were going next. Where was his stand? She didn't recall seeing a minstrel's booth. A woman brushed past and Gilly said, "Mistress, have you seen a minstrel in here?"

"Only one who claims to have been to Erov." The woman paused and gave a harsh laugh. "I wasted good coin listening to his idiocy. Black skinned people, indeed. I've heard more plausible tales from my children." She pointed a thumb across the room. "His booth is beside the scarf seller."

Giddy with relief, Gilly was about to take off in that direction when the woman snagged her sleeve.

"Don't waste your money listening to his lies, missus. If you want to hear a good taradiddle, the Rycan Warriors spin a better tale about Prince Keegan's daughter arriving in Perm. At least they spout their nonsense for free."

Gilly shook off the woman's hold, and then wondered if that's why there were so many Horsemen in this chamber today. Why they refused to allow anyone to loiter. Were they on the lookout for Keegan's daughter? If so, she wished the young princess safe travels.

Crossing the chamber didn't take as long this time because the crowd was definitely thinner. She hardly bumped into one person. *Means I'm running out of time.* If people were leaving, the market must be closing soon. If she didn't return to her tent, the gates could shut and she would be trapped inside Perm with nowhere to go and Horsemen on patrol everywhere she turned.

Her impromptu dash brought her to Cullen's booth.

It was empty.

She gave a defeated sigh and leaned against the stand, a painful stitch springing up her left leg. Where could they all be?

After a moment, she sensed someone watching her. *A Horseman?* Slowly, she swung her gaze to her left. The scarf seller from the booth beside this one was eyeing her with intense interest. Dread collapsed and hope reared. This man might have spoken to Cullen. She pushed herself away to hurry over to him. "Sir, did you see the minstrel Cullen? Will he be returning soon?"

He shook his head. "Just started my shift. No one's been over there since I arrived. You look like you could use a pretty scarf to cheer you." He held out a silky blue confection. "This one's from Tibor. They breed the best silkworms along that coast where the weather is warmer and humid. If Prince Keegan's daughter was here, she would wear this material. You can have it for a steal, missus."

Gilly absently waved him away and asked the next person who strode by about Cullen, and the one after that. A young boy said he'd listened to the minstrel earlier this morning but the booth had been empty for a while.

Defeated, Gilly returned to Cullen's booth and sank onto his chair. Nothing left now but to return to her tent and hope Anna was there with her family. Or Tom had returned to look for her. That last hope got her back on her weary feet.

The room was almost bare now. So sparse, in fact, that even the scarf seller was shutting down his booth. The nearest Horseman, about eight paces away on her right, seemed to be eyeing her with suspicion for loitering. Time to leave. A cry rose in her throat in protest at that admission of defeat, but she swallowed it down. Her sore leg protested but she doggedly hobbled across this large chamber repeating a silent mantra.

Anna is safe. The children are safe. Tom is safe.

There was a crush to get out the front doors and when she finally exited onto the cobblestone street outside, the sun was low on the horizon. Her steps halted and her stomach clenched in rejection of crossing the road to the portal through which she and Anna had entered Perm. Once those giant gates slammed shut behind her, Anna would be trapped inside Perm, with Gilly locked outside. The stretch of road before her yawned as wide as the forest through which she had trudged with baby Anna in her arms, leaving behind two siblings and her mother in the cottage to perish.

She choked back a cry before it broke free. *Think.* If everyone was leaving the market, there could still be time before the gates shut. If she hurried to the tent, and found it empty she could slip back into Perm. What if she misjudged the time? *Ask someone the hour.*

The sound of a hammering drew her distracted gaze to an open window. A man was working with a small round block of wood that had leather stretched over it. The friendly smell of tallow drew her near him until she spotted buckles and lacing hanging on wall hooks, a row of curved blades and awls, along with rags and a blackening pot scattered along a long worktable. A tall shelving unit behind him had sandals, boots and shoes neatly arranged in pairs. A shoemaker.

With his shop this close to the exit he must be familiar with the routine of the guards who manned the gates. "Sir, how soon will the gates close?"

Without looking up, he said, "Sunset."

"I need to know precisely how much time I have."

He glanced up then with mild annoyance. After checking the sky, he said, "I'd wager you've an hour and a half."

The tension in her shoulders released. Plenty of time to check the tent and return to Perm. "Thank you, thank you, thank you!" She took a few steps into the street when another idea struck her. There was one person she hadn't searched for yet. Talus had come into Perm to visit with the King's Warriors. She hurried back to the shoemaker and found him by the window watching her intently. "Sir, apologies for disturbing your work again but where are the . . ."

"Name's Ned," he said, with wide-eyed curiosity now, his gaze fixed on her legs. "You limp, missus? I can make you shoes that would make your walk easier."

She warmed at his kind suggestion, and if she had time, she might have taken him up on his offer. "I'm looking for my family. Can you please direct me to the warriors' encampment?"

His kind gaze narrowed.

Realizing how easily that question could be misconstrued in this city where both the King's Warriors and the underground Rycan Warriors resided, she added, "I meant the King's Warriors, of course. No other Warriors. I must speak with the King's Warriors."

She was babbling. Her fear for Anna, Marton, the children and Tom had left her thinking fuzzy.

"You're from Erov, aren't you?"

Gilly's pulse shuddered. "What makes you say that?"

"Hagan's put out the word to keep an eye open for a woman with red hair who limps."

The news terrified her. Who was Hagan and why was he interested in her? Could he be the local Captain of the King's Horseman? She was too frightened to ask. "I don't know anyone in Perm, so no one from here would be looking for me."

He leaned out the window to check up and down the street. Gilly checked, too, unsure for whom but terrified it was for someone in a green cape.

Ned, the shoemaker, then whispered, "Missus, the King's Warriors aren't your friends. They will not help you. Hagan will. Best you speak with him."

"Look, I don't know this Hagan. I'm seeking the King's Horsemen." She shut her mouth in shock. Had she said the King's Horsemen? This Ned had her so rattled. She took a deep breath to calm her nerves. "I meant to say I'm seeking the King's Warriors. I'm not looking for the Horsemen and they're not looking for me. Also, I don't know any Hagan. Will you please tell me where the King's Warriors are?"

With reluctance, he gave instructions – follow the main street on her right until she arrived at a red roof with a door lintel depicting two crossed swords. The minute she turned away from his window, he slammed the shutters closed. That action returned her suspicions. What if he was lying and sending her to this Hagan's home instead?

There was a way to verify his instructions. Jarrod had given them a map of Perm. She dropped to the ground and rifled through her sack but the scroll wasn't there. When she packed this bag to come with Anna, she must have left out that map. The better plan would be to return to the tent, to ensure no one was there, and then return to Perm.

Hardly anyone was about now. Heeding an instinct to be cautious after hearing this Hagan was looking for her, she stepped behind a tall wagon and quietly chanted a spell to make her movements inconspicuous.

Hide me, save me, keep me out of sight.

Drops of Light sparked around her and then winked out as she hurried back to the tent. She might be panicking for nothing. Anna and her family could have returned to the tent and were at this moment worried about Gilly's whereabouts. That hopeful thought spurred her steps past the open gates and up the pathway.

The tent was empty.

Gilly died a little as she surveyed the inside in the fading light. Articles were scattered about because everyone had been in a rush to leave this morning. Only Cullen's spot was tidy, his bedroll neatly folded. She spotted her map and rushed to spread it out.

She could hardly see the sketches, so she lit a lantern. She'd need light soon anyway, when she returned to Perm. Once the flickering light shone across the map, her shoulders sank with disappointment and relief. The place the shoemaker gave her directions to was marked here as a private home. That was a close call. He must have been sending her to this Hagan's home.

It suddenly grew darker and Gilly's pulse jumped thinking Hagan had found her. A glance outside, however, showed the sun had finally set over the horizon. She was out of time. If she didn't hurry, Perm's gates would close. She rushed back, her sack in one hand, lantern in the other, only to see a guard shut the doors on her.

"Wait!" Dropping her *hide me* shield, she waved to the guard. "I must go back in. My family is inside."

"Sorry, missus." The guard's disembodied voice came from the other side, followed by the metallic sound of the gates being barred. "You'll have to wait for sun-up."

"But they don't belong there," Gilly said. "They live in a tent out here."

"Should have left earlier then, shouldn't they?" His footsteps clomped upward. Once he reached the top, he leaned over the wall and shouted, "Now get on about your business before I tell the Horsemen you're making trouble."

Stunned by the turn of events, Gilly stood beside the closed gates with the glow of her lantern spilling about her feet. Her sister had specifically asked her to come to Perm to guard her. What had she done? She'd lost her. The old horror that she was responsible for her family's destruction returned full force, tightening its grip on her chest and making her tears swell.

I swore I'd never let my family down again and here, I've done it a second time!

"Name's Hagan," a voice said, "heard you were looking for me."

Gilly let out a startled yelp and swung around.

A short stout man stepped out of the shadows of nearby bushes. The scar running the length of his right cheek chilled Gilly's blood. Her *Hide me* spell tingled on her tongue but she held it in. A quick check upward showed the guard watching them.

"I'm not looking for you."

"Ned said you asked about the warriors," he said in a whisper. "I'm their leader."

A shiver began deep within her. Why would the leader of the Rycan Warriors be interested in her? An absurd answer related to that rumor about the royal daughter being in Perm popped into her head. She flicked it way like an annoying fly. *I am no princess.* Her sister would laugh at the idea. *Anna! Where are you?* "I was looking for the King's Warriors."

And then she shuddered. Talus was a King's Warrior and he had helped to decimate the Rycan Warriors. She took a cautious step back, closer to the wall, and prayed that guard was still up there watching them.

Hagan kept his distance, and she breathed a sigh of relief. He wasn't going to hold her ill-advised statement about seeking the King's Warriors against her.

"Heard you limped." His head tilted as his gaze roved over her left leg, turning that knee to mush and forcing her to rely more on her right side. "Thieves sometimes fake such ailments to garner sympathy."

"I'm no thief!" This was wasting her time. With the gates closed, she was prevented from searching inside Perm. That left searching there from without, which meant using magic. In Nadym, she often cast a hearth spell to check on Anna's whereabouts. Similar to the one she used in Erov when she sought Aton's killer. This would be safer, for she was only looking for Anna, not searching far and wide for a culprit. Still, it required quiet, so she could focus her thoughts. "I have to go."

Hagan resolutely blocked her way. "If you're not looking for me, are you perhaps seeking your family?"

The question sent her pulse racing as her fear, already on high alert, spiked. Could he have anything to do with their disappearance? At this point, she didn't trust anyone. Certainly not a rogue who was so interested in her limp his gaze kept slipping to her lame leg. She defiantly raised her chin. "I have no family."

"You told the gatekeeper your family was inside."

"I thought he'd let me in if I said that than if I was separated from friends."

"Then you're out of luck." He stepped aside, leaving her path back to the tent wide open. "I won't keep you."

Her stomach in a tight knot, she wanted to scream in frustration. He knew something about Anna, her family and their friends' whereabouts. His lips appeared on the verge of smiling as if he enjoyed a private joke at her expense. Had he or one of his men seen the Horsemen take Anna? Why didn't he just tell her then? What payment did he want for that valuable information?

Silence stretched uninterrupted until the guard on top of the wall shuffled away, his footsteps fading into the quiet night.

Gilly's patience snapped. "Where are they?"

"Who?"

She clenched her fingers until her nails bit her palms. "If Anna or the children are hurt because you refused to help me, I'll make you sorry."

"Will you now?" He shifted to again boldly block her path. "For someone who doesn't have any family, you seem extremely attached to this Anna. As much as to a sister."

He toyed with her. He suspected she limped and that Anna was likely her sister. If she told him she could cast spells, she half feared he'd say, "I already know." She was well and truly beaten and if she wanted to discover what he knew, she had to admit that. "What do you want?"

Satisfaction flickered across his craggy face before it slithered under a gleam of innocence. "I want to see you walk."

What Gilly saw were the flames of fury. Her ears were scorching with the heat of her temper. She had no more time for games. Besides, Hagan wasn't about to tell her anything she couldn't find out on her own. What if all he was going to tell her was that Anna and her family were in the Horsemen's custody, or worse, been executed. She gulped past her swollen throat. Better to cast her spell and locate Anna so she could decide how to rescue her.

"You want to see me walk? Fine, then you may see my backside do the deed."

She marched around him and toward the path that led to the tents, entirely conscious of the distorted rhythm of her stride. At the edge of the clearing, she stopped and looked over her shoulder. Hagan was smiling in triumph.

As much as she wanted to storm away, her legs refused to budge until she asked the question. She had done as he asked, he owed her. "Do you know where they took my family?"

"How did you get that limp?"

She shouted in frustration and, a fist clenched around her lantern and the other holding up her skirts, she ran limping down the pathway, away from that infuriating man. If necessary, she would blaze the sky with Light to find her sister.

Chapter 11

Once out of his sight, Gilly cast her *hide-me* spell. Then she took the long route, close to the rushing stream, coming the back way to the blue tent to ensure no one noticed her. She slipped inside and held up her lantern. She was alone. A bittersweet reassurance, for she would have dearly loved to see Anna's cross face as her sister berated her for being gone so long.

With a flick of her wrist and the command, "Open no more," she secured the tent flap. She then dropped her hide-me enchantment and shuttered the lantern, drenching herself in darkness. She did not wish anyone to see her shadow and question her odd movements as she went about protecting the confines of this large tent. At least this time Cullen wasn't around to spook her.

Retrieving her tiny spell stones from her pack, she made her wide circular walk, muttering the warding incantation. When she stumbled across a scattered item that someone had carelessly left behind, she vented her frustration by viciously kicking it out of her path until her toes ached at their abuse.

Each of her tiny spelled-pebbles hit the ground and sparked with a release of Light. Once the circle was complete, a faint glow emanated as a much-needed reassurance that her incantation held.

She sat in the center of the tent and took several deep breaths to calm her racing thoughts. With eyes closed, she raised her arms to shoulder height, palms facing up. She'd taught herself this *seek-her* spell after arriving in Nadym - a safe way to keep an eye on Anna without following her.

She sent a string of thought into the darkness outside, searching for her sister's familiar specter. Bright sparks winked in inky blackness. Like distant night stars, souls of people made themselves visible.

One Light was brighter than the rest, emanating a sense of familiarity. She swooped toward that beacon and as she drew closer, the Light split in two. One was large, bright and warm like the sun, the other its moon. Then the moon split again, one bigger than the other. That second Light seemed to recognize her, staring directly at Gilly. *Bevan?*

Then the largest of the three clustered Lights winked and Gilly received a distinct impression of warm, healing energy. Joy infused her. "Anna!"

"She is safe, for now."

Gilly stifled a startled cry and snapped open her eyes. The tent was no longer dark. A candle was set directly before her and its glow highlighted a pair of legs. Hagan stood inside her protection circle, with arms crossed and wearing a triumphant grin. *He's seen me work Light.*

Why was he not concerned about her use of magic? Anna said the people of Perm were more accepting of the forbidden craft. Also, the Horsemen wanted Hagan almost as much as a magic user. So, he wasn't likely to run and tell on her now, was he?

Her pattering heart slowed and thumped at a steadier pace, as rising anger at this man's imposition replaced her fear.

"Your wards would work better," he said, "if you check who is inside your enclosure before sealing the circle."

"I did."

"Ah, well, I snuck in the back way after you shut down the lantern light."

She scrambled to her feet. "How dare you intrude!"

His gaze flew to her fist and his eyes widened with alarm. He held his hands up. "Hear me before you strike, lady."

Gilly checked her right hand. Crescents of Light shone between her clenched fingers, dazzling as the three harvest moons riding in sync. She hefted those fiery balls to shoulder height and drew back.

Hagan's worried gaze met hers and he dropped to his knees. "Hold, I beseech you. I come with good intentions."

"You come uninvited." The power in her fist vibrated through to her bones, stirring molten satisfaction in her core, as if some long-lost part of her had finally returned home.

"Only because I have waited my entire life to meet you, lady." Tears spilled over his lower eyelids. "I needed to be sure, you see. It is difficult to believe when one's dream appears to have come true. To see what I've fought for, seen my men die for, is actually real and not a delusion born of my desperation."

Hagan, leader of the Rycan Warriors, then bowed his head and stretched his arms toward her as if in supplication.

His odd reaction confused her. He did not look afraid. Fear, she understood. This man acted as if he was in awe at being in her presence. "I ask again, what do you want? And don't say to see me walk."

He looked up, wiping his wet face with the back of his sleeves. That hard uncompromising stoniness crept back across his shoulders. "You know what I desire."

She backed away in rejection, but an unwanted idea rose to confront her, along with a remembered exchange from the marketplace.

If you want to hear a good taradiddle, the Rycan Warriors spin a better tale about Prince Keegan's daughter arriving in Perm.

She lowered her arm and shook out her fingers, using that as an excuse to break eye contact. Droplets of Light flitted around her body until, one by one, each blinked out. A part of her sighed with regret at that power's passing. Quietly, she said what should have been obvious even to the blind. "I am no princess."

Hagan rose, all resemblance to abject humility lost with his upward surge. "The legend says you are."

"What legend? Marton said you were mad and I believe he might be right."

"I've never met Marton." Hagan sounded offended. Then he seemed to reconsider his assertion. "Okay, once maybe, when I tapped him on the head. Hardly reason to call me mad."

"You hit Marton?"

"Barely touched him."

Gilly hissed her frustration. "I am not Prince Keegan's child."

"Yet you grasp magic as if you are its master, as he and his beloved Mamosia did. You passed through Erov. No one enters that magical city unless Erov wishes it. You also carry the mark of your father's death in your walk."

"My limp doesn't mean I'm his offspring. There are countless women who have such deformities all across Ryca."

"Why deny it?"

"You're not listening to me."

"Are you afraid of Ywen? He will not touch you while I draw breath. My warriors will see to it."

There was no reasoning with this lunatic. She decided on a direct tack. "Do you know where my family is being held?"

"I have them."

"You?" That answer brought profound relief the Horsemen didn't have her family, followed swiftly by hot burning hope in her belly that she might be able to coax this deluded creature into letting Anna and the others go. *Please let this not be another useless wish.*

"Hagan." She softened her voice, aiming for a reasonable tone. "I wish you the best of luck on your quest, but I cannot help you find Keegan's daughter."

"Lady," Hagan replied, implacable in his determination, "you are her."

"Then take me. Let everyone else go, I beg of you. They mean you no harm."

"I will release them. Once you admit who you are."

She racked her brain on how to convince him to relent. He returned her regard with stubborn silence. *Well, what do I have to lose by listening to his crazy ideas?* In fact, by showing him the error of his thinking, she might be able to convince him that he was wrong.

She nodded and sat down. "Very well. Convince me."

He sat facing her with a pleased expression, his compact body folding neatly, the whites of his eyes bright with excitement in the dim candle glow. "Little Skye and I had a long talk earlier today."

"Likely without Anna's blessing."

He flashed an unrepentant grin. "Children are more honest than adults. What she told me was astonishing. Erov sounds like a marvel to behold."

"The Erovians are a remarkable people."

"Never heard of a Telling Ceremony. Wish I could have been there. Quite the tales the three of you were asked to relate. The one this woman, Mayla, spoke of is Ywen's official account. A host of lies, of course."

Agreeing with Hagan wasn't her plan. "You don't know that."

"Everything Ywen says is a lie," Hagan replied in a hard voice. "Skye tells me Lord Jarrod named you 'Defender of the Light.' Do you understand what that means?"

"I believe he was referring to magic but I'm not that person either."

"Full of denial. What are you afraid of, lady? Ryca needs such a defender. There are many masters of the guild trapped in the king's dungeons these many years, tortured past bearing."

"That's merely gossip...if true, I feel for them. However, I am not the one to rescue them. Look at me, Hagan, I can barely walk straight without straining and you expect me to oppose the king's might?"

"You would not walk alone, my lady. The people need a symbol as much as they need a leader. Your presence alone could help us conquer Ywen's forces."

When she shook her head, he leaned forward with a crazed intensity in his eyes, bringing a whiff of his meaty dinner on his pungent breath. Gilly held her breath.

"How do you think you got that limp?" Hagan asked.

"I fell down a well," Gilly said through clenched teeth. *Someone pushed me!*

"Wrong!" His eyes gleamed with excitement.

What did he know that she didn't? She'd recited what she remembered of her fall, and Jarrod had affirmed she spoke the truth. *The truth as they remember it.* "My mother never said how I was injured."

"Then she's as much a liar as Ywen. Because she knew."

"How dare you call her a liar!"

"And foolish."

Gilly slapped him, hard.

For several heartbeats, her white hand print remained visible on his tanned cheek, and the smacking sound rang in her ears. Her glance swerved to the tent wall that was a good ten feet behind him. Could anyone outside have heard that? Aside from the strike, they had been yelling, too.

"My men cleared the area and are standing guard," Hagan said, tenderly rubbing his cheek. "No one will disturb us until I say we're done."

He had come prepared. She met his gaze with reluctant admiration. Taking a deep breath to calm her raging temper and racing heart, she squashed the desire to apologize. He deserved that slap. She'd wanted to do it ever since he first opened his mouth by the gate. Mam wasn't a liar.

Or was she?

The first crack formed in her firm belief in everything her mother had said. Because if Mam lied about Gilly's injury, what else had she hidden from her children?

"Tamarisk was the one who gave you that limp," Hagan said, "when he hurled you over a corridor railing in the castle at Tibor."

Gilly's body grew cold as her mind painted a picture of the awful moment of being suspended in air.

"He taunted your mother before he dropped you."

Gilly raised her hands to cover her burning cheeks and Hagan took hold of her fingers and lowered her arms.

He's afraid I'll slap him again. That was the last thing she wanted to do because with each word, Hagan was pulling back a veil that had lain over her since that horrible night.

She squeezed his hands, drawing strength from his solidity as her world shook, shattered and reshaped. The memory of her fall became as clear as if it were happening right this moment. She was dropping, face down, hands flailing, air rushing past her. Then so swiftly she barely had time to take in a breath for a scream, she hit the marble floor, fast and hard.

She cringed from the awful impact and the familiar blackness returned to comfort her, to lie to her. This time, Gilly saw the edges of a dark field that shielded the memory. It undulated with specks of Light.

She took a shaky breath and, in her mind, touched the blanket shielding her past. Instantly, she received a clear impression of Mam. They were in the woods with Gilly's siblings kneeling around her.

"Mama, is she going to die like Papa?" Thirteen-year-old Tamara whispered.

"Shush," her mother said. "I must concentrate. I can't heal her properly while she is in such pain. You and Garren, go keep watch, and come find me quietly if anyone approaches."

As the children left, with tears in her eyes, the queen, still in her bedclothes, roamed her hands over her daughter's broken body as Gilly moaned and writhed in agony.

Forget, little Saira. Forget what was done to you. Forget what you saw as you lay cuddled beside your papa this night. Forget your sister and brother playing with you in the courtyard. Forget the life that can be no more. Forget me.

"No!" Gilly tore the blanket, ripping it to shreds. Hagan's fingers slipped from her grasp as Light pulsing from Gilly flung him backwards. He thumped against the tent wall and slumped.

In that instant, a floodgate opened, sending Gilly bittersweet snippets of memory from her childhood in another life. She wept for the loss of her papa, seeing his blood spraying across her face at the moment of his death. Her mama pulling her back into her distended belly as a dagger slashed toward Saira. Mam thrusting an arm outward and Uncle Ywen being thrown backwards. She grabbed Saira's hand and they ran to a side door. "Hurry, we have to find Tamara and Garren and get away."

"You would have died that night," Hagan said, returning to squat before her, "your bones cracking as they did. Except the queen cast a spell to save your life."

"Why?" Gilly shivered in shock and remembered pain. "Why would Uncle Ywen want to harm us?"

"You remember that? Good!" He nodded, looking pleased. "My guess is Tamarisk poisoned his mind against his brother. I don't know the whys or hows. All my mother said was that Tamarisk lusted after your mother. He wanted her from the first day your father brought her to the castle. One night, he tried to assault her. Her magic helped fend him off long enough for her to race to Keegan. Your father would have destroyed him. Ywen stood up for his boyhood friend, and testified it must have been someone else. That Mamosia, in her fright, had been mistaken. He swore Tamarisk had been by his side all day."

Hagan stayed silent a moment as if considering his words before continuing. "Keegan was ready to call his brother a liar. Your mother held him back. She had a kind heart and persuaded him to ban Tamarisk from the castle instead. A mistake. It cost Keegan his life."

No matter what lies Mam had spun her, she was not responsible for Gilly's papa's death. "That wasn't her fault."

"It was!" Hagan said in a harsh voice. "Do not make the same mistake. Tamarisk cannot be trusted. He cannot be ignored. He must be destroyed."

She didn't need Hagan's admonition. She had no intention of trusting Tamarisk. When and if Anna dragged them to Tibor, Gilly didn't plan to court the Royal Magician's anger. Despite this incredible revelation, Mam was right.

What's past is past. Best she forget the life that can never be. Her breath hitched in her chest. She pushed aside the pain of her decision, but her returned memories she savored and squirreled away. For a time when Anna was safe and Gilly was free to think on all they had lost.

When she didn't respond, Hagan continued with his tale. "Ywen and Keegan had been at odds ever since their father announced Keegan would rule after him. The boys were identical twins, born moments apart. When Keegan turned five, his magical ability manifested. Once both boys reached adulthood, and it became obvious that Ywen possessed not a shred of talent to wield Light, the old king proclaimed that upon his death, Keegan would rule."

It was so odd listening to this tale, knowing Hagan spoke of her family. All that running her mother, *the queen*, put them through, while heavy with Anna and grieving her husband's death, finally made sense. A shudder rippled through Gilly at the horror Mam must have experienced.

Hagan met Gilly's gaze. "From that day forward, Ywen spent every waking moment plotting his brother's death. Once he finished off Keegan, he killed their father. The story goes that the old king died of a broken heart after hearing of Keegan's death, but I know better. He was poisoned."

Gilly was stunned by how much Hagan seemed to know. Few in Ryca were aware of what really happened in Tibor over twenty years ago. What made this man so different that he dedicated his life to fighting for her family's right to rule this land? "How do you know all this?" *Why do you care?*

"My mother worked at the castle, lady. She was your mother's maiden at hand. Ywen had her killed after the assault on your family, but I knew the whole story. She'd sent me away when the tension in the castle built to a confrontation. Before Ywen came for her, she wrote to me about what happened that night."

Gilly's mind flitted back to the Telling Ceremony. "Tom said Tamarisk was in the castle the night the prince," *Papa,* "died. How can that be, when Tamarisk had been banned from there."

She recalled once asking her mother, *Mama, why can't I play with Uncle Tam anymore?*

He's a dangerous man, Saira. You must never be alone with him. Promise me?

"He was there to help Ywen kill your father. To counter Keegan's or Mamosia's protection spells." Hagan took her hands, his rough callused palms grazing her skin and keeping her grounded. Which brought to mind why they were having this discussion at all. *Anna.*

"My sister is in the dark about all of this. She doesn't know we're related. She wants to go to Tibor to beg King Ywen's forgiveness." Gilly shivered at that once foolish-seeming plan, now seeing how truly dangerous it was. "We must stop her."

"Why?" Hagan gripped her hands tighter. "Her plan works nicely with mine. Tibor is exactly where we must go."

"No." She pulled free from his tight grip, his calluses scraping her skin. "If she goes there, our uncle will kill her."

Hagan grabbed her upper arms and pulled her forward until they were inches apart, his earthy scent imprinting on her, and the candle hot beneath them. "He won't harm her," he said in a deadly voice. "Because I will kill him first. For my mother. For my queen."

"But..."

"And you," he continued relentlessly, "will kill that slop-sucking rat, Tamarisk. For yourself, and for the good of the Light."

Gilly pushed him away and put as much distance between them as the boundary of the large tent allowed. At her abrupt movement, the candle flickered and went out. In the darkness, she lost sight of Hagan but sensed he stood where she'd left him.

She took several deep breaths to cleanse herself of Hagan's presence, but she couldn't shake off his words. He had accomplished his goal, convinced her that she was Prince Keegan's daughter. Her chest tightened at that incredible realization.

Mam was Queen Mamosia. I am a princess of the realm. Uncle Ywen wants me dead.

Along with returning memories came the realization that Hagan intended to lead Gilly and her family to their certain deaths. She could never kill a powerful sorcerer like Tamarisk. Not if, as Hagan maintained, the sorcerer was drawing strength for his spells from those poor magical guild members in the castle's dungeons. He had more experience, access to an unlimited source of power, and was ruthless.

He helped Uncle Ywen kill Papa. Desolation swamped her. *How could I have forgotten you, Papa?*

Resentment toward her mother flared but she shook it off. Mam always had a sound reason for doing what she did, just as she had been right about how best to deal with Tamarisk.

Run and hide.

Running had saved her mother, for a time. Staying out of sight had kept Anna and Gilly safe for all these years. She had no interest in killing Tamarisk or overthrowing Uncle Ywen or becoming a queen. Anna was the one who had Papa's fighting spirit. If her sister learned of her family connection, she might insist they take back what rightfully belonged to them.

"You can't let those sorcerers rot," Hagan said. "They're your people."

The arrow struck its intended target and Gilly faltered. She shelved her rising compassion and clung to reality. "You can't seriously believe those guild members are still alive? No one could survive being drained of magical energy for decades. They are long dead." *Please be dead.*

"They're victims of your family's wrath," Hagan said through clenched teeth. "Stuck in their prison, tortured, because your uncle hated your father. Your family destroyed their lives. Can you not find it in your heart to give their families peace? If there's anything left of them, they deserve a quick end and a decent burial."

She covered her ears, her insides quivering. Even knowing Hagan twisted her emotions to gain his way, the possibility of such devastation was too horrible to bear.

Focus on Anna. Not on people who may or may not be alive. If something could have been done to defeat Tamarisk and Ywen, Mam would have done it. Instead, she hid both herself and her children. If Gilly hadn't been so slow to warn Mam...

"Mamosia. Say it, Saira. Mamosia." Papa knelt with an encouraging smile.

He had blue eyes like the desert sky over Erov.

"Mam." I stomped my foot. "Mam mam mam,"

"You've lost this battle, my love." Her mother chuckled and hugged child and father.

Gilly turned her back to Hagan and surreptitiously wiped a tear that wet her cheek. So that name hadn't been another form for mama, but rather a long forgotten nickname. Why had her mother allowed her to keep using that name when she had wiped everything else from Gilly's past? Unless her magic had been too weak. Or little Saira's stubbornness too strong.

"It's time to go," Hagan said, his voice gruff.

That sounded as if he was softening. Gilly swung around, but his stern mouth refuted her assumption. He indicated the tent flap, reminding her she still had her seal spell on it. Once she released her binding, he opened the flap and invited her to step outside and into disaster.

Her shoulders sagged with defeat. "Why didn't you ask Anna to lead your fight? You already had her."

He gestured to her leg. "You are the marked one. You are a better symbol for our people to rally behind than your sister. I will work with her instead, if need be. Your choice."

"No choice at all," Gilly said, as an ethereal noose settled around her neck.

"Then you agree?" Eyes lit with excitement, he finally met her gaze. Gilly glimpsed his madness. Neither she nor her sister would stand a chance against Ywen's forces but Hagan only envisioned glorious victory.

"Have you ever tried to rescue these guild members?"

"I've tried six ways to Tver but the King's Warriors always cut down my troops."

"Yet you are certain we will succeed this time?" She layered her doubt with sarcasm.

"This time, we have you."

"A lame girl who can magic a ward or two?"

"Keegan's daughter who survived Tamarisk's assault. You will unite Ryca. If people see you alive and riding to Tibor to demand the throne, they'll be behind us six thousand deep."

"With you at the head?"

"It is my destiny."

The trap was set. No choice but to walk in. She had to protect Anna from both her sister's impulsive behavior and Hagan's bloodthirsty plans. She came closer. "I want Anna and her family to remain here while we travel to Tibor."

"No. She's all I have to ensure you cooperate."

"Then please keep her in the dark about our intentions to overthrow the king. Anna wouldn't want her children involved in a fight and might interfere with your plans."

"Why would you want to help me?"

For a madman, his faculties were sharp. "I don't want my sister involved in a fight with a powerful sorcerer like Tamarisk or a murderous king."

He was quiet as if he considered her suggestion.

She held her breath. Anna's life depended on his answer.

"All right," he said.

She released her pent-up breath. *Yes.* A tiny win, but at this point, she treasured every victory.

"Once we reach Tibor," Hagan said, "I'll find a safe place to stash them. Let's go."

She nodded and ducked under the tent flap to step outside. The horizon was light. A new day was upon them. The Rycan Warriors gathered to greet her.

More like a gathering of shopkeepers than a squadron of fighters. They may carry swords and shields, and one or two wore chainmaille, but these men with their friendly faces belonged in the city. They should be taking care of their business, playing with their children and eating meals with their wives. No wonder Talus and his King's Warriors had decimated them. These men were no more prepared for battle than Tom.

Hagan presented her. Each man stepped up, fist circling her forearm, smile wide and cheerful. Gilly was at a loss on how to convince them that what their leader intended was beyond their capabilities.

Bells rang then, signaling the gates were opening. Morning already. Together, they trekked into the city. Hagan led her along the exact route the shoemaker had given her, attesting that he, too, must either work for the warriors or, more likely considering the state of the Rycan Warriors, was one of them.

They entered a home built into the mountain and a warrior shouted, "Breakfast for the princess."

General agreement followed.

Hagan led her in silence to an underground kitchen. Shelves had been chiseled into the rock walls to house pots and pans and supplies. A tall circular stone chimney in the center of the room over a blazing hearth drew smoke upward, allowing the room to stay warm but not smoky.

Ned, the shoemaker, was eating breakfast at the table – *what a surprise* – as well as the gatekeeper who had refused to allow her into Perm last night. Did their wives know what these "warriors" planned?

"Where is my family?" Gilly stayed rooted in the doorway.

"You must learn to trust me, lady." Hagan sat at the table and drew a plate to him. "They're comfortable. Sit."

Despite her seeking spell's reassurance, a part of Gilly still feared her past was repeating itself. A tortured corner insisted she had been too slow to save them. Again. What if while she had argued with Hagan, the Horsemen discovered where this madman had put her family? "I want to see for myself."

He gave her an exasperated look, and then pushing his plate away, led her through a side door and through a series of underground corridors. She stooped as they walked through even though there was plenty of headroom. She forced herself to straighten, but traveling deeper into the mountain with rock in every direction wore on the mind. They turned down so many corners, she feared even if she knocked out Hagan, she and her family might never find their way out to safety.

Finally, he stopped at a door, unbolted the bar and invited her inside. Her family and Tom were there, under guard. No Talus or Cullen, but Tom was here. *Safe.* A hot flush of relief swept through, leaving her trembling and wanting to cry with joy.

Tom's eyes seemed to mirror her relief. *He was worried about me.* The thought tasted sweet and delicious.

With a cry of happiness, Anna ran toward her, but a man with a sword gestured her back. Marton slipped his arm around his wife's waist, hugging her close. Their children were also safe and close by, appearing less agitated than their parents. All whom she loved were accounted for and unharmed.

She thanked the Light for this mercy and her horror of losing her family as a child receded into a long-ago memory, where it belonged.

Bevan seemed unusually carefree as he waved cheerfully to her. Considering he had seemed to look right back at her during her *seek-her* spell, exactly how powerful had her nephew's awareness of Light grown lately? Could the boy have kept track of her after she broke contact?

"Gilly, what's going on?" Anna asked.

Her sister drew Gilly's distracted gaze and she became spellbound. Her heart thumped like a runaway horse and her breath caught. With her beautiful blond hair and blue eyes, Anna was a female version of their Papa.

Chapter 12

"Gilly, speak to me," Anna said. That impatient tone, the commanding stance. Anna was definitely her father's daughter.

Her sister pulled away from Marton and defiantly shoved the Rycan Warrior with the sword aside and ran to Gilly and hugged her. "Why are you crying? What did he do?"

Hagan waved away his man and his understanding gaze met Gilly's teary one. *He knew.* Jarrod, too? One look at Anna and they would have realized she was Prince Keegan's daughter. There had been no reason for Hagan to make Gilly go on and on about her limp, unless he, like Jarrod, had been trying to jog her memory.

"Are you all right?" Anna whispered.

"Yes." Gilly wiped away her tears, unable to tear her gaze from her sister. Papa might as well be standing before her.

"That man is Hagan, the leader of the Rycan Warriors." Keeping a firm hold on Gilly's fingers, Anna dragged her toward her family.

"I know." Gilly resisted the urge to hug and kiss Anna all over her beautiful, memorable face. Instead, she cleared her throat and said what she had been practicing since leaving their tent. "Hagan is going to help us leave Perm, Anna. The King's Horsemen are coming, so we must leave. Fast. He's agreed to provide us with horses and an armed escort to Tibor."

"Gilly, you can't decide something like that. Who comes with us is up to Marton." She gestured for her husband to join the discussion.

"It will be safer if they accompany us," Gilly said.

Bevan's laughter drew her gaze. Hagan had gone over to join the children and was tossing the young boy in the air. Bevan squealed all the way down.

Marton gave their abductor a suspicious look. "Why would he want to help us?"

"I agreed to do something in exchange."

"What could he possibly want from you?" Anna asked.

"I'd like to know that, too." Tom moved closer and took her hand.

Gilly squeezed his fingers, taking silent comfort from his touch. There were so many unanswered questions in his gaze that she could never answer.

Skye laughed as Hagan tickled her.

"Children, come away from him," Anna said. "Don't play with that man. He's dangerous."

"Anna," Gilly said, in a warning undertone. "This is not the time to make a fuss."

"He captured us, hit my Marton on the head and kept us locked up here all night. If that doesn't warrant fuss, I can't imagine what does."

As Skye and Bevan ran over, Gilly turned with concern to Marton. "Are you all right?"

"Never mind him," Anna said, dismissing her husband's injury as swiftly as she'd brought it up. "What does Hagan want?"

Hagan returned to the doorway and leaned nonchalantly against the wall.

Gilly's stomach clenched. This was the unpredictable part of her plan. Her gaze flitted nervously between Tom and Marton, as she said, "Hagan knows about the magic."

"What magic?" Marton said.

"I can wield Light," Gilly said. "That's how I helped Anna escape back in Nadym, and kept Skye from being injured from a fall."

His eyes widening, Marton pushed Anna and his children behind him.

Tom remained silent, his hold steady, as if he were indifferent to her revelation. To him, this was not news. How much did he know about her?

Anna patted Marton's arm. "Magic is not bad."

"I thank you for saving Anna and Skye," Marton said, "but I will not have my family exposed to that forbidden practice. Since it's the Horsemen's job to track those who use it, you have put my family in jeopardy. I thought you cared about us."

Each word stabbed Gilly in the chest. "I do."

"You don't act like it. Anna isn't going anywhere with you or him." He pointed to Hagan.

"Anna and Gilly will do as I say," Hagan said, straightening his stance, arms crossed. "This is the time to rise up and strike against the King."

Gilly moaned at that foolish admission. After he promised to keep silent. She had to stop him before he spilled all of her secrets.

Marton stared at Hagan open-mouthed and then turned on Gilly. "I can understand him spouting nonsense, but I thought you had sense."

"Please let me explain, Marton." She glared over her shoulder at Hagan. "Alone!"

He remained stubbornly by the doorway, and then with a shrug, left the room with his warrior. A lock clicked.

Gilly faced Marton. "As he said, he wants to go to Tibor to overthrow Ywen. He believes because we were in Erov, we are a symbol he can use. He refuses to let us go, unless I help."

"I don't know if I believe a word you say anymore," Marton said.

His words hurt, partly because they were true. She was lying, but she was also trying to save him, his wife and his children. "I have a plan." She motioned everyone closer. "I have a potion that will put Hagan to sleep for a long while. It will give us a chance to get away."

"No magic," Marton said.

"Marton, magic isn't evil," Anna said.

"But Mama, everyone says it is," Skye said.

"They're wrong."

"No, they're not," Marton said. "She's bewitched you, Anna." Appearing both repulsed and curious he stared at Gilly. "Are you a witch?"

"She's the same as you or I," Tom said.

"I don't know what I am," Gilly said. "I've always been able to cast spells and set wards. Marton, I love Anna like a sister and would never harm her."

Anna gave Gilly a startled look, and then turned to her husband. "If Gilly is evil, so am I."

"What do you mean?" he asked.

"When we were at Erov, Gilly tried to find out who killed Lord Aton by casting a spell."

"And you didn't tell me?"

"I didn't want to alarm you." She took his hands. "There's more. When she was in the middle of the spell, something attacked her." She sent Gilly an apologetic look. "Her whole face was scorched. There was blood and burned skin and her eyes, oh Marton, they looked horrible."

He drew her to him and muttered soothing sounds. "But, Anna, Gilly's fine now."

Her sister's description sent shock waves through Gilly. Had she been hurt that much? She remembered the pain but the next day her face was normal. If her sister was right, then not only did magic run in both their blood but her sister was more powerful than either of them imagined. Even their mother had not been able to heal Gilly so well and so fast after her fall.

"Gilly's fine because I healed her," Anna said, sounding confident and leaving Gilly amazed.

She glanced at Bevan with new speculation. If his mother was this powerful, what did that say about her children, about Bevan and his bright Light that had outshone all others?

"You, Mama?" Skye asked.

"Yes, me," Anna said.

That exchange drew Gilly's distracted thought to the present, but she was left shivering in wonder.

Tom, squeezed her hand, his gaze worried.

She didn't know how to address his concern.

"I held my hands over her face," Anna said, "and prayed to the Light to heal her and the redness disappeared and her eyes were normal again. I thought maybe I'd imagined it. That Gilly hadn't really been hurt, but now I think back, Marton, her face was completely burnt. I know it. I didn't imagine it. Something attacked her, tried to kill her."

"This is the reason why magic is banned, Anna," he said. "Don't you see? You must never do it again."

"Marton, how can it be evil if it saved Gilly's sight?"

He shook his head and sat down on a nearby bench, holding onto Anna. "I don't understand any of this."

"Gilly has another secret that could explain it better," Anna said. "I've thought about it a great deal." She turned back to Gilly. "About your story of being in charge of me and carrying me to safety. You weren't just my keeper, were you?"

Gilly gulped. She had been waiting for an opening like this to tell Anna they were sisters. How could she share anything now? "I've told all I can."

"You missed one important point," Anna said. "You left out that we're kin."

Gilly's head snapped around. Anna knew?

Marton said, "That's why..."

"...we can both wield Light," Anna finished. "I know in my heart that Gilly is my sister."

There. It was out and not from her lips or Hagan's. Her sister looked defiant, as if daring her to deny their connection. The thin line of Anna's lips said how hurt she was at Gilly's silence and Gilly's heart melted. She was done with denials. Now she knew how much Anna resembled Papa, denying her would be paramount to denying him. "I'm sorry I didn't admit it before, Anna. I spoke the truth when I said you have your papa's temper. You are also his spitting image."

Anna's eyes welled with tears and Gilly opened her arms to the child who had longed for a family and invited her back into hers. Her sister ran to her without hesitation.

All Gilly's worry that Anna would be furious at her numerous lies and evasions and abandonment vanished as her sister clung fiercely to Gilly, claiming her with the same uninhibited love she bestowed on her husband and children. "I knew it!"

Gilly basked in her sister's acceptance. She could have held her like this forever. As long as Anna had wanted a family, Gilly had been missing hers. A tear fought free of her tightly clenched eyelids and warmed her cheek.

Skye and Bevan's arms wrapped around them and Anna laughed as she included her children in the family gathering. Gilly wiped her cheeks, which grew moister with each hug.

"It's all right to hug Gilly, huh, Mama?" Skye asked.

"As if my strictures ever stopped you," her mother said, but her indulgent smile robbed her words of their sting.

"If this is to be a moment of truth," Tom glanced at Marton, the only one who still stood far from Gilly with his arms crossed, "and it seems it must be if we are to trust each other, I, too have a confession." He looked at everyone in turn, and finally his sorrowful brown gaze met Gilly's. "I did kill Vyan in Nadym."

"I knew it!" Anna shouted, this time with fury, but then she fell silent as Marton shook his head. She hurried to her husband's side, dragging her children along.

Gilly ignored Anna's gesture to join them. Of all the things she had expected Tom to confess, this was not one of them. "And Aton?" she asked in a quiet voice that barely squeaked out of her tight throat. *Please say, No.*

"No," Tom said, reclaiming her icy fingers within his warm hold, "I didn't kill him."

"Why did you kill Vyan?" Marton shuffled Anna and his children to the bench's far side as if afraid that Tom might lunge at his family with a knife. He had given her the same look a few minutes ago when he learned of her wielding Light.

Gilly took a deep calming breath and faced Tom. He was right. Time for truth to blaze away all of their fears and insecurities. In her heart, she held onto the man she had known most of her life. The one who was silent, who watched her with haunted eyes, whose touch made her tremble with odd desires. He had saved her life in Nadym by killing Vyan and been beaten savagely for that service.

"What happened, Tom?" Gilly asked.

"He was about to tell the Horsemen about a baby who was once found at the temple," Tom said. "And about a young girl with goats who appeared shortly after. I could see his intention in his eyes whenever his gaze swept over to Anna. I had to stop him, so I threw that knife from the front window."

"That would have been over twenty paces away," Anna said, in a scoffing tone. "You could not possibly have hit him from that distance. Not as drunk as you were back then."

"As a lad, I used to practice knife throwing with my father," Tom said with a slight frown and flexed his right hand as if he, too, were surprised at how well he had done. "This time Gilly and Anna's lives depended on my hitting my target. That seemed to give my throw power and aim."

"Why would you care what Vyan told the King's Horsemen?" Marton asked. "Enough to want to kill him?"

"Jarrod was right," Tom said. "I am from Tibor, the boy responsible for Prince Keegan's death."

"You ran for help," Gilly said, and gently stroked his arm. "Tom, he must have put a spell on you. You are not responsible for what happened that night."

"What does any of this have to do with Vyan and Anna?" Marton asked, shaking his head in obvious confusion.

"I'm coming to that." Tom's anxious eyes were fixed on Gilly. "In the corridor outside Prince Keegan's room, I came to from the blow to my head in time to see Tamarisk drop one of the royal children over the railing. Princess Mamosia screamed and cast a spell to stop her daughter's fall, but it was too late."

"Enough." Gilly placed a warning hand on his, seeing where this was leading. Tom was about to say Gilly was that child, and if that were the case, and Anna was her sister...

"Let him speak," Marton said. "Since you are now a part of my family, you will abide by my rules. That means no more secrets. Go on, Tom."

"Princess Mamosia fled down the stairs with her other children. Tamarisk was about to go after her so I tripped him and he stumbled and fell. I ran away before he could come after me and took the back stairs. I reached the courtyard in time to witness the royal carriage leave. I followed on foot."

Gilly listened to his tale and the last puzzle piece that was Tom fell into place. He must have followed her family, not only to the cottage in the woods, but trailed her and Anna to Nadym. What a resourceful, determined boy. She held herself back to keep from hugging him. He had been her invisible shield and sword from the moment Papa died. She had never been alone.

"The hardest part was after the Horsemen found the royal family hiding at the cottage," Tom said. "I wanted to warn them, but Princess Saira, Gilly, arrived ahead of me. When she left with the baby and a few goats, I followed her."

"Lady Saira-Gilly," Anna said. "Lord Aton called you that. He knew who you were, who *we* were all along." She abruptly sat on the bench behind Gilly, her face ashen. "We're Prince Keegan's children."

Gilly met and held her sister's stunned gaze. This was the revelation she feared. How would Anna respond? Would she charge into Tibor to demand her birthright? She hoped not.

"I should have waited to make sure the princess and the other children left safely," Tom said, regaining Gilly's attention. "When they didn't follow, I went back to check on them."

"You found their bodies?" For so long she had berated herself for not going back to check. Fear of leaving Anna alone or taking her into danger had kept Gilly away from the cottage. "Did you give them a proper burial?"

"They weren't there, Gilly," he said. "I checked the whole area. The Horsemen were gone, and so were your mother, bother, and sister."

Legs shaking, Gilly stumbled over to Anna and sat beside her, her mind numb. The Horsemen hadn't killed her family? Anna threaded her fingers through Gilly's and held tight.

"I did the only thing I could," Tom continued, his beautiful brown eyes solemn as a gathering thundercloud, his face lean and intent. "I followed Gilly. You covered your tracks well, but I was determined to find you. I searched village after village. Then in Nadym, I hit gold. I heard of a baby left at the temple steps and about a lame young girl who cared for goats. I knew I'd found you."

"Why?" Gilly thought of all that wasted time. The countless nights she's spent alone, out on the moors with her goats, staring at the dark sky and wondering about her past. All that time, Tom had been nearby, watching her. "Why didn't you tell me who you were?"

"You didn't trust anyone. I tried to talk to you a few times but you always ran away. When you grew older," he began and then hesitated, breaking eye contact.

"He didn't think you liked him," Marton said. "I told him you would be lucky to call him your man but he said he wasn't worthy. I never understood then, I do now. He feels responsible for your father's death."

She covered her cheeks as a rush of heat coursed through her body. Had Tom been interested in her as more than a duty, even back then, in Nadym? Why couldn't he have said so?

There was something important she was missing in this conversation. What had he said about her missing family members? They weren't at the cottage when he went back to check. Why would the Horsemen have taken their bodies? *Oh no!* Could they still be alive? She cried out.

"Gilly, what's the matter?" Anna put an arm around her. "Talk to me! Don't shut me out again."

"If the Horsemen didn't kill Mam, Tamara and Garren, would they have taken them to the castle? To the dungeons. For Tamarisk to drain them of power as he does the magical guild masters?" Gilly clutched her sister by the shoulders, "Oh, Anna, they could have been suffering all this time. While I've been hiding, that monster could have been torturing them.

• • • •

GILLY AND TOM HERDED the children outside to give Anna and Marton a chance to speak in private. She could well imagine the thoughts racing through sensible, practical, Marton's mind, now he had discovered his wife was a princess who wields magic.

As am I!

Her mind wrestled with the absurd notion. Yesterday, she was a lonely goat herder. Today, she belonged to Ryca's highest station.

And Mam might be alive!

Bursts of joy spiraled up besides waves of dread at what her family might have gone through these past two decades trapped in the dungeons of Tibor castle. Underpinning those swirling emotions was a quagmire of overwhelming guilt for not returning to the cottage in the woods when her family didn't show up at the appointed time. For assuming they were dead.

Mam would come for me if she was alive.

The foolishness of such a false belief tasted as sour as week-old milk. Tamarisk the sorcerer held Princess Mamosia captive.

She *couldn't* come.

Heat washed over Gilly's face in shame at the safe life she had lived in such complacency. No more. The time for hiding was over. She wanted to storm out of Perm right this minute and straight into whatever horror Tibor held so she could rescue her sister, brother and their mam.

Not so Anna. She had her family's safety to consider.

How their perspectives had switched in the space of a few hours. Anna now understood why the King of Ryca, *their uncle*, wished to eliminate her family. Seeking clemency was no longer an option.

Skye wandered ahead along Perm's main road with a stone wall on one side, and houses built into the mountainside on the other. With happy abandon, the girl poked her head into store windows or chatted with the people on their doorsteps. Bevan, more cautious by nature, clung to Gilly's side, occasionally swinging on her right arm.

One of his wilder swings tipped her sideways and Tom's arm snaked around her waist to steady her.

Gilly's breath caught in her chest at that casual yet intimate gesture. Did he hear her heart speed up?

"A full-scale war against Ywen is out of the question." Tom said.

"What?" Gilly asked, confused by the abrupt return to their earlier topic while she was still grappling with what to do about his hand at her waist. "Oh, right. Yes. I mean, No, that's not what I have in mind."

"Good. A frontal assault would be sheer suicide. Better to mount a secret invasion of the castle, release those trapped in the dungeons and get out fast."

Amazing how his mind worked so in accord with hers. "We must convince Hagan of the wisdom of that plan."

Odd, so openly strategizing with another person. After years of planning, taking action and worrying in secrecy, discussing her best option with Tom was as unsettling as his thumb absently stroking her midriff.

Pounding hoofbeats from ahead halted Gilly's steps, and her thoughts scattered as terror spiked. Before a single horse came into view around the mountainside, Tom pushed her and Bevan in through a nearby open doorway. Luckily, the room was empty of inhabitants.

"I have to get Skye." Gilly swung back to the door.

Tom's arm blocked her while he peered outside. "I don't see her but we have unwelcome company."

Gilly squeezed in front of him and spotted horses galloping down the street toward them. The King's Horsemen with One-Eye from Nadym at the lead had arrived in Perm.

She desperately searched for a sign of Skye. People were scattering to get out of the Horsemen's way. Then Tom pointed straight at One-Eye.

The captain was leaning down to pluck Skye up by the back of her dress. Holding her suspended in mid-air, he slowed his mount to a walk. "Come out, witch!"

"You're not going," Tom said in a fierce whisper.

"I must." Terror for Skye overrode her sense of self-preservation. She tore out of his painful grip and limped outside, straight toward One-Eye. "Release her."

The captain's grin was insolent.

As she drew closer, Gilly's tongue tingled as she wove a *Come-to-me* spell that would yank her niece out of his grip.

He forestalled her by opening his fist. Skye tumbled down with a frightened cry. Gilly leaped forward to catch her and they both sprawled onto the cobblestone street. She was straightening when a net landed over her.

Pain streaked across her back. Skye screamed in agony while Gilly shuddered. Everywhere the net touched was excruciating. She huddled Skye close to shield her from the touch of that scorching net. The girl cowered beneath her and softly whimpered.

A crowd was gathering to watch the spectacle, but Gilly did not expect much help. They looked like visitors who lived outside the walls. None were the shopkeepers she'd seen here or one of the Rycan Warriors that Hagan had introduced to her. Those men were probably hiding. Smart.

Gilly trembled and then her muscles seized tight. Her skin began to itch and her strength leached out of her. That was when she noticed the netting sparkle as drops of energy were sucked out of her body. No, not energy. *Light*. It drew her magic out in little glinting beads that slithered over the lines before sinking into the knots of the cross links. Is this how they had captured her powerful mother?

One-Eye lowered a sword to Gilly's throat. "Order me again, witch," he said in a deadly tone, "and it will be your last words." The sword's nick at her throat was akin to a pinprick compared to the net's torment, but a wet droplet trickled from her throat and slid wetly down her chest. "Where are your kin?"

She took a rasping breath. "At Tibor's castle."

"Don't play games." He jumped down and stooped to speak. "Where are they?"

"Captain!" a man called out.

Talus? Was he in league with the Horsemen? Was that why these butchers were here? Gilly had liked Talus. Begun to trust him.

Disappointment lay as heavy as that tormenting net. Another failure on her part.

"What seems the trouble here?" Stomp of boots announced Talus' arrival at their side, but Gilly was unable to move her head to see him. He whisked the netting off in one swift move.

She sucked in a breath as profound relief washed over her in a blessedly cool wave. She hadn't been wrong about him. He was a friend.

Gilly scrambled up, and ignoring the armed Horsemen, shifted Skye and herself behind Talus. Whispers grew among the crowd watching this spectacle.

"What are you doing, Warrior?" One-Eye asked in a deadly tone. Metallic swish of weapons being drawn rang through the air. "This is none of your business."

"I'm making it mine." Talus's tone was hard and uncompromising. "These two are under my care. What is your business with them?"

"The woman and her kin are wanted by the king." One-Eye motioned to one of his men to come forward and then he mounted his horse. A black stallion this time.

A Horseman dismounted and with his drawn sword held out, he cautiously approached Talus and extended his free hand, gesturing to the netting.

Talus tossed the accursed contraption to him.

The captain nodded and sheathed his sword. "The woman travels with this child, the child's brother and their parents. Do you know the others' whereabouts?"

Gilly tightened her grip on Talus's tunic in warning.

Talus crossed his arms and leaned back on his heels. "I repeat. What is your business with them?"

"For starters, she stole my horse."

"And you admit so in public?"

A Horseman behind One-Eye snickered and a few in the crowd chuckled. The captain swung around and glared at his men, trying to spot the culprit. Everyone quieted, displaying bland faces.

One-Eye slowly returned his attention to Talus, and Gilly trembled at the fury in his gaze. She recalled from Nadym that when in a temper, this captain lashed out at anyone nearby, even his own men. Then his malicious gaze settled on her and he pointed. "That one's accused of practicing magic."

Gilly's pulse lurched as the crowd released a collective gasp. Their quiet mutters grew into a din.

One-Eye raised his hand in a commanding gesture. "Silence!"

At once everyone quieted.

Talus said in a calm tone, "She's been in my care for many days. I've never witnessed her casting a spell. We are on our way to Tibor. When I report in at the castle, I shall inform the king of your concern. You may leave." With an outstretched arm, he swung around and shepherded Skye and Gilly ahead of him in a clear sign of dismissal.

"Hold, Warrior!" One-Eye said.

Talus kept walking, forcing Gilly and Skye to hurry.

Behind them horses nickered nervously and hooves thudded closer.

"Run!" Talus pushed Gilly's back before he swung around, sword drawn. A frantic glance over her shoulder showed the crowd surging back, with some people wisely running for cover with their children. Shockingly, the vast majority stayed, perhaps hoping to witness the spectacle of a battle.

This was no entertainment to Gilly. Picking up her skirts, her heart pounding in terror, she ran limping away with Skye flying ahead. Steel met steel and her fear for Talus's safety surged. Out-numbered, he wouldn't be able to hold them off for long. Hoofbeats suggested the chase was on. She cursed her left leg for lagging as she and Skye pounded down the street.

Suddenly, Hagan was there, running toward her and shouting, "Rycan Warriors, fight, fight, fight!"

All along the street, doors were flung open and the shopkeepers of Perm, with weapons drawn, stormed out. Tom was at their lead carrying what looked like a stout club.

"Gilly, over here," Anna shouted from a nearby doorway, Bevan and Marton beside her.

Snagging Skye, Gilly veered their steps toward her sister, weaving her way through a crowd to get to that doorway and safety. As soon as they were inside, Marton shut and locked the door. The blacksmith had a sword in hand, and stood braced and ready to use it if anyone broke in.

Chapter 13

"Marton, open that door," Gilly said. "I have to help Tom!

"No, you don't." Anna hugged her two children. "If we must have a killer in our party, we should at least be allowed to put him to good use in our defense."

Outside, the fighting raged to the sound of grunts, cries, thuds and the occasional sword clang. Unable to budge Marton, Gilly went to a window and flung open the shutters. Most of the crowd had retreated to either ends of the street, leaving the fighters in the center, blocked on all four sides. Though these people weren't scattering, nor did they help. As Gilly's frustration at their inaction grew, she wanted to shout at them to do something, but fear clamped her tongue in silence. What if they turned against her side?

"If you won't let me out," Gilly said to Marton, "then you're going to have to put up with me using magic."

Arms crossed, the blacksmith stood his ground though the scowl on his face said he disliked the bargain.

Drawing on Light, Gilly chanted out the open window. "Come wind, come rain, and batter these Horsemen."

Clouds gathered, darkening the sky and thunder rumbled. Lightning flashes littered the sky. Those on the street who overheard Gilly's chant spread apart to either side of the open window, and then looked upward.

"Oooh," Bevan breathed, mimicking their audience's awe. He came out from behind his mother to watch dark clouds gathering in the sky.

Tom ran to help Talus fight off Horsemen and was joined by Rycan Warriors. Together they beat back half a dozen foes.

Seeing One-Eye ride up sword raised behind Talus, Gilly shouted, "Look out!"

Hagan heard her warning cry and jumped onto One-Eye's horse, jarring the captain's aim. The two men fought until a nearby Horseman galloped forward and stabbed Hagan's side. One-Eye then pushed the wounded man to the ground and in one deadly swing, hacked off his head.

Hagan's blood splattered along the street mingling with the falling rain. Horror washed over Gilly in a cool wave and her bile rose. The crowd moaned at the sight and beside her, Skye cried out. Gilly shushed the girl with a hand over her mouth. Too late. One-Eye's focus swung toward them.

Rain fell heavily now and resounding thunder began to frighten the horses. Instead of going forward as urged, One-Eye's mount shied. He pulled on the reins but at a second thunderclap, the beast bucked, almost unseating him.

Unable to contain herself, Gilly let out a crow of triumph. The sight of One-Eye in trouble seemed to energize the crowd, too, and people surged forward, beating Horsemen with their fists or throwing rocks.

Seeing the fight turn from his advantage, One-Eye called a retreat and rode off toward the gates. His men scrambled to follow. As they left, shouts of victory rose.

Gilly heard Tom's voice above the din, giving an order to shut the gates once the Horsemen had departed.

Marton finally relented and allowed Gilly out of the house. Overwhelmed that this fight had ended with her family and friends unharmed, a tearful Gilly limped outside, her throat swollen with unspoken gratitude for Talus, the Rycan Warriors and the scores of people who had assisted them. By defending her and her family, the people of Ryca had thrown their lot in with hers against their king.

Talus nodded to her as she passed him, silently wiping the blood off his blade and sheathing his sword.

Gilly's attention never wavered from Tom, who had stopped along with the crowd near Hagan. He gently closed the man's eyes and moved the head closer to his body.

"We need a new chief," a man said in a sorrowful tone.

The Rycan Warriors turned as one to Tom.

He shook his head. "I'm no leader."

The shoemaker reached over and raised Tom's hand. "Who agrees that 'Tomas the Brave' should be the new head of the Rycan Warriors?"

The description surprised Gilly until she realized that Anna's stories by the tent this morning and Cullen's tales in the marketplace about their visit to Erov must have spread around town. That would explain why all these people had stayed to watch this fight and then finally came to their aid. Anna had suspected the people in Perm might hold a different view of magic than the King's Horsemen. She was right.

Half-amused and half-terrified, Gilly observed Tom tug at his captured hand. Instead, the Rycan Warriors lifted him up onto their shoulders to cries of "Tomas the Brave."

"Never thought I'd live to see such a scene," Anna said coming up to her side.

"Put me down," Tom ordered in a harsh voice.

He was instantly set back on his feet.

Watching their gentle handling of Tom, Gilly realized these men already saw Tom as their new leader.

"This is the time to see to our wounded and bury our dead," Tom said, straightening his tunic. "The fallen Horsemen, too. And keep the gates closed."

As she listened to his commands, the impetus to flee nipped at Gilly's heels. With the Horsemen at the city's doorstep, now was the time to flee Perm. Which way would Anna go, back toward Nadym with her family, or toward Tibor with Gilly? She prayed it would be the former. That was much safer for the children and Anna. It was the sensible thing to do. What Marton would want to do.

In a quiet resigned voice, Gilly asked, "Have you both decided on your course?"

"How can you even ask?" Anna said in a cross tone. "Of course we're all going to rescue our family in Tibor."

Gilly stood shocked at that flat uncompromising statement. Had Marton, who was as wary of magic as the Horsemen, agreed to this?

Talus approached them then, and right there in the middle of the street in front of everyone, he knelt with elaborate ceremony before Anna and Gilly and put hand to heart. "I swear my allegiance to Prince Keegan's true offspring."

She stared at him in shock and wonder. Gilly hugged him tight, uncaring that her tears wet this brave warrior's face.

A deafening cheer had her standing up straight and looking in astonishment at the crowd. Apparently, if the news about Erov had stirred these people's passions about the existence of magic enough to fight the Horsemen, knowledge that Prince Keegan's offspring were amongst them set the townsfolk on fire. Every man, woman and child crowded closer and lining up behind Talus, they all knelt as one and swore fealty to their prince's offspring.

Tom stood by himself beside Hagan's body. Then with a grim smile, he, too, knelt and bowed his head.

Anna hugged Gilly close. Marton's arms wrapped both women closer to him. Gilly's heart warmed. Perhaps he didn't hate her and her magic so much then. Anna's children ran to be included in that family moment.

From that point onward, nothing Gilly could say would dissuade the Rycan Warriors from accompanying her and her family to Tibor. Anna looked on with a wide satisfied grin. "We'll have help for our quest then. Good."

Gilly gave in with grace. Mainly because she had no choice in the matter. "If we're to set off for Tibor, we had better do so before the Horsemen rally and return with reinforcements."

Tom gave her a nod of encouragement before he, too, left to get ready for the journey ahead.

Soon Gilly stood alone on the quiet, empty street. Heart hammering in excitement, she whispered, "Hang on a little longer, Mam. We're coming for you."

••••

WHEN IT WAS TIME TO depart Perm, Cullen was nowhere to be found. He might have returned to their tent outside the gates when the fighting began and found himself locked out. Just as well, Gilly decided. He had shown no liking for magic and in all likelihood, would have turned against her and Anna.

At hearing the news about Cullen's absence, Marton muttered, "Good riddance," reflecting most of the group's feelings on the matter.

Gilly nodded, but a tiny part deep inside her wondered if Marton would say the same if she disappeared.

At nightfall, the Rycan Warriors escorted them into an underground tunnel. A torch held at the lead and one at the back highlighted their eerily silent trek through the mountain's interior. The warriors promised this path would save them two days travel overland and leave the King's Horsemen in their dust.

It was an interminable never-ending journey. The moment they reached fresh air, Gilly took a big relieved breath. Her neck muscles were stiff from stooping even though there had been ample room to stand straight. She rolled her shoulders to relieve her lingering tension and then caught sight of their location.

They were on the side of a narrow mountain trail, so high up that if she reached out, she might touch the sky. Having lived on flat plains most of her life, being this elevated had her hugging the side of the mountain she had just been itching to get out of.

Tom was at her side, pulling her close to his chest and it was the most comforting feel Gilly had ever experienced. As she rested her head on his shoulder, he whispered, "You're safe."

Within his arms, she felt safe. How odd. A brand new experience. Even while she stood on a precipice. Slowly, together, they followed the rest of her party on the trail downward. Thankfully, no one asked her to mount a horse while up here. Though she might have allowed Tom to pull her away from the mountainside, she wasn't ready to have her feet leave the ground. The downward trek was harder on her leg than climbing up to Perm.

Once the trail widened, they mounted horses before continuing the journey. Tom stayed nearby the whole time. His concern warmed her heart and made the ride almost pleasurable, as long as she did not look to her left where the track seemed to drop off into a valley far below.

By sunset, having ridden for hours, Gilly's left leg was seriously stiff and beginning to cramp as they entered a resting spot near the mountain's base. Tom went to speak to the warriors about setting up a perimeter watch.

"Are you all right?" Anna asked, coming up to her side. "You look as white as the mountain top."

"Didn't you find it hard being so high up?" Gilly asked.

"Loved it," Anna said with a wide smile. "I can see myself living up here one day. I suggested to Marton that mountain cities needed blacksmiths, too. He didn't say, *No*." She leaned in and whispered, "I think he liked Perm."

As that startling news sank in, Gilly wondered how she would fare living up a mountain for the rest of her life. She shivered, her body rejecting the alarming thought. Still, it would be far from Tibor and the king, and if she could be with Anna, she should have to give the idea serious consideration. Leaving her sister was not an option. Their future depended on how this rescue mission fared.

Another worry instantly reared. One she had been mulling over since that terrible destructive fight in Perm. Once they reached Tibor, the Rycan Warriors would need to defend themselves better than they had in their home city. She was unwilling to witness Tom's or anyone else's head being hacked off as Hagan's had been. That vision still haunted her.

However good her new friends' intentions, well-trained King's Warriors could slay these shopkeepers faster than she could swat flies. So, Gilly asked Talus to give Tom and the other men lessons in swordplay.

To her surprise, since it had been Talus' kind who slaughtered their comrades during the Makakala Wars, the Rycan Warriors were all on side to train with Talus. As the King's Warrior began the first practice session, it soon became obvious what the Rycan Warriors had wanted. A chance to fight Talus. The men soon discovered, however, that overwhelming Talus was easier conceived than achieved. They learned why Talus and his comrades had so successfully beaten down the Rycan Warriors.

Everyone, even Talus, went to bed looking bone weary. Gilly and Anna exchanged knowing glances, and by mutual consent, kept their opinions to themselves. Best to let the men work out this issue for themselves. Over the course of the next week, as Talus pinpointed and worked on everyone's strengths and weaknesses, the practice sessions evolved into true training exercises, rather than a chance to batter each other at will.

• • • •

AS THE DAYS WORE ON, the group worked its way out of the Makakala range of mountains. The surroundings changed from hilly to flat rolling green terrain that stretched far ahead. According to Talus, in less than two weeks they would reach the east coast of Ryca.

Like the landscape, Tom, too, seemed to be changing. His wounds healed, and lack of the brew brought a healthy gleam to his face. Regular exercise added muscle to his figure and one day, Gilly realized he had transformed into the warrior Jarrod named him in the Telling Ceremony.

Surprisingly, even though Tom's training had been her idea, Gilly grew resentful of his busy schedule. He'd not said a suggestive word or approached her intimately since Perm.

In fact, he seemed to have forgotten her. For a man who had purported to follow her his whole life, could he not ask how she fared? Did her leg hurt? Was she comfortable? He seemed more concerned with training with the warriors than spending time with her. He even spent all his time riding glued beside Talus, peppering him with questions about training techniques.

Most nights Gilly sat in a secluded place to care for her leg. Each stroke of her hand evoked delicious memories of Tom's touch. Whenever Marton gave Anna a hand up from the campfire and led her off to their sleeping pallet, Gilly's chest tightened with longing for Tom to do the same with her.

Of course, she was being silly. She had decided a long time ago that the life a woman enjoyed with a man could never be hers. Given a choice between a sound woman and one hindered by a deformity, what strong healthy man would choose the latter?

The self-pity in that thought irked, so she shook it off. Then turned back to the same topic and blamed her obsession with Tom on him, too. She wouldn't be considering the possibility of a relationship between them if he hadn't run his hands up her leg so wantonly that one night. Why couldn't he have left her in peaceful ignorance of the reaction a man's hands could arouse in her body? Now, instead of tossing at night in fear of attacking Horsemen, she slept fitfully dreaming of Tom's hands roving up her calf and over her knee.

Lack of sleep was also making her bad tempered. If she kept this up, she wouldn't have to worry about any man wanting to spend time with her. No one would. One night, annoyance turned to frustration, and Gilly rose to seek solace in privacy.

Her self-appointed bodyguards jumped up to follow. With a sigh, she strolled into the night ignoring their quiet shuffle behind her. She sat by an outcropping to stare at the midnight sky. Before long, their soft snores reached her.

She smiled with indulgence. Their devotion to her safety was rather sweet, if short lived. Few people had shown her such caring. When she lived at the cottage with Mam, most of her time had been spent alone at Lookout Point. In Nadym, the women in the village shunned her and the men didn't notice her. Now, family, friends and warriors surrounded her at every waking moment. Strange then that she still felt so alone.

Soft tones of sleeping drifted in the breeze. It would be easy to step away now but she couldn't do it. Although her guards believed they watched over her, over the course of the last few days, she'd begun to feel as if it were she who guarded them.

At the clip of boots on rock, the snores abruptly ceased. They were no longer alone. Mumbled voices were followed by the sound of her guards retreating.

"So much solitude can't be healthy for a soul." Tom sat beside her bringing his heady male scent with him.

She felt light-headed until she realized she had breathed him in too deeply and was now holding her breath. Her breath gushed out in a sigh. "Hardly solitude, with three such stalwart guards."

"I know you could have lost them if you wished," he said, "but it makes them feel good and it makes me feel better to know you are not alone."

Gilly gave him a side-glance, noting his frown. She hadn't thought he'd noticed her at all lately.

"Your sister misses your company," he said, when she didn't reply.

"Anna? Did she say so?"

"She didn't have to. Her gaze rarely wanders from you. Even the children have mentioned that you seem not to like them anymore."

"Of course, I like them."

"It's hard to tell when you speak no more than one or two words a day."

She went quiet. He was right. She had unconsciously distanced herself from her family. Perhaps partly due to Marton's harsh reaction to learning she could cast spells, hinting he didn't want her to be a bad influence on his family. If she were honest, it was also due to her secrets being exposed. She had always hidden from people and emotional ties. It had been a necessity of life. Now, there was nothing to hide behind, leaving her exposed.

"I'll speak to them," she whispered, her chest tightening at the idea that she might have inadvertently hurt those she loved.

"What about the rest of us? I worry as well. It isn't good to spend so much time alone." He laughed softly but there was a harsh edge to it. "Don't want you getting ideas about going off on your own. We're all in this together."

She looked away. "You needn't worry that the princess you've guarded all of your life will leave without warning, Tom. At least, not yet."

He took her hand and wove his fingers through hers. "Not ever."

His strength had increased; she felt it in his touch. It was intoxicating. Did he expect to guard her forever? She had been hoping for more between them. There was that hateful word again. *Hope.* Her mouth soured on the word as if she'd bitten into a rotten apple.

She pictured Tom, married with children of his own, coming every day to keep an eye on old Princess Saira-Gilly, unmarried with just goats for company. It was more than she could bear. She pulled free. "Once we find my mother, she will become your primary responsibility. Then it will be time for you to let me go."

"Is that what you want?"

"What I want doesn't matter."

Abruptly he stood. "You've been alone so long, Saira, you've forgotten how to love. It involves touching and talking, giving and taking. Let those who love you know when you're ready to remember."

He retreated to camp and in moments her guards returned to their post. She continued her contemplation of the stars, trying to ignore the tears that slid down her cheeks and the ghostly feel of Tom's fingers threaded through her heart.

She slept fitfully that night, dreaming of Hagan's disembodied head glowing amid a dark cloud and then Tom walking away, holding another woman's hand as he had held hers tonight.

She awoke with a start, heart pounding, the cry, *Come back,* on the tip of her tongue.

Jarrod was sitting beside her bedroll.

When she would have spoken, he placed a slender black finger across her lips. He gave a head tilt, as if to say, *Follow me*, and then stood and walked away.

Gilly pulled on her boots, excitement at seeing Jarrod and a bit of lingering fear from her recent dreams coursing through her. Why was he here? Did trouble brew nearby? Jarrod was far to her left now, a silent silhouette.

She stood, trying to be both careful and quiet. Astonishingly, she didn't trip over anything as she left. Even her ever vigilant guards didn't notice her passing right beside them.

Could Jarrod's magic be at play? His people were incredibly talented at moving through Rycan society without leaving an impression. Hopefully the Light magic he used was the kind Tamarisk could not trace.

By the time she caught up to him, the dark horizon had hints of lightness in the east. Once they were both out of earshot, she touched his arm and asked "Are you real?"

"Gilly," he turned to face her, "your sleep was troubled."

She wiped crusts out of the corner of her eyes and cheeks, and then ran a self-consciously hand over her hair. She had no wish to discuss her confusion over Tom. "I seem doomed to be the cause of death to all leaders I meet, Jarrod. It's not wise to spend so much time in my company."

"A defeatist attitude. After such a resounding victory in Perm."

"How long will that lucky streak last?" She leaned back against a large boulder and stared out at the lonely landscape. Still a sennight's journey before they would reach the coast and Tibor. "The King's Horsemen are after us, Jarrod. We're heading for the king's city, where, notified by the Horsemen, he will no doubt have a contingent of his warriors waiting to capture us. It would be simpler to let the Horsemen take me."

"On that we agree," he said.

"Oh." Her attention swung back. "Are we doomed?"

He came over to rest against her boulder. "It isn't only the King's Warriors that will greet you in Tibor. The king's royal sorcerer, Tamarisk, uses a deadly black cloud to protect himself. He's been reinforcing it lately, probably in anticipation of your arrival. It is capable of destroying anything it touches."

Gilly stared at him in stunned silence. What was there to say to that? A slow anger burned in her chest. "How can you stay so calm and tell me my entire family and all my friends are about to be destroyed? Have you no feeling?"

"I care, Gilly. Deeply. Why else would I be here?"

"Then you have a plan? To defeat this cloud thing."

"Only you can destroy it. All I can do is warn. Even that violates my people's laws of non-interference."

She grabbed at Jarrod's tunic and pulled him closer. "Would a weather spell conquer it? Can a ward keep us safe? If I blow on it, will it dissipate?"

Jarrod tipped his head back and laughed.

Thoroughly disgusted, she pushed him away and moved around the boulder until she had her back to him. "I'm glad you find my dilemma amusing."

His laughter faded into a quiet chuckle. "No, merely your turn of mind. I cannot laugh at your troubles, for they are indeed grave. Be wary of what lies ahead in Tibor."

Gilly contemplated the moon. The first had risen this night, smallest of the three sisters. The Horsemen behind her, a deadly cloud ahead. No idea of how to defeat either. She supposed she should be glad Jarrod had come to warn her. It gave her party an opportunity to re-assess their chances of survival. Especially, Anna and the children.

She turned back to him. "Jarrod, will you..."

He was gone. As quietly as he'd arrived, the Chief Councilor of Erov had taken his leave. The man was a mystery, both in his manner of arrival and departure, and in his knowledge of coming events. Yet, she trusted him. If he said, beware, that was what she planned to do.

A tremor went up her back. She'd never heard of anything as destructive as what Jarrod described. Danger had stalked her steps all her life, yet it had been of the variety she could see and touch. Men with weapons and a leader bent on her family's eradication. This cloud thing she couldn't explain or reason away and she had no idea how to defeat it.

Her first instinct was to take her family and run away. This time she couldn't. Not with Mam and her brother and sister relying on her to save them. So, what could she do?

An idea instantly formed but it was a dangerous move. One she'd tried before, and failed at abysmally. Did she dare do it again? *Yes!* For there could be no more running away.

Gilly walked back to camp, her thoughts battling between a plan to cast an enchantment alone or ask her sister for help. Before she arrived at the camp, she heard a sentry call out, "Missus Gilly is returning."

It was not quite light yet. What could have aroused everyone? She turned a corner and arrived back at camp to find everyone dressed and ready to leave. Even the fire had been put out. Instead of heading east, though, they were facing west, the direction in which she had walked off with Jarrod.

Looking into everyone's concerned gazes, her decision solidified. Tom was right. She had family and friends who wanted to be a part of her life. Time she let them in.

Anna, with arms crossed, watched her return with a narrow-eyed stare that would have normally set all of Gilly's alarms ringing. This time, she faced her sister with her chin raised. She needed Anna's help. Correction, she needed everyone's help.

"I plan to try and contact Mam," she said, addressing everyone. "Tamarisk might trace that seeking back to me, so I need Anna to help if the backlash hurts me. All of you must watch over her, in case she's harmed."

The resounding silence after Gilly laid out her plan had her on edge. Her toes curled waiting for someone, anyone, to speak their mind.

Finally, Tom said, "Well, this saves us following you to wherever you planned to cast this spell in secret."

"Yay!" Skye clapped her hands and jumped up and down. "I want to help, too."

"No, you won't," Marton said in a firm tone. Then he put his arm around Anna. "She will, and I will watch over her."

"We will all watch over *both* of you," Tom said in that quiet firm tone of a leader he seemed to have acquired during their trek across Ryca.

Gilly's throat closed up with intense gratitude and she silently nodded her thanks.

Chapter 14

Taking a shaky breath, Gilly laid out the reasoning she'd been marshaling since Jarrod left. "There's no point going further if we're not sure Mam is even at the castle," she said, her gaze trained on Anna. "We need to know, now, before we enter Tibor and risk our lives more than we already have."

"The last time you did a seeking spell was in Erov, wasn't it?" Anna asked.

"I have done one since."

"When Hagan captured us," her sister said. "That was you I felt."

"Yes, I was worried and wanted to make sure you were alive. Also on the night we were together in the alcove in Erov. I tried to seek out Aton's murderer."

"You were almost killed, certainly blinded," her sister finished.

"I plan to be more prepared this time." She then mentioned what Jarrod said about this dark cloud Tamarisk used. "It will be a chance to check on its composition and see if it has any weaknesses we can exploit."

Marton rubbed his wife's hands thoughtfully. "This sounds dangerous. You said any use of magic draws the Horsemen to us. Will this seeking risk the children?"

"They're already at risk," Anna said. "Especially if we go to Tibor without knowing the facts."

Talus, who had remained silent during the discussion, spoke up. "I don't like this. It puts Missus Gilly, and you, Mistress Anna, in danger. Tamarisk is not a man I would cross. He is a most powerful sorcerer. If he lashes back with magic, there is nothing I, Tom or the guards can do to help."

"You're going to do this regardless, aren't you?" Tom asked. At her nod, he said, "Then how can we strengthen your protection?"

"The tools I need are in my satchel."

With that, preparations began. As Gilly laid a circle of candles, Anna followed behind, setting power stones between each candle. "You surprised me today."

Gilly glanced back at her sister. "How so?"

"I saw you leave with Jarrod. Strange no one else saw him, not even Marton or Tom. They just saw you, walking off alone. Tom sent a warrior to keep an eye on you. If you didn't return soon, I intended to follow, too."

Anna had seen Jarrod? A smile teased at Gilly's lips. "I'm glad I threw you off track by coming back."

"Tom was set to tie you to a tree to keep you in his sights, but I said it would be better if we followed you rather than forced you to stay with us."

"Tom?" Gilly was truly astounded now.

"He knows you better than I," her sister replied. "Or hadn't you realized?"

Gilly continued to place the candles in a circle, but her thoughts were on Anna's revelations about Tom. He had followed her all her life. Silently watched over her from afar, as she had done her sister. She knew Anna as well as any sibling could, perhaps better. Not far-fetched then, that Tom knew Gilly as well. Unsettling maybe, but unsurprising.

Once the ring was complete, she backtracked, chanting. Anna followed, scattering herbs to strengthen the boundary. The aroma of rosemary wafted up, strong and protective, rising like giant trunks of a circular pine forest.

She nodded to Tom and Marton. They were ready to begin. She motioned for Anna to enter the circle. Inside, Gilly sat in the center, right leg tucked in and left stretched out. A snap of her fingers sealed the barrier. A dome of protection vibrated around and over them. Satisfied Anna and she would be as safe as she could make them in here, she cleared her mind in preparation for her mental journey.

"What should I do?" Anna whispered.

Eyes closed, palms held up, Gilly said, "Sit across from me and lay your hands over mine."

Her sister's touch was as gentle as a breeze. In an instant though, the breeze turned into a gale that pulled them both straight up. So powerful! Gilly eased away from Anna and the level of energy diminished. Interesting. For exploration later. Right now, she had a job to do.

She shut out Anna's presence and gazed at the world around her. The draw of magic was everywhere. The calm soothing melody of the land was ever present and old as the sky. Sparks of Light scented with power lay in every direction. Some brighter than others. Normal people and those with the ability to wield Light? Was this how Tamarisk tracked his enemies? Did he send his Horsemen to kill any Light that sparked too brightly in this darkness? If so, why were so many bright ones still lit? She may not have been the only one hiding.

Perhaps, too, his vision was not as clear as hers. Draining the power of others against their will could have distorted his sight, the way dark magic destroyed the land. Sensing her thoughts wandering, Gilly re-focused on her goal.

Find Mam!

Within this vast Light show, how was she to locate her mother? It would take all eternity to check on each spark. She needed another way. Focus on what was wrong in this picture. She tuned out the humming warmth of the land, the sparkling glow of individual Lights, and sought that which felt abused. Immediately she sensed a draining from one side of the world.

"Anna, stay back," she warned.

"Be careful," her sister said but then she withdrew.

Once Anna's Light was a tiny spark in the distance, Gilly followed the dark pull. It led her to a place where the land gave way to an abyss. In the midst of the dead area was a black pockmarked wave. A festering wound that sucked energy from everything in its vicinity. What Light it drew into itself did not fill its emptiness, merely enlarged the wound. This was a true distorting of what Light was meant to do.

She could not imagine her mother living in the middle of this horror pit. She was the person who taught Gilly magic was meant for good, to heal wounds, to protect against evil and help people evolve to the best of their ability. This stank of Tamarisk's handiwork. Therefore, a good candidate to where he was holding Mam.

Gilly skirted the abyss, looking for a safe entryway. There were none. It was complete in its pulsing self. As she drew closer, she heard its call. It hungered for more Light. Her instinct was to run the other way, but Gilly quelled the urge to run and instead released her will until she melted into the darkness. She was pulled and stretched and torn apart until she and the darkness became one.

They were an inky stream. The screams of countless souls assaulted her, and came from her. Their terror, pain and fear, were her terror, pain and fear, multiplied a hundredfold.

There can be no calming of our angry energy. We flee hither and yon, without purpose, focus or intent. Drift aimlessly, unknowing the passage of time, waiting for the Master to call. To use us to do his bidding.

An imperial summons came.

We excitedly cluster together to form a shaft and soar across the sky like a phoenix.

Search for her. Find her. She must not escape.

Where is she? Where is her Light? So much darkness. Our darkness. We extinguish Lights. We remember when once, the night was bright with starlight. Now only darkness. Darkness that feeds our needs. Too dark. We need more Light. We need her Light.

Find her!

There, Master, in the mountains. We cannot see. We sense her presence. She is there. Too much Light to be any but the child of your beloved, Master.

We soar through the sky, an ebony shaft with new purpose, a fresh goal. Must consume that Light. A barrier! The clash reverberates through our shaft. Draw back!

Clever girl. Not clever enough. Take her!

We circle the candles. Two Lights inside, Master. What are they doing? Can't see past the flames. Too hot to touch. Will scorch our darkness. We cannot reach her.

Horsemen. Must send Horsemen. The Master departed.

No, do not leave! The shaft scattered, dissolving into a wave of energy, returning home without purpose. Lost again.

Pain. Terror. Horror. Hate the Master. Master shattered us. Need him to be whole. Love the Master. Come back. Make us whole again. The pain. Must be whole again. Master. Come back. Come back. Make us whole, if only for a moment. Where are we? Why are we here?

Darkness everywhere. Eternity of darkness. Pain. Loneliness. No hope. Must please the Master to be whole. Master is looking for someone. The child of his beloved.

You are the Defender of the Light. Jarrod's voice.

Who is Jarrod? No Light here. No Defender. No Light. No Defender. Wait. There is a Light. We see a Light. Deep within us. We see a Light. Where is the Master? Must tell Master. Tell him about Jarrod. Tell him about the Light.

No, cried a single objection.

Yes! we reply, burying the dissenter's protest. Jarrod might lead the Master to the Defender. Was the Defender the child of the beloved? Must tell about Jarrod. Tell about the Defender. We have a purpose. We are whole. Tell the Master. Where is the Master?

Find the Lights. Search for the Lights. Three of them.

The darkness scattered. We have a new purpose. Find the Lights. Must find three Lights. Why? Where?

Find the three Lights.

Don't know why. Must find the three Lights. Who is Jarrod? Defender of what?

Find the three Lights.

Some of us see lights. We converge, circling the faint Lights. We shatter and are hauled together again.

Stay focused. What have we found?

We have found the three Lights. Here they are. Bright as sunlight. Long forgotten sunlight. What was sunlight? We press closer. This sunlight is tainted. Not so bright. Sunlight is dying. Found the three Lights. They are dying. Why search for these Lights?

Focus is gone. Ahhhh! The pain. The horror of separation. The darkness of eternity alone.

Gilly pulled back from the mass and sped toward the warmth of her sister. Candlelight surrounded her, offering comfort, security. From somewhere energy flowed into her and sealed the wounds in her soul. Slowly she became aware of her sister's fingertips pressing into her palms. The physical pain of nails digging into her tender flesh brought Gilly out of her stupor and she stared at Anna in horror.

How close she had come to losing herself in that blackness, becoming a prisoner of the Master, for all eternity. She hugged Anna, savoring her solid arms, her familiar scent, the softness of her worn clothing, the silkiness of her hair. All real.

"You are not lost," Anna was repeating. "You are home. Safe."

"I found them," Gilly whispered breaking into her sister's refrain. Finally, they had confirmation their family really was alive. Shock waves coursed through Gilly as that realization sank in. Her insides began shivering uncontrollably. "I used the dark cloud to find Mam and our brother and sister. They're dying."

"We will save them," Anna said in a hard tone. Then she pointed to Tom and Marton outside the circle. The men were pacing back and forth. "Let them in."

Gilly broke the protection circle and Tom rushed in and lifted her into his arms. She stayed in his embrace, savoring being held, soothed, and comforted.

Slowly, she drew back. "We have to leave. The Horsemen will be arriving here soon."

"I'll have the sentries return and we'll ready for our departure," he said, but didn't release his hold.

"Now." Gilly pulled away, anxiety overtaking shock.

With a nod, he hurried off to confer with Talus.

Marton and the children were hugging Anna as though they had feared never seeing her again. The sight shook Gilly. There was such apprehension in Marton's eyes. Love made one so vulnerable.

In silence, Gilly gathered her candles and various rocks and branches of dried herbs. She couldn't shake one thought though. Not only was her family in need of saving but countless others. It wasn't right, what Tamarisk was doing to those magic guild sorcerers. They were the dark cloud Jarrod warned about. She had to do something about them.

They all mounted and left the camping spot in short order. Talus, looking worried, led the way. The Rycan Warriors were right behind him. For a change, Tom chose to ride at the back with Gilly. Marton, Anna and the children crowded close. At Talus's curt order, a handful of warriors dropped back to act as a rear contingent, watching their backs.

"Tell us what happened," Tom said.

"My family is at the castle but they are dying."

Tom nodded. "Talus tells us that within a few days, we will be on the outskirts of Tibor. We'll get to them soon."

"Something else frightened you," Anna sounded certain. "What was it?"

Gilly took a deep shaky breath, trying to put her impression of the horror she had experienced into words. "He has many sorcerers' souls trapped and broken. They don't even know who they are or what has happened to them. They live for the moment he appears to give them a sense of purpose. That purpose is always to search out others who wield Light. They don't realize what they've destroyed and yet the more he twists them to his bidding, the darker their souls become, sucking from the Lights around them to simply survive."

"Oh, those poor things," Anna said with abject sorrow.

Skye and Bevan were wide-eyed and speechless, while Marton's mouth turned grim.

Tom simply took Gilly's hand.

"Even if Mam wasn't there, I would have to go to Tibor now to release these souls from that suffering." Gilly wanted to bury that memory away forever, but she refused to. They needed saving and she intended to be there for them.

"They'll all be free before long." Tom gave her hand a bolstering squeeze.

Gazing into his direct stare, she believed him. His quiet words held strength of purpose that mirrored her resolve. If she didn't love him already, she did now, with all her heart. The realization floored her and she rode on in silence, cherishing his firm hold, as if he never intended to let her go.

• • • •

SIX DAYS LATER, BY mid-afternoon, they reached the River Qiqi. They were now within a few hours travel to Tibor.

Time for the next dangerous part of their plan. Gilly informed the warriors that storming the castle was out of the question. She was unyielding on this point. They were not here to overthrow King Ywen. They were only on a rescue mission for her family and the imprisoned magic guild members.

There was surprisingly little argument over her plan. She suspected that after practicing with Talus, these men must have realized they would not stand a chance if they were pitted against trained King's Warriors in their home city.

What they needed was a way into the castle dungeons that wouldn't draw attention.

Talus asked Ned, the shoemaker, to tell everyone about Hagan's plan to enter the castle. Apparently, during their sword practice sessions Ned had mentioned a secret doorway.

As a child, the late Rycan Warrior Chief had been smuggled out of Tibor castle by his mother. Ned was the only one to whom Hagan had spoken to about the passage and where the door was supposedly located in Tibor. He'd even shown him where he'd kept the key hidden in Perm.

Ned held it up for all to see. "I know he would want us to use it," he said, sounding a little choked up.

They decided that along with Ned to guide their way, Tom and Talus should go first on a scouting mission to locate the site. While they were gone, Talus ordered the warriors to practice moves he'd taught them. It would be their last chance to improve their skills before any fighting might be required.

Marton agreed to stay behind and keep an eye over Anna, Gilly and the children.

Tom then firmly took hold of Gilly's arm and marched her into the woods, saying, "I have something for you."

Worried about letting him go into Tibor alone, Gilly absently accompanied him, scouring her mind for a good reason she should accompany the scouting party.

Once they were alone and out of earshot, Tom placed a crossbow in her hands and insisted on teaching her how to use it. "If Horsemen come before I return," he said as he positioned her to hit a tree trunk, "you'll need a physical weapon to fight your way free of their magic-binding net. You must never go anywhere without this weapon. Promise me?"

With his arms around her and his breath in her ear as he showed her how to aim, her pulse skipped with joy. She was ready to promise him anything.

Twang.

She missed the tree entirely, the arrow sinking into the ground several paces past.

He reloaded and made her aim again. "Focus."

By the third try she grazed the side of the wood, purely by chance. It made him smile though and that warmed her heart. He ran to retrieve the arrows and returned to reload. In his gaze was the stature of a King's Bodyguard, front and center. Behind that intense focus lurked his fear about leaving her.

In the distance, Talus called out, "Tom, time to go."

Even though she doubted the weapon would be of much use, when he offered her the arrows, she accepted them and gave her word to always keep the crossbow with her.

On impulse, she reached up and said against his lips, "I'm ready to remember how to love," and kissed him. It was her way of wishing him goodbye, but it turned out to be the sweetest touch she had ever experienced.

The forgotten crossbow and arrows slid to the ground, thumping by her feet. Gilly didn't notice as she roved her hands over this adorable man. Once she began kissing him, she couldn't stop. How had she survived so long without holding him like this?

At first he stood stiff in her arms and then he pulled her close, claiming her in return. It was a long while before he pulled back enough to give her room to breathe. Or to think. She only noticed he'd moved her when a tree trunk pressed against her spine. Then he chuckled, ruining the mood.

"What's so funny?" She thumped him on his chest.

"If I'd known all I had to do to win your favor was give you a weapon, Saira," he murmured against her ear, "I would have showered you with bows and arrows when you reached eighteen summers." Then he rained kisses all down her neck and under her chin. Gilly lost her train of thought.

Talus called out again, this time followed by him stomping through the underbrush toward them, "Tom! If we don't leave soon, it'll be sunset."

Unwilling to let go, Gilly snuggled close, wrapping her arms around him. "Don't listen to him. It's barely sunrise."

"It's almost noon," Tom said and kissed her.

"Promise to come back?" she asked coming up for air.

"After this send off, try and keep me away." He retrieved the crossbow and pressed it into her arms. "Keep this close, always."

She nodded and hugged the wooden weapon to her chest, her throat aching. With a wave, he ran to meet Talus. Gilly returned to camp slowly, her thoughts a confused whirl of happiness and sorrow. The riders were already out of sight by the time she arrived. Anna was seated with her children and husband.

Her sister's gaze skirted away from hers, appearing guilty. Had she sent Talus after Tom? Which meant Anna had been following Gilly's movements. Because she didn't approve of Tom or because she was worried about Gilly? If something was bothering her, why didn't she speak up? Unusual for Anna to be so reticent.

As she'd reached out to claim Tom, perhaps it was time to connect with Anna, too. "I'm going to catch up on washing," she said and set the crossbow down to gather her clothes. "Want to come with me, Anna?"

"Yes!" Her sister jumped up and began to sort through her family's clothing.

"I can come, if you wish," Marton said tentatively, as if washing clothes wasn't his favorite activity. "It may not be safe to go to the river alone."

With an understanding smile, Gilly picked up her crossbow. "I'm taking this with me." She then nodded to where her ever-present guards were watching their friends practice. "And we won't be on our own."

Marton nodded, satisfied, and returned to playing a game with Bevan that involved tossing rocks into a circle to hit the opponent's pieces. Anna conscripted Skye to help her carry her pile of clothes.

By the water's edge, Gilly took off her shoes and sloshed in. She chose a large flat rock to pound her clothes against, dropped her bundle beside it and fished out soap from her satchel. Anna settled nearby with the same purpose. Skye dropped the clothes and ran back to watch the fighting practice.

Her sister didn't speak and Gilly, trying to think of something to say, was flummoxed. Then she remembered her sister's interest spiking when she mentioned their father's temper. Now some of her memories had returned, she could share a little about him and maybe draw Anna out

"Mam didn't talk much about our papa," she began, looking up to see Anna's reaction. Her sister stiffened, but her gaze remained fixed on the clothes she beat against her stone. The action had more force than earlier though.

Good sign.

Gilly rubbed soap onto a stained bit of dress hem. "Mam said papa liked to play the Light game with me, where I'd chant a spell to move an object and he'd block me."

Anna's glance was filled with curiosity. "How could he do that?"

"When High Magic works, specks of Light dance around. Anyway, Mam said Papa would knock the specks away and make me drop what I was trying to move. She said it would make me mad and happy all at the same time. That I would stubbornly move a spoon or pot no matter how hard he made it. I vaguely remember laughing so hard the Lights flew about the room shaking everything."

"I wish I could have known him," Anna said in a wistful tone. "Do you think Papa was training you to become a strong sorceress? Pushing your limits?"

The idea surprised Gilly. "I don't know. After Mam first told me that story, I spent hours at Lookout Point trying to shift branches and stones. It never worked."

"You're good at casting spells now," Anna said.

Gilly nodded. "Mostly Hearth Magic. I can influence the weather. Set wards. Coerce animals to behave in a certain way. Even do a seeking. Not move inanimate objects though. Except once, when Skye was in danger."

They continued washing in silence, then Anna asked, "What was she like?"

"Mam?" At her sister's nod, Gilly shook her head. "I don't truly know. She loved us, I'm sure of that. She tried to make a normal life for us, though we were always on the watch for Horsemen. I think she missed Papa. Sometimes, late at night, I'd cry out and she'd come to cuddle me and tell me I shouldn't be scared. That Papa was with us all and he'd never let anything bad happen to us."

"I wish he were here now," Anna said. "I'm scared all the time, for Skye and Bevan and Marton. To think I wanted to go to Tibor to offer my services to King Ywen. That would have meant my death and that of my children. Instead of turning back, we're still headed toward him."

"You don't have to come." Was this what was worrying her sister? "I said so in Perm. Better if you, Marton and the kids find someplace safe to hide."

"While you go to the castle to rescue our family?"

"I intend to be careful," Gilly said.

"You always think this is your fight." Anna's face was flushed now and her eyes wide and sparkling with temper. "It's *our* fight! Yours and mine. I may have been a baby when we lost our mother but I'm now grown up. She's as much a part of who I am as you. Do you think I care any less for her because she never cuddled me at night?" A catch in her sister's voice spoke of Anna's hurt at missing that treasured experience. "How could I desert her after she risked her life to save mine?"

"She wouldn't want you to put your life or your family's in danger."

Anna flicked that concern away with a wave of her hand. "But she'd want you to risk yours? Would she be proud of me if I let you do this alone?"

"Better if only one of us jeopardizes her life."

"Then you've done more than your share. You stay behind and I'll find her on my own."

"Anna," Gilly began gently.

"Don't Anna me," her sister snapped. "I've had as much as I can handle from you and everyone else taking care of me. Whether you like it or not, Gilly, I'm sorry I treated you badly in the past. I intend to make up for it now."

When Gilly would have spoken, Anna held up an imperious hand. "There's nothing you can say to change my mind. We're sisters and we're in this together. Resign yourself to that. Now, I've been thinking about Tamarisk. He's likely draining our mother's powers to use against us, as he is these sorcerers. That means two people who meld their powers, can become stronger. I felt that when I touched your hand during your searching spell. Didn't you?"

Gilly nodded reluctantly. In fact, after touching Anna, her powers had soared. That might have been what triggered Tamarisk to come looking for them.

"Well, if we both have the ability to use magic," Anna continued, "why shouldn't we try to join forces?"

"Because Tamarisk has been doing this for twenty years. He has imprisoned magical guild members to draw from. Also, he is better at it than us."

"We're younger."

"Inexperienced."

"We have surprise on our side." Anna shook Marton's soggy shirt with such force, he was in danger of losing his one spare shirt. Dark clouds gathered overhead.

A smile tugged at Gilly's lips at her sister's show of temper. She liked the person Anna had become. "Your children need you, Anna. Mam would say the children are more important than our wish to save her."

"And she'd be wrong," Anna replied with grim purpose. "The time for hiding is over."

Odd, but the exact thought had crossed Gilly's mind in Perm.

"If Tamarisk had you in that dungeon, what would our mother do?" Anna asked, driving home her point. "Wouldn't she do everything she could to come for you? Or me?"

Gilly didn't know how to answer. She knew Mam through the eyes of a child. Her mother told ten-year-old Saira that hiding was the answer to their problems. Gilly didn't know the reasoning behind that conclusion. As an adult, she couldn't guess what drove Mam to abandon her former life instead of fighting Tamarisk.

Hagan had said that Tamarisk was too powerful for her mother. She'd run to her husband when she felt in danger. When Keegan died, she no longer had anyone to turn to for help. If he'd taken one of her children captive, would she have risked her life to face him, knowing he could overwhelm her? What manner of woman was Mam? The child in Gilly believed she was wonderful. The adult knew her not at all. Perhaps it was time to build a cornerstone of belief all her own.

She pushed her wet laundry away and turned to face to her sister. Anna was right. Time she opened herself to change. No longer was she Gimpy Gilly, the lonely goat-herder of Nadym. Nor Saira, a wounded child, staring out Lookout Point day after endless day. She was now part of a family who rode together, loved each other and fought side by side.

A long forgotten mischievous streak rose in Gilly. She held out her wet soapy hands. "All right, let's give it a try."

"Try what?" her sister asked, hesitant, suspicious.

"To join our powers.

Chapter 15

Anna splashed closer and reached for Gilly's hands.

"Nothing too elaborate," Gilly warned glancing around. The wind seemed to have died and not a bird chirped. The sound of trickling water from upstream faded away. The silence felt expectant.

Heat emanated from Anna's fingertips. It built up, came in contact with Gilly's power and flecks of light rose to dance around their clasped hands. Gilly chuckled in delight. All of a sudden, a powerful wave of energy swooped into her body and surged up to tingle her scalp, and then swept down to curl her toes. Laughter lit up Anna's eyes. The sweep of power must have touched her, too.

"Something small, you said." Anna turned toward Marton's wet shirt on the rock beside her. It slithered across the stone's surface.

Gilly smiled as she added her focus to her sister's and the shirt flew high into the air. Her grin widened with glee. She hadn't expected such a swift response. She often wondered if her mother had made up that story of her father testing his daughter's ability to move things. Apparently, she hadn't.

Her gaze met Anna's and with mutual silent agreement, they drove the shirt into the water and pulled it out dripping, and repeated, as they would have if they were actually washing it. Gilly laughed out loud as they twisted the shirt mid-air until all the water was wrung out. When it untwisted, the wrinkled shirt no longer dripped.

Anna pulled away but Gilly tightened her grip on her sister's fingers. Anna raised an eyebrow in question.

Gilly glanced up toward the cloudy sky. Dark clouds were still there from Anna's earlier temper tantrum. She dispersed those clouds and the sun shone bright and hot over both of them and the shirt. In moments, the material was steaming dry. Anna's focus shifted to the shirt and she began to fold the material neatly before lowering it over by the riverbank. They simultaneously released their grip.

"Well, look at that," Gilly said with satisfaction, placing her hands on her hips. "If we can't overthrow Tamarisk, we can at least do his laundry."

A movement caught her attention. The guards assigned to watch her had observed this magical practice, more interested in that than in their comrades' swordplay. Word would soon spread that both sisters could work magic. More proof they were Keegan's kin.

"Enough for now," she said, then her gaze narrowed on the changes around them. She pointed to the shoreline where it was no longer dry and grassy, but filled with green saplings "Look at what we've done."

Anna swung around. "But we weren't trying to do anything with plants." She went over and swiped across the new growth. The branches sprang back. They were so tall even Marton's shirt was hard to find buried among them. "What does this mean?"

"It means combining our powers must have been High Magic." Worry swamped over Gilly's good humor. How could she have been so foolish as to work High Magic so unnecessarily? Doing laundry no less. "The Horsemen are likely to follow that spark straight to us."

"Oh no!" Anna said and then shook her head. "Maybe they won't come here. We decided they can't pinpoint locations so easily, right? They could have been transported far away. We might have time to leave, except we can't go until Tom and the others return." She glanced around. "Gilly, *we* did this. I have to say I'm impressed."

Gilly took in the changed shoreline from her sister's perspective. "The land looks healthier," she said softly. "How can magic be evil when it recreates nature so wonderfully?"

Anna's gaze caught and held hers with grim determination. "This suggests we can stop Uncle Ywen and Tamarisk."

Gilly shook her head. "Moving a shirt and stopping those two monstrous men are two entirely different things. I will write in Jarrod's book to tell him about combining our powers and the effect it seems to have had on the land. Maybe he can suggest a way this discovery can help us with our rescue mission."

"In Erov, he called you the Defender of the Light." Anna said as she collected her things. "Did he mean magic?"

"Yes, but I can't imagine why he thinks I can be that. I don't know how to defend Light, and from what?"

"Not what, whom. Tamarisk. If he's abusing those sorcerers in his dungeon, he's also misusing their powers."

Arms full, they started back to camp, both of them deep in thought.

"Even with our magic combined, we're not up to defeating Tamarisk," Gilly said, inserting a note of caution into their thinking. "Most of what I know of magic I learned by trial and error. Mam spoke little of how Light works. She did say it was like a trade, each individual good at one kind or another. For instance, your special ability is to heal."

"I've seen you do many different types of magic." Anna stopped and dropped her bundle of clothes. She held her hands over them. Gilly sensed she checked if she could do more than just heal. Her sister's effort vibrated in the air. The clothes stayed put.

Anna lowered her hands in disappointment. "You try."

Gilly dropped her bundle and held out her arms, calling the clothes back. Her laundry jumped into the air and landed in her arms. The crossbow she'd forgotten by the riverbed then flew over to rest on top. Had she called to that? "How odd."

"You said you could do this as a child. Maybe you needed my help to remember how. Also, if Jarrod is correct, and you are the Defender of the Light, this explains why your talent is not so specialized and limited like mine."

"I suppose."

"Let's go back. I need to warn Marton the Horsemen will be coming."

"Yes, sentries will need to be posted further away." Before her sister could retrieve her fallen laundry, with a twitch of her finger, Gilly raised Anna's clothes to rest gently across her sister's arms.

"Thanks," Anna said, with a grateful smile. Then, she asked, "Do you feel different?"

"How so?"

"Despite us traveling for days with little rest, I feel thoroughly energized. As young and vibrant as those plants."

Gilly nodded. "I feel the same way."

They hurried back. While Anna went to speak with Marton, Gilly doused their fire to prevent anyone locating them that way, then picked up her quill and opened her book. She wrote Jarrod's name prominently at the top of the page. She spent an hour detailing all her questions. Satisfied she'd asked the right ones she shut the book and went to help Anna. If they must leave once Tom returned, they had better start packing everything they'd unpacked.

By late-afternoon, when no Horsemen thundered into camp, Gilly breathed a sigh of relief. Maybe this once, their magic hadn't been noticed. Or what she and Anna did together was a different type of Hearth Magic the Horsemen couldn't track. Like when Anna healed Tom. No Horsemen had come then.

Her sister was playing a sticks game with the children. A few warriors were polishing their weapons nearby while others patrolled the perimeter. Diligently carrying the crossbow Tom had given her, Gilly wandered in the direction Tom had gone this morning. Why wasn't he back?

Just as she was ready to give up, a call sounded in the distance. The men were returning. She was racing toward Tom without thought to how her impulsive dash might look to those around her, or to Tom himself.

Talus was the first to reach her. He jumped off his horse and bowed over her hand. "Well met, Missus Gilly. We've much news to share. Our trip was both frustrating and fruitful."

"I'd expected it to be as much." Gilly had to smile at his formal address. "Where's Tom?"

"Coming," Talus said. "He stopped to ask one of the sentries how all of you fared while we were away. Would you like a ride to camp?"

Gilly absently shook her head, her thoughts circling around seeing Tom ride toward her. Perhaps she could steal another kiss. She walked across the clearing toward the woods, stretching her neck to spot Tom. "I'm happy to walk, thank you."

Talus mounted behind her in a clatter of metals. Suddenly he wrapped an arm around her waist and swung her up high. She let out an involuntary squeal and then regretted it when Tom came galloping out of the woods.

Talus settled her in front, with his arm firmly holding her in place. "Ladies do not normally refuse when I offer a ride on Padion."

Perhaps the ladies he accosted didn't mind their hips being twisted to sit on top of a saddle. Gilly found the experience not worth the time saved. Her temper flared. As if picking up on her mood, the horse shied and bucked.

Talus tightened his grip on her waist.

Tom had slowed to a stop, an angry frown overriding his concerned expression. Then, to her shock, once he had made sure she was safe, he rode past without uttering a word.

"Have a care, missus," Talus warned as he focused on controlling his horse.

Watching Tom's stiff back as he left her behind, Gilly released her tight hold on the horse's mane and settled against Talus in disappointment. She shouldn't take her bad temper out on his horse.

Tom's rigid posture, his silence, and the speed with which he headed off all spoke of anger. No, not anger. His expression was similar to Marton's when Anna flirted with other men. Could Tom be jealous? That was too silly, but if true, amazing!

She had always envied Anna when Marton appeared jealous. This suggested Tom cared enough to be upset by Talus showering his attention on her.

Deliciously warm happiness infused Gilly and on impulse, she gave Talus a kiss on his cheek. "Thank you."

"What for?" Talus asked, with a surprised chuckle.

"For showing me that Tom cares for me."

He glanced from her to Tom who had now dismounted and was glaring at them as he brushed down his horse.

Talus's grin grew wider. "Ah. Since you care how he feels, then it is he who is the lucky one," he said gallantly.

With a happy smile, Gilly slid off Padion and was about to go toward Tom when she noticed her left hip wasn't in pain. After being swung up on a horse, twisted around and on dismounting landed hard, she should be in agony. Why wasn't she?

Then she remembered the magical play she and Anna had engaged in this morning. When they joined their powers, could her sister's healing touch have fixed Gilly's twisted hip? The idea was astounding. Why hadn't she noticed this change?

She took a few steps, conscious of her odd walk, and realized her left hip rose higher than the right more from habit than necessity. As Talus trotted away to join Tom, she purposely took a few steps in the sensual natural way

Anna walked. It felt awkward but possible. Instead of going to Tom, Gilly turned her steps to her sister's side.

When she was beside Anna, Gilly sat cross-legged. She no longer needed to stretch out her left leg. The words to tell Anna of this miracle clogged in her throat. She wanted to savor this joyful discovery.

She glanced around at all those who were gathering to hear the men's news from Tibor. No one paid her any attention. As if they hadn't noticed her walking normally to this spot or sitting down just like them, with both legs crossed.

Tears of happiness gathered. Her friends and family had not noticed she no longer limped. Because they didn't see her as Gimpy Gilly? Her heart swelled with pleasure at the thought.

They just see me.

Marton called out to Tom and Talus. "Hurry up!" Once they approached, he said to Ned, "We're all here. Tell us what you discovered and don't leave out a detail. Did you find the secret entryway?"

"Yes, indeed, sir," Ned replied, "exactly where Hagan said it would be, hidden behind overgrowth. It blends into the shadows so well, if I hadn't explicit instructions, I would never have seen it. The gate was rusted but my key worked."

Talus strolled toward Gilly but Tom rushed ahead and shoved him aside before planting himself beside her. Gilly's heart warmed at his possessive hold on her hand. She raised their clasped fingers and kissed his knuckles. His eyes lit up until Marton cleared his throat and speared Talus with a pointed glance waving him to sit.

Once a few of the men made room, the King's Warrior sat down and the discussion began.

"Was my mother there?" Anna asked, looking anxious.

Gilly held her breath. *Please let them be alive!*

"No, they were not among the guild members and I was glad." Tom's hold on Gilly tightened. "They must thankfully be housed elsewhere."

"What we found was worse than anything I ever imagined," Ned said. "Hagan was right. Many of those magical guild members need to be put out of their misery. The few that can be saved will need all of our help to carry them out of those horror chambers. The three of us could do little. This will require all of us to work together."

Gilly's heart sank at the news. Beside her, Anna was shaking and Marton pulled her close, their children huddled between them.

"We talked over what we needed to do and decided to check at the harbor before returning to camp," Ned said. "One of Master Hagan's contacts there owns a vessel."

"Why do we need a vessel?" Gilly asked.

"For the prisoners," Anna said. "If they are as ill as Ned suggests, we will need a way to transport them out of Tibor. Taking them by road would slow us down and get them captured again."

"Exactly, Mistress," Ned said, nodding his head. "Since we are not storming the castle, and this is a straight rescue mission, we would need an escape route. We have one. We've arranged for a vessel to be on standby to take us to the coastal city of Emba come tomorrow morning."

"Tomorrow?" Gilly asked, in alarm. "So soon?"

"Our rescue must happen tonight," Tom said. "I'm not sure what's keeping those prisoners alive, likely Tamarisk's magic, but the sooner we get them out, the better."

Gilly let this alarming news sink in and then asked something that had never crossed her mind. "How are we to pay for passage?"

"The citizens of Perm authorized me to promise any sum needed to save the imprisoned guild members," Ned said. "Saving them was Hagan's dearest wish and they want to honor him with this gift."

Gilly nodded her thanks, grateful to Hagan once again. He might have upset her the whole time she had known him but he had also come to her rescue when the Horsemen found her in Perm.

The discussion veered toward plans on how the group should travel through Tibor without raising alarms. After a great deal of discussion, it was decided they should go after dark and in groups of no more than three to five.

"Best if you and Anna stay here," Tom said.

"No!" Both Anna and Gilly answered in tandem. Glancing at each other they nodded, in perfect agreement.

"If the guild sorcerers are in as bad a shape as you say," Anna said, "my healing ability will be needed to get those we can help into a fit state to travel."

"And I can counter any wards set in place," Gilly said.

"We cannot take the children there," Marton said.

"You can bring them to the vessel and meet us on our return," Anna said.

He refused point blank. "I'm not allowing you to go to this unholy castle dungeon without me."

In the end though, he reluctantly agreed Skye and Bevan's safety must be his top priority.

The discussion wound down soon after. They had a couple of hours left before twilight. Wanting to give Anna and Marton time alone, Gilly whispered to Tom that she wanted to take Bevan and Skye to the clearing in the woods where he had taught her how to shoot her crossbow.

"Alone," she added, when he offered to come. "I need to teach them a magical trick or two while we're all away. Will you keep Marton away from us? He won't like me teaching his children magic."

He nodded but then pulled her close and kissed her soundly on her lips. Right there in front of everyone. As she pulled away, breathless, he whispered, "That's so everyone here knows you belong with me now."

By everyone, he no doubt meant Talus. Gilly stood on shaky legs. She would have preferred to take Tom into the woods to have her way with him.

Instead, she went to collect Bevan and Skye. If they were leaving in a few hours, she had to teach the children a way to defend themselves and their father. Anna gave her nod of consent and Gilly suspected it was for more than her proposed walk with her children. Marton's gaze flicked from Gilly to Tom. His approving grin said that for once Gilly had done something right in his eyes. By the time she reached the woods, her cheeks were still hot from blushing.

She began the children's lesson with a simple distress call. Skye enacted it easily, sending a clear signal. Gilly smiled cherishing the distinctive voice of her niece inside her head. Bevan's call remained as silent as he had once been with his words.

With a sigh of disappointment, Gilly turned to the next spell. How to build a protection barrier. Skye could erect the barrier, but she could not seem to hold it.

On the girl's tenth try, while Bevan watched with wide curious eyes, the barrier wavered. Gilly instinctively reached to strengthen it, but then held back. The girl would not have help when the time came to use it. Propping her now wouldn't do any good. On Skye's next try, as the spell began to collapse again, Bevan raised his arms and the barrier shot straight into the sky.

Aunt and niece watched, heads tilted up and mouths open, as shimmering light reached for the heavens in a circle around them. It took a lot of coaxing to convince Bevan to lower the shield and let them all out again. When he finally complied, she realized her nephew might one day be as powerful a sorcerer as his grandfather had been.

"Better not tell your papa about our practice," Gilly suggested. The blacksmith had enough to contend with, realizing his wife was a powerful sorceress who was about to go into danger without him by her side. This news about his children could wait a day or two.

As they reached the edge of the clearing, Gilly spotted Jarrod leaning casually against a tree, watching her. Excited, she nodded to him and bent to take Bevan's and Skye's hands. "I want you two to go back to the campsite without me. Bevan, tell your mama I'll be back shortly and not to worry. Skye, tell Tom that he holds the key to my heart and always will. Will you both do that for me?"

They nodded and raced away, hand in hand. Then Bevan turned back and shouted, "Bye, Jarrod."

"That boy is gifted," Jarrod said from behind her.

"Yes, more than I ever imagined." Gilly studied the Chief Councilor of Erov in silence as they strolled back to the woods. "Thank you for coming." She took a seat on a log and sensed waves of worry emanating from Jarrod though she couldn't identify the cause. He wanted to talk to her but held back.

"What was your impression of the black cloud?" he finally asked and sat beside her.

"You knew about my journey? Of course you did. That cloud's filled with tortured souls. Is there nothing you can do to help them?"

"An atrocious aberration of the Light keeps them trapped. My people are simply recorders of history, Gilly. It is neither our place nor within our ability to alter the course of events. We can, if we are careful, direct the right people to the right places to affect a desired outcome."

"Is that what you're doing with me?"

He nodded. "Light has been decreed wicked in the land of Ryca. Yet, only Light can save us all now."

"All? I thought it was only those lost souls trapped in the dungeon and my family who were in danger."

"The black cloud's hunger is unending. It reaches its dark tentacles toward the city itself. Increased disease, famine and plague are but the beginning signs of what ails Tibor and will soon consume the rest of Ryca if that cloud is not annihilated."

Gilly shuddered. "All I plan to do is to release those trapped in Tibor's dungeons. Will that end the cloud's spread?"

"The darkness must be banished from our land." Jarrod's tone left no room for argument. "The man who controls the cloud must likewise be vanquished. As Defender of the Light, it is your responsibility to right the wrong done to the Light."

"How can you expect me to banish Tamarisk? The last time we met, he almost killed me." She couldn't believe she'd said the words. It made it feel so real. "Why?"

"Do you mean why destroy Tamarisk?"

She shook her head. "Why did Uncle Ywen kill my father?"

Jarrod nodded. "You are wise." He opened his arms and Falcon's Tomb appeared there.

Gilly sat stunned at such casual use of magic.

He flipped open the book and leafed through pages. After a few moments of rapid paper shuffling, he found the annotation he wanted and turned the book toward Gilly. When she remained where she was he tapped the page impatiently.

Gilly slowly inched over until she was right beside him. Her eyes scanned the page, reading the words as if in a dream. As darkness fell, the words began to glow.

Behold here the Tale of Tarrius Ryca. King Tarrius, a powerful sorcerer, was the first King of Ryca.

"This is the story of my ancestors." Gilly said.

"Yes. Read on."

The story spoke of a betrayal by the king's brother who brought about Tarrius and his entire family's demise.

Before Tarrius passed away, he placed a curse on his brother's descendants. Not one in that family line would wield Light as powerfully as Tarrius could. With each descendant the ability to wield Light would be diminished until the day a set of twin princes were born. The elder will be stripped of the Light that made Tarrius the greatest king of all. The younger will be born with the key to resurrect the Light lost in preceding generations and break the curse set upon the family. To release the confined Light, the gifted and cursed must merge.

"I don't understand," she said. "If father and Uncle Ywen were these brother princes, why did my uncle kill my father? This was our family's one chance to regain the magic lost by the curse."

"Discover that, and you will know how to vanquish the black cloud," Jarrod said.

"No," Gilly jumped up and faced Jarrod. "You are not going to be cryptic about this. You can't expect me to go blindly into that castle with no idea of how to accomplish all you want me to do. I need your help."

"You were planning to do this before I arrived."

How could he be so calm? "What I planned was to rescue my family and those poor lost souls and leave." Jarrod did not respond but looked vastly interested. "I had no intention of going against Tamarisk or Uncle Ywen. In fact, I had every intention of avoiding them."

Jarrod was now rapidly writing in his book.

"What are you doing?" she asked.

He glanced up before returning his attention to his work. "I knew your plans, but not your intentions. This is good. The history of this journey wouldn't be complete without both the intent and action properly recorded."

"Jarrod!"

"Yes?"

"This is my life, not a story."

"This is history in the making, Gilly." A frown appeared between his dark brows. "You understand why it must be recorded?"

"Well, Chief Councilor, why tarry?" she asked. "You've accomplished your goal to record all pertinent points. Why waste time helping me to defeat my uncle, vanquish Tamarisk, and save the world as long as you've obtained your research."

"Who are you talking to?" Anna came out of the bushes.

Gilly swung around and then back to the log where Jarrod had been sitting. It was empty but for a single sheet of paper resting there. She picked it up. It was the legend of King Tarrius.

"What's that you have?" Anna asked coming closer.

Gilly folded the page and sighed. "A new intent."

"Bevan said Jarrod was here. Was he really?"

Gilly nodded. "And he has plans we must discuss."

"Such as?"

"He believes Tamarisk's twisting of Light to his favor is a threat to all of Ryca. If we don't stop him, that black cloud will consume all who live and breathe on this land."

Anna sat abruptly on the log. Gilly joined her. Her mind was starved of ideas.

"What can we do about it?" Anna asked.

Gilly shrugged and gave her the paper Jarrod had left. "He said this holds the key to Tamarisk's downfall. If it does, it is beyond me. What do you make of it?"

Anna did a quick read. "Keegan and Ywen were twins?"

She nodded.

"But our father is dead. They can no longer join to release this 'gift.' Without that, I don't see how we can defeat Tamarisk."

Gilly was unprepared to face Tamarisk, let alone her uncle, the man who had killed her father and hunted her entire family for years. Even with Anna's added powers, she was no match for them.

What distressed her most was the thought of destroying those souls in the cloud. How could she bring herself to end the existence of so many? The same ones she'd planned to rescue?

Gilly retrieved the sheet from Anna and tucked it folded inside her clothing. "I think it best we stick with our original plan. Once Mam is safe, perhaps she can help us find a way to handle Uncle Ywen, Tamarisk and those condemned souls we can't rescue."

Chapter 16

Tibor lay with its feet submerged in the shores of the sea of Tver. At the top of a hill, the king's castle had been erected to oversee the entire city.

Gilly, Anna, Tom and Ned were the first to enter the Tibor. The next group would be a quarter hour behind them. Then the next, and the one after that. Seven in all. Hoping to be less conspicuous, they left their horses behind in the woods.

She'd never been to a place this large or with such strange habits. All the streets they'd trekked through were illuminated with torches and lanterns at regular intervals. For what purpose would a city need such illumination kept up all night long?

Her party hoped to sneak through to the castle and certainly didn't need anyone noticing their passage. At the center of town, a hundred steps led up to twin monuments that reached to the sky. Large ferocious stone beasts with furled wings guarded the entrance to those two buildings. She'd never seen that kind of an animal. Did it even exist or had they been designed from someone's fevered nightmares? Now she thought on it, all the lighted main streets led up to these two central towers which were situated halfway between the city and the castle.

With a sigh she followed her sister and friends, putting Tibor and its peculiarities out of her mind. Perhaps on her next visit to this fascinating place, she could think about learning more. Her only concern tonight was gaining access to the dungeons. Still, as they continued their journey, she couldn't help glancing at the night sky half-expecting something with leathery wings to swoop down.

After they passed the towers, the lanterns were fewer and most were unlit. Sensing an evil presence in this darker section, Gilly soon called a halt. Voices whispered to her but she could spot no living thing nearby other than her party. Everywhere, the ground was parched. She touched a plant and it crumbled as if fire had recently consumed it, leaving behind a skeleton of dust.

"The door is close by," Ned whispered, pointing down the lane.

Nowhere did Gilly see any sign of a door. The street they had stopped at stretched long and narrow. All the plants were dried branches as if it were winter instead of midsummer.

Suddenly, Ned vanished from sight. Then he reappeared around a side of the wall that she had at first taken to be a crease. On closer inspection, she noted an emptiness that must be the start of a tunnel. Her sister and friends ducked under a knot of bare dead branches and vanished from sight.

The sense of a dark presence was everywhere. Gilly looked up and then ducked. The sky felt as if it began two feet above her head. Darkness loomed over her like a malevolent mist. She forced herself to straighten and then reached up. On her fingertips' contact with the throbbing darkness, Light shot up from her hand, drawn upward.

The cloud shrank, as if her magic scorched it. In the instant of contact, Gilly received a clear impression of the spell used to create this cloud. She breathed in a breath of admiration. Pattern laid upon pattern. A more convoluted spell than any she'd ever woven.

This was the dark cloud she'd mentally visited. A master sorcerer held these souls captive. The bindings used to keep them trapped in place appeared to her, drawn like a treasure map. She instantly understood not only how this trap had been crafted, but how it could be dismantled. Like a puzzle to be unhinged, layer by layer. Had Jarrod known she could decipher a spell by simply touching it? Was this why he labelled her Defender of the Light?

"Gilly!" Anna called from inside the tunnel.

"I'm coming," she ran to catch up. Past a short corridor Ned held an intricately carved wooden gate open while Tom fashioned a rope knot to keep it hinged that way. Smart. The others coming in their wake wouldn't need Hagan's key to get in.

She brushed her hand over the vines etched into the gate. "No wards are placed on this structure."

"Thanks," Tom said absently, focused on his work.

"What kept you back there?" Anna asked.

"The dark cloud is directly above this location," Gilly said. "I touched it and it retreated. It was afraid of me."

"Why?"

"Perhaps because on contact I saw how it could be destroyed."

Anna's eyes widened in shock.

Once the door was stable, they traveled on for a long distance, following a passage that twisted and turned moving ever upward. Scurrying and squeaks suggested vermin and insects frequented here.

Tom and Ned lit torches posted along the walls. Talus and the rest of the Rycan warriors coming after them would have an easier time coming through here. After a sharp bend, moans came from up ahead. They were approaching inhabited grounds. Anna took Gilly's hand and squeezed tight.

"Prepare yourselves for the stench," Tom said.

In her next breath, a whiff of dank and musty air assaulted her, and Gilly gagged at the rank smell of decay and death. The smell warned her of what was ahead but nothing could have readied her for what they encountered when Ned opened a door along the corridor.

She'd visited with these lost souls inside the cloud and knew of their hopelessness. Now she understood their suffering. Beside her, Anna retched. Once she stopped, Tom put his arm around them both, drawing them closer, forcibly shutting out their surroundings from their horror-stricken eyes.

Gilly held her breath but couldn't keep out the cries of pain, which continued unabated.

Her body shrank even as she recalled Hagan's words. *They are your people. If there's anything left of those poor sods, they need to be put to a quick end and given a decent burial.*

Anna straightened. She looked terrified, yet drawn toward the pain and suffering. Within the safety of Tom's arms, Gilly watched Anna push the door wide open and enter. There were at least ten bodies in this chamber alone. The odor of fecal matter and urine assaulted them in a wave.

Her sister touched the man nearest her and a host of flies scattered into the air and rats dispersed. Anna pulled back but then, shuddering, she knelt near the closest man and laid her trembling hand on his forehead. He flailed, grabbing at her.

Tom approached and held him down so Anna could work. Gilly watched from the doorway, listening to Ned's harsh breathing.

Like the others, the person Anna tended was almost naked and had open sores. His ankles were bound by a rope. No, not a rope, but the same kind of cord that formed the netting One-Eye used on her and Skye. Every prisoner's ankles were tied with the same material. The drip, drip of Light draining off these men and women glinted in the darkness.

"Anna, don't touch that cord by his feet," Gilly warned before turning to Ned. "Remove the cords from all the prisoners and pile them in a corner outside. We'll destroy them later."

He hurried to do as she bid. Even as he released each prisoner, no one moved.

"Doubt there's much she can do for him," Ned muttered as he left with the cord that had bound the man Anna was helping.

He was more right than he realized. Anna's healing worked on the man's wounds, but his eyes remained blank.

Footsteps of several people, followed by Ned's relieved voice, suggested the next group had arrived.

"I'll get them to help us free others in adjacent rooms," Ned said from the doorway.

She nodded before crouching beside Anna. With a nod to Tom who struggled to hold the writhing patient still, she laid her hand on the patient's forehead. She searched for his consciousness and found emptiness. Swallowing back her loathing at what she must do next, she kept a thread connected to his body and reached toward the black cloud roaming above the castle. Somewhere in there was this man's soul.

She hesitated at the edge of the inky cloud, dreading entering the darkness and losing herself within. How could she hope to find this man's spirit within so many lost ones? She didn't even know his name.

Bran, a voice whispered.

It had come from the body. The soul had been removed, but the body knew its name.

Bran, she called and sank into the cloud. Would this disembodied soul remember its name? *Bran, answer me.*

Bran, the souls took up her call. *Bran*, they repeated, chanting over and over in a mindless melody. A lone voice whispered, *Bran*, in counterpoint.

Gilly followed that whisper. *Come home.*

Home, the chanting began.

Bran, come home, she said.

Bran, come home, the voice whispered.

Bran, the mindless voices shouted.

Gilly untangled the spell that held this man's soul captive inside the cloud, enough to allow Bran to follow her. She acted as the conduit, drawing him toward his body, enticing him, calling to him until in a swoop Bran's spirit settled into his body.

Bran sat up with a gasp and cried out in pain.

"You've done it," Ned said in wonder, peering back into the room.

Bran howled in agony.

Gilly felt him slip back out. She held him in place, speaking in soothing tones, assuring him about the safety and necessity of staying. Warmth emanated from Anna as she healed the man's wounds.

Stay, Gilly said, *Bran, stay, you're home.*

"Oh, please let him die." Ned said. "It's better to die than face such suffering."

"Die," Bran cried, his gaze coming into focus. "I want to die."

Heat radiated from Anna's fingertips and spread over Bran's body.

"You're burning me," he shouted. "Mercy, you are burning me."

Anna slumped back, exhausted. The fiery light dissipated, leaving behind red and blue skin, swollen in patches but no longer open and oozing.

Gilly let go of his head. Was it too soon? Could he keep hold of his life?

Tom gently released the man's arms.

Bran sat still, his face contorted in a look of unimaginable suffering. His shallow breathing deepened. His pallor receded from his cheeks, replaced by a healthier glow.

Ned approached and offered a sip of water from his leather flask. When Bran stared blankly, Ned tipped it to the man's lips and tilted his head up. Water dribbled around his mouth and then with a gasp Bran took a gulp. Ned took the bottle away. Bran flailed toward him, seeking more.

"Slowly," Ned said. "Or you will harm yourself."

Bran made a cackling sound and then another.

Gilly looked at Tom. Had they released a mad man?

A smile broke out on Tom's lips. "He's laughing, Gilly. Ned made him laugh."

He was right. Bran was laughing at Ned's suggestion he might harm himself. After what he'd gone through, the thought was rather funny. She let out a laugh herself, relieved to see him in his right mind.

Her laughter died when she looked around the room and down the long corridor. How many others were in Bran's recent state? Anna was exhausted simply healing one man. What were they going to do?

"She can't heal them all," Ned said, as if reading Gilly's mind.

Gilly turned to Anna. "Remember what happened when we tried to merge our powers?"

Her sister nodded. "We can do more together."

"Tell the others, Ned. We'll need to gather all those who are still alive. You must fetch them closer to Anna and me. If we try together, Anna, we might be able to bring them all back in one trip."

"Is that possible?" Tom asked with awe.

"I don't know," Gilly said. "It's the only chance we have. Trying to heal one at a time will exhaust us and take too long." She helped Anna stand. "It's our best chance to find Mam and Garren and Tamara. Lingering here will draw Tamarisk to us. May already have."

Everyone except Gilly, Anna and Bran, who still couldn't stand, scattered to gather all those who were conscious. Tom cleared the entryway outside the room and around the corner of debris, so Gilly and Anna could work there.

In the end, they gathered close to four dozen people. Many others were beyond hope. Through it all, there was no sign of Gilly's family. She wasn't sure if she was happy or sad at the news. Death was preferable to the existence these sorcerers had endured for so long. Then again, perhaps Tamarisk housed her family in more congenial quarters than the rest of his prisoners. After all, rumor was he had loved her mam. For now, they would do what they could to help these prisoners.

She and Anna sat surrounded by the guild sorcerers. Gilly reached out and took Anna's hands and heat jump up her arms. Faster than she could think it, she was within the black cloud, surrounded by lost souls. The names of men and women swirled through the blackness and they assembled around her. She sensed the confusion and anger of those whom she had not called.

With words and pictures she wove a future for those she could help, herding them toward their bodies until she was alone with the dammed. The ones who had no body left alive to return to. They pulled at her, pleading with her to stay. Gilly promised to return and followed her sister's call.

Screams of loneliness followed her out of the cloud. Anna's eyes were wide with fear. Her sister was afraid she could not save so many. Gilly had no such doubts. She'd experienced the incredible bounty of Anna's power within her. Her turn to share that wonder with her sister. She sent her Light into Anna, who sat up straight as the rush of power swept through her.

Anna's tears fell as she sent their joint Light flitting across the room until it swamped each and every prisoner. A haze of red surrounded the entryway. Slowly, the screams of pain subsided. The raging red aura changed to mauve to orange to yellow, and finally a blinding white. With inexplicable joy, Gilly watched Anna as her sister realized she had indeed healed all these people.

When her sister released her hands, Gilly returned to the cloud above. Tamarisk could not help but notice their work this night. She had one more task to perform before bidding farewell to the souls left in limbo. Jarrod's wish that she vanquish the dark cloud was foremost on her mind. Now she knew how to fulfil that promise. When she had physically touched the cloud, an idea had come to her.

She needed to help them remember who they once were.

The moment she entered the cloud, voices swamped her, sending her impressions of confusion and panic.

I promised I would return and here I am.

We miss the ones who left. We're alone and afraid.

Gilly gathered them and then merged with them until they were one.

Where are they? We are alone. The Master is gone. We are alone. We will die.

We are not alone.

We are alone. We will die.

We are not alone. Yes, we must die.

No! The Master will save us. The Master is calling to us.

Leave the Master. Come this way.

The Master will save us. We are alone.

We are not alone. We are together. We will save the world. Save our people. Come this way. See the wonder. Touch the spirits of your descendants. See who we have become. See what we do to our world. Understand the blessing of our curse.

Together they roamed across Ryca. Visited the fields of Tavdar, touched the villagers sleeping in their cottages. Felt their worry about the Horsemen. They traveled through the Kocheya Basin to Erov. Watched in wonder as that city flitted from place to place. The people saw them and shrank in fear.

Why are they afraid? We love them. We are them. Why are they afraid?

A bright Light waved a welcome.

They settled near it and it began to diminish.

It is dying. The Light is dying. Why?

We are killing the Light.

They alighted and sped away.

We are afraid. What are we? Why do we kill the Light? Light is good. Light must be preserved. The Light is the world. We are killing the Light.

They flew over the Makakala Range. Perm welcomed them. Women and children dreamed of their missing men. The Rycan Warriors who would save this world. Their men would save this world. They would free the imprisoned sorcerers. Those poor souls. Those tortured souls. They must be freed from imprisonment.

Free the sorcerers, the call went out. Free the sorcerers. They must be released. They must be set free. Who dares hold us prisoner? Who takes the Light from the land? The sorcerers are the Light of the world. Their Light must be preserved for the world to flourish.

Tamarisk holds us prisoner.

Tamarisk is the Master. We hate the Master. We will never answer the Master's call. Where are we? The Lights are afraid.

The land is scorched. All is darkness.

No! The Master lives here. This is true darkness. Here, Light is dead.

We are the Light and we are dead.

We are the sorcerers and we destroy our land.

The Master uses us to find the Light and we are the Master's vassal.

The spell. We see the spell the Master weaves to hold us prisoner. The spell must be dismantled. We must destroy the cloud. We must destroy the Destroyer of Light.

Not yet. Wait.

Wait. Why wait?

Wait for Tamarisk.

Wait for the Master. We will not leave before the Master is entwined within our arms. Go! Bring Tamarisk to us. Bring us the Master.

Satisfied, Gilly withdrew from the cloud.

•••

THE RYCAN WARRIORS left the tunnel, each small group leading a handful of sorcerers out of the dungeons. Gilly gave Ned strict instructions. If she, Tom and Anna did not return to the ship by daybreak, they must depart for Emba immediately. If they saw trouble approaching, the newly-released sorcerers' safety was their primary concern.

It was only when they were about to head into the castle, Gilly noticed Talus was not among them. "What has happened to Talus?" she asked Tom.

"He didn't want you to get your hopes up, or to worry about him in case he failed. He's gone to the King's Warriors' compound to speak to his friends. He hopes he can turn some of them to our cause, so if a fight breaks out, we will have help."

Foolish as the move was, his action touched Gilly. Talus might get himself arrested, or worse, killed, but she could not blame him for turning to his friends for help. This meant they were on their own. She couldn't ask for two better companions than Anna and Tom.

Tom led the way. This far down in the dungeons, no guards were posted. Gilly supposed there was no need. The poor souls who resided here held little hope for survival let alone mischief. She had seen evidence the men were fed occasionally but the servants who tended them were probably too frightened to tarry.

Considering the prisoners were his main source of power, she was surprised Tamarisk did not take better care of them. It showed him as a man who had no compassion or caring, and who valued human life less than his possessions.

She couldn't imagine what Tamarisk looked like. According to Hagan, she had known him when she was a child. Now she knew the truth about her past, why would her mind not reveal the details? Any bit of information could be invaluable in finding her mother.

They reached the level in the dungeons where ordinary prisoners were kept. Here, guards were everywhere. Tom was about to brave a fight, when Gilly held him back and softly chanted a spell of confusion. As the guards looked around for noise in one direction, she, Tom and Anna moved in another. They passed through the corridors, avoiding maids, footmen and guards alike. They were hiding behind a tapestry near the main stairway when Anna peered through a hole in the material and drew in a harsh breath.

Footsteps halted. "Who goes there?"

Before she could stop her sister, Anna peeked around the tapestry. "Cullen, it's us."

Tom swung aside the tapestry and held his sword to the minstrel's throat.

"Never thought you'd make it to here," Cullen said sounding impressed.

"You knew we were coming?" Gilly shifted past Anna.

The slender man looked none the worse for his disappearance. His smooth cheeks and strong straight nose looked as cheerful as ever and his smile was back in full display. He eyed her with interest. "Is it true? Are you Keegan's daughter?"

"We missed you in Perm." Tom lowered his sword. "Where did you disappear to?"

"Friends took me for a meal and talk. By the time I heard Horsemen were in the city, the story had circulated you were Keegan's offspring. I didn't know what to think. I am vocal about my support of my king and my disapproval of magic. Still, after we journeyed together, I considered you friends. Therefore, I chose not to do anything. I hope you understand Mistress Anna, Missus Gilly?"

"Will you turn us in now?" Gilly asked.

"Of course he won't," Anna said. "You heard him, he called us his friends."

"Indeed," Cullen said. "Also, since returning, I have been disturbed by the blackness above the castle. During the day, Tamarisk raises the darkness so travelers may enter the premises. Quite a sight walking toward the walls with that thing hovering like a deadly thundercloud. At night, as a defense, he lowers it." He looked at them with curiosity. "How did you get past?"

"We had help," Anna said.

"No time for that now," Gilly said, hoping to waylay her sister before she revealed all their secrets. "If you're not going to turn us in, will you help?"

Cullen stepped back and held up his hands. "Whatever you have come to accomplish, don't involve me. In return, I will pretend I never saw any of you."

"That we can do," Tom said and put away his sword.

They checked the stairway and were about to ascend, when Cullen asked, "What is it you are looking for? Perhaps I've seen what you seek."

"Our mother," Anna said, before Gilly could stop her.

"Princess Mamosia is here?" Cullen asked in surprise and avid interest. "Now that, I had not heard. Horsemen have been seeking her and her children far and wide. If only they knew to look closer to home. I am sorry, Mistress Anna. I have not seen the princess. The servants from the upper eastern section have reported strange goings on. I took the liberty of asking the king about it and he warned me not to question it. That area is Tamarisk's domain."

Cullen was on close terms with King Ywen? Enough to question him? Gilly's unease tripled and she would have left but Anna and Tom wanted Cullen to tell them the direction to the section of the castle Tamarisk occupied.

Cullen looked up the stairs. "It is difficult to direct you from here." He looked over his shoulder as if expecting Tamarisk to pop out of the shadows and strike him. "I could take you part way, I suppose."

"Any help you can provide, we will gratefully accept," Anna said with relief.

With a nod, Cullen led the way. Gilly lagged until she was at the rear. She cast no spells. There was no need. Cullen, being a regular visitor in the castle, was not questioned when they traveled with him. That was something else that worried her. All was not well with this picture but she could not put her finger on what was wrong.

She sensed danger around each corner and inside every doorway. They were probably walking into a trap but there was no way out. If her family was held up here, they had to find them. Tonight. She, too, had laid a trap for Tamarisk. Time to spring it.

They moved up many stairs before Cullen stopped and pointed toward a darkly lit area. "The sorcerer lives down that corridor."

"Thank you," Anna said.

"Yes, thanks," Tom said. "We can take it from here. Best you return to your quarters."

Cullen hesitated. "After coming this far, I'm curious to see if your mother is indeed at Castle Tibor. It would be quite the tale for a minstrel. I would have first telling of it. I'll come a little further. After you, Missus Gilly."

"I prefer to take up the rear," Gilly said. "Stay between Tom and me, and if trouble starts, keep out of the way."

"You have changed," he said, giving her a backward glance as he moved forward. "I recall a young lady who once hid behind bushes and refused to face a stranger in the night. In my line of work, I've told many a tale of Princess Mamosia. The tales say she was courageous. If so, you have her spirit."

Despite his curiosity, he was probably frightened of Tamarisk and his magic. People often hated that which they feared most. She, too, was frightened of Tamarisk. The man was evil, no other description fit the deeds he'd done to his victims in the dungeons. Cullen had reason to be afraid.

"Go on," Gilly said.

Once they reached the upper floor, they proceeded without interruption. This worried Gilly. It was a definite sign they were in Tamarisk's territory. The feelings she picked up along this corridor were alarming.

On one side, the wall housed closed doors. On the other, a balcony railing looked straight down to the ground floor, some five stories below. She peeked over and her head spun. Never good with heights, this place frightened Gilly like none other.

"Long way down." Cullen leaned over beside her.

"Careful." She pulled him back. "You might fall."

He gave her an appreciative smile. "Thank you. So considerate." Concern replaced his gratitude. "Missus Gilly, you look pale, is something troubling you?" He glanced to the floor far below. "Are you afraid of heights, by chance?"

"Keep moving." Tom said. He and Anna had stopped ahead and waited for them.

Gilly backed up to the wall, her legs trembling.

Tom hurried back to Gilly's side. "I've been here before, too. Saira, you're remembering this spot."

"Why, how obtuse of me," Cullen said. "Of course, these quarters used to belong to Keegan. This must be where you..." he stopped talking and just mimicked with his arm rising up and dropping over the railing.

"Enough, Cullen," Tom said.

Gilly plastered herself against the wall.

"I'm so sorry, Missus Gilly," Cullen said. "It's still hard to believe you are Keegan's special girl. You don't look the least bit royal in that common dress with the ragged hem. Perhaps that's why I didn't make the connection right away."

Anna hurried over and put her arm around Gilly. "We don't need to talk about this. Where is the room you're leading us to? The one belonging to Tamarisk?"

"That one." Cullen pointed. "I heard Ywen gave this suite of rooms to Tamarisk after Keegan's death as a reward for his friend's role in injuring one of Mamosia's spawn. Excuse me, Missus Gilly, I meant one of her children. Oh, dear, it's so hard to forget a lifetime of teaching."

Tom reached for the handle Cullen had indicated and pushed the door open.

"Well?" Anna asked. "What's in there?"

He turned back, his face ashen and opened the door wider so the women could look inside.

Chapter 17

Gilly couldn't take her eyes away from the three still figures crouched in a corner of the room.

Oh, Mam, Gilly's heart cried. *Thank the Light you are alive. Tamara and Garren, too.*

Beside her, Anna sucked in her breath.

Gilly took her hand so they could enter together.

"Wait," Cullen said.

In a daze, she barely heard him. Only his steel grip on her upper arm stopped her.

"What now?" Tom asked.

"Shouldn't one of us stay out here to keep a lookout for Tamarisk?" the minstrel asked. "We wouldn't want to be surprised while we were rescuing the royal princess."

"Good thinking," Anna said. "One of us should stay out here. I...I guess I can. My mother doesn't know me."

"No," Gilly said. "Mam would want to know you're safe."

"You're not going in there without me," Tom said.

Gilly took another look into the room, willing herself to think clearly. This was no time to be overcome by emotion. Something was wrong with her mam. Her family was caught in some sort of spell.

"I might need Anna's help to release them." She turned to Cullen. "Will you stand watch?"

"I'd be honored. Problem is, although I've visited the castle often, I've never met Tamarisk. I've no idea what he looks like. Do you?"

She shook her head.

Tom shifted and she turned to him.

He nodded. "I know what he looks like. But I'm not letting you go in there alone."

"They won't be alone," Cullen said. "I'll go with them. Will you give me your sword?"

Tom hesitated and then gave him his dagger instead. "I doubt you know how to wield a sword with efficiency but this may come in handy." He turned to Gilly and drew her to him. "I'll be right outside. Call me if trouble erupts. Promise?"

"Yes." She pressed her face close to his heart, suddenly not wanting to leave him. He held her in a fierce hug, as if he, too, worried they may not have another chance to hold each other. At Anna's pleading look, she reluctantly let go of Tom and entered the chamber. Cullen shut the door behind them.

Her mother, brother and sister stood poised, as if ready for an attack. Mam still wore the dress with flour dust on her apron from working bread dough. Thirteen-year-old Tamara, skirts falling to just below her knee, hair in a scarf, carried a jug of water in her arms and a pack of food on her back. Five-year old Garren in short pants and a tunic, his father's heavy sword raised part way, stood protectively before his mother and sister.

Gilly approached slowly, circling the three figures, noting the fear clearly written on their faces. She couldn't believe she'd found Mam. Her heart beat rapidly and the happiness that threatened to overwhelm her skimmed close to the surface.

A glow surrounded them, like the radiance that appeared when she cast a spell, only dimmer. In fact, the Light seemed faded in places as if someone had made inroads into it.

"Remarkable, isn't she?" Cullen asked, as if in a daze.

"She never grew old," Anna said, speaking the words that eluded Gilly.

Her sister was right. Whatever spell held these three in place, had frozen them within time itself. Garren and Tamara were still children. Mam, well, she was as young as she had been when Gilly left her in the cottage. In her early thirties. The same age Gilly was now.

"We must act," Anna said. "Tamarisk could return at any moment."

"The longer we linger," Cullen said, "the more chance we will be interrupted. Do you know how to release your mother?" He reached up as if to stroke Mam's cheek and then withdrew his hand before it connected.

"Check the other room," Gilly said, "while we work."

Cullen nodded and headed off.

She waited until the door closed and held out her left hand for Anna's. "I don't trust Cullen. If we're to do this, let's do it now and get them out of here."

The minute Anna's hand touched her palm, heat soared into Gilly's body. The shimmer around the three captives drew her focus and Anna followed suit. Light erupted, swirling until it enveloped the figures. Gilly inched closer until she melded with the wavering glow.

The swell of power almost carried her off her feet and a forgotten sweetness enveloped her. This spell's complexity and strength were amazing.

Mam had cast this spell herself, Gilly was certain of it. The pattern of the spell was clear. This was meant to hold these three safe. If Mam was capable of such incredible weaving of Light, why had she been afraid of Tamarisk? Surely someone so powerful could defeat a man who stole his power from others? No time to speculate. She dismantled the spell, one layer at a time, until it collapsed entirely and the three captives took a collective breath.

Her mother raised her hand.

She was going to attack. "Wait, Mam!" Gilly said. "It's me, Saira."

Her mother paused, hand half raised and stared at Gilly as if unbelieving. She shook her head. "This is a trick."

"No. I swear, it's me, Mam. Don't you know me? I watched out for all of you at Lookout Point. I tried to warn you about the Horsemen coming, but I was too late." She knelt by her mother's skirts and clutched at the material, tears streaming down her face. "I'm sorry I didn't get to you sooner. I'm so sorry. Please forgive me. I couldn't run any faster. I tried. I really tried."

Her brother and sister peered at them from behind Mam's skirts.

"My Saira?" Mam asked, looking confused.

Gilly nodded, thankful her mother recognized her after all these years. She wiped at her wet face and tried to explain. "After I took the baby to the cave, I wanted to come back, but I was afraid to leave her alone. If I returned, the Horsemen might take me and then what would happen to her then? She was so tiny and helpless. If I brought her with me, we might both get caught. I wasn't a match for anyone with this leg." She bent her head and sobs shook her body at the remembered horror of her decision to leave her family to fend for themselves. "I should have come back to find you. I should have come for you, Mam."

"No, you shouldn't!" Anna placed her hand on Gilly's shoulder, a bracing touch that shoved a ramrod down Gilly's spine, straightening her shoulders.

Her sister looked furious as she glared at their mother. A mother she didn't remember holding her, rocking her to sleep.

All to defend me?

"She did the right thing." Anna waved a negligent hand at her estranged family. "You'd cast this fine spell to protect yourself and your children. You couldn't have helped her. She would have been killed if she returned or captured like you. Perhaps me, too. Then I would not have met Marton. Or had his wonderful children. I don't care if you think I'm selfish for being glad I'm alive, or for living the life I did in Nadym, but I am. Gilly saved me, took care of me and watched over me for years."

"Years?" Mam said. "And who is Gilly?"

Gilly hurriedly stood. "I'm Gilly. This is your baby, Anna. You're in the castle at Tibor. You were captured and kept here for twenty years."

"Twenty three to be exact," a man said

Gilly started in surprise at that familiar voice. A man she knew, yet didn't know, watched them from the inner doorway, a fond smile curling his lips.

"Tamarisk," Mam said and Gilly's pulse leaped with dread.

Anna gasped and backed up next to their mother.

Before Gilly could react, a black lance leaped off the floor and flew toward them, surrounding her and her family. Binding them in place. Pain coursed through Gilly where that deadly cord touched her and she recognized it as the same vile material One-Eye used. Her hopes of rescuing her mother shattered.

"Thank you, my dear." Tamarisk moved further into the room. He looked older than Cullen and his voice was raspier. His balding dark hair had receded since the last time she saw him but his hooked nose still overshadowed his thin lips.

Bevan had been right. His smile did not reach his eyes.

"I've been trying to crack your mother's spell these many years," he said, "and in a few heartbeats you undid it. I sensed you could. That's why I didn't kill you in Erov. Though I was tempted a time or two."

His tone at once complimented and tormented her. By untangling her mother's time spell, she'd made Mam vulnerable to this horrible man's power.

"What a clever child you've grown up to be, Lady Saira-Gilly. Good thing that fall didn't kill you, I suppose."

"Damn good thing," a second gravelly voice said. A bent old man came out of the back room. His shoulders looked as if they had been broken and mended in an unhinged fashion. His neck was stretched unnaturally to the side and his legs and hands were atrophied. He was clutching Tom's dagger.

"Come in, Ywen," Tamarisk said. "Come wish your family well."

"Watch your tongue, Tam. I'm still your king and I'll thank you to show proper respect."

"Of course, Your Majesty." Tamarisk bowed low.

The crippled old man pushed the sorcerer aside and approached his family.

"About time you woke up," he said to Mamosia. "Held us off a long while, you did, royal sister. As you can see, I have not fared well in the interim years."

"Your deeds reflect your image, Ywen," Mamosia said. "What you did to your brother and father was an abomination against nature and nature bestowed its judgment on you."

"It was the magic that cursed me thus," he said. "But I intend to have the last laugh." He turned to Gilly. "Did you notice how it transformed Tamarisk, niece? Made him look handsome? It's going to do the same and more for me, once I have all the family's power."

The idea of what Tamarisk had done to twist Light to his own use was difficult enough to stomach, but Gilly was unwilling to consider what this bitter old man would do with such power. She would die before letting her uncle abuse the Light so. With all her might she reached to throttle him. All her efforts ended in vain. She couldn't move a muscle.

"Tom," she shouted, "Cullen is Tamarisk, go for help."

The door handle wriggled but refused to open.

"We wouldn't want the boy disturbing our little party, would we?" Tamarisk asked. "Shout all you want, little Saira, all it will do is alert my guards to take our brave Tom to the dungeon."

She instantly regretted calling out. If she'd stayed silent, Cullen might have forgotten about Tom. No, Cullen, Tamarisk, whoever he called himself, wasn't the forgetting type. No doubt he had plans for Tom and her warning might have saved Tom's life. If he ran to find Talus, there might be a chance some of them could get out of this alive.

Tamarisk circled them. Why could she not break this binding, when with a touch she could see how to tear apart the black cloud? She concentrated on the cord, trying to find its weakness. She sent a pulse of Light to explore its composition and arrows of pain stabbed her head. She almost lost consciousness.

"It is useless to fight it," Tamarisk said. "The more you do, the weaker you will become. This is a toy Ywen gave me years ago. As a boy with no powers, he haunted the docks, eagerly seeking items shipped in that could interfere with the use of Light. A cord was brought to our shores from a foreign land. Been very useful to me ever since. Ywen is an enterprising man, though, and as an adult, he sent me to acquire more." Tamarisk reached under the wire and pulled her brother free, easily knocking the sword out of his hands.

"No!" Mamosia cried. "Leave Garren be."

"Now, now, dear," Tamarisk said, "no need to upset yourself. Ywen merely wishes to have a few words with his nephew."

Her uncle's chuckle was pure evil. Speaking to Garren was the last thing on this twisted old man's mind. He pulled the frightened boy toward him and raised the dagger to the boy's throat.

Mam cried out.

Gilly saw her father's death happening all over again. Then she remembered Jarrod's story of the twins. "Kill him, Uncle," she said, "and you will surely die."

Dagger raised, he hesitated.

"Do it," Tamarisk said, "she's trying to distract you."

"He was wrong before," Gilly said. "Didn't he promise you would be as powerful as my father if you killed him?"

Her uncle's gaze stayed trained on her. She'd hit a nerve.

"The spell was not completed with Keegan," Tamarisk said. "I had not counted on this boy being magical as well. You needed to kill both of them."

"He's wrong, Uncle. Listen to him and it will be the end of you. Did he tell you Jarrod from Erov named me Defender of the Light?"

Her uncle regarded her in silence, his gaze drenched in envy.

"It took me awhile," Gilly said, "but I now understand. I know how Light works. Kill Garren and you will die."

"What is she talking about?" he asked Tamarisk.

"She is reaching at anything to prevent you from killing her brother," Tamarisk said. "Kill him and you will become the most powerful sorcerer in all of Ryca."

"Wrong," Gilly said. "I carry the family's magical gift. You killed your brother for nothing. Look at you, you were ravaged by the power that was released from my father. Make the wrong move again, and it will kill you."

Uncertainty crept into his gaze.

"For the last two decades," she said, intent on feeding that spark of doubt, "Tamarisk has ensured he is the only practicing sorcerer in the realm. Would he now step aside to a more powerful sorcerer, stronger than him? Do you truly think your dear friend is that altruistic, Uncle?"

"You would let her turn you against me with a few words?" Tamarisk asked.

Ywen's gaze flew between friend and niece as he tried to decide whom to believe.

A thump on the door, followed by a second and third one, suggested Tom was attempting to break in. The foolish man would put out his shoulder soon. Why didn't he go for help?

"Haven't I stood by you all these years when everyone else turned away?" Tamarisk asked.

"Who failed you all these years, Uncle?" Gilly asked. "Have you never wondered why?"

"What proof do you have of what you say?" he asked.

"Release me and I will show you," she said.

"No," Tamarisk said. "Don't be a fool. Kill the boy and be done with it."

Gilly speared the sorcerer with a scornful glance. "Afraid you can't handle me without your toy? You were so brave when I was a child. The years have drained you of your courage as you drained those poor sorcerers of their powers."

"She has a point," her uncle said, smirking. "If she tries to trick us, you have access to all the power you need to retaliate. Let her go. I want to see her proof."

Pressed tight against her family in one corner of the sitting room, Gilly crowed in silent triumph. Her plan was working. Once released, all she had to do was stall long enough to regain her strength by wedging a deeper break between this unholy pair. Then she was ready to pit her power against Tamarisk and he wouldn't have his cloud to back him up.

She scanned the room for possible weapons. There was little furniture other than cushioned benches positioned against the walls. The only other item was the cupboard her uncle leaned on for support while he held young Garren prisoner. Nothing to use as a weapon. Then her gaze fell on her father's sword that Garren dropped. Tamarisk had kicked it across the floor.

She suddenly noticed the silence in the room. The door to the corridor remained shut but Tom's pounding had ceased. Had he gone for help? She hoped so.

Tamarisk approached, his furious gaze screaming murder. Had she pushed him too far? Instead of killing her, a twirl of his finger and the cord twisted away from her but kept the rest of her family imprisoned.

"Saira, be careful," her mother cried. "Don't trust either of them."

She nodded to her mother but speared the sorcerer with a curious glance. He'd surprised her. She'd pegged him as crafty and suspicious. Nevertheless, he'd obeyed his king's order to release her.

The relationship between these two men confused her. The old feeble king was an easy match for Tamarisk. Yet, since she'd seen the two together, her uncle continued to order Tamarisk around as if he were a servant. The sorcerer bowed to the king's wishes even though he was stronger. What was Tamarisk waiting for? What did her uncle have that he wanted?

Had she read the sorcerer wrong? Was there a deep abiding friendship between these two? If so, why did her uncle so easily suspect Tamarisk of tricking him?

Gilly took a deep breath and let it out slowly, assessing the new situation. The draining effect of the cord receded leaving an aching where it had touched her. She was free. She needed time to regain her strength and to remove Garren from the king's grasp. Her family remained vulnerable while the magic-deadening cord bound them. If she attacked Tamarisk directly, he might turn his anger and vengeance on her family.

What was that cord he wielded so casually? He never touched it, controlling its movement from afar. Could she, too, now unbound, move it from afar? Thus far, she'd only tried to attack it while confined.

"Come here, girl," Uncle Ywen said. He held young Garren by the throat. The frightened boy struggled in his grasp.

She'd missed her little brother. Tamara. Mam. A part of her, empty for so long, filled with love for the three members of her family she'd thought long dead.

"Quickly!"

Gilly approached the twisted king. Tamarisk followed.

Too close. "Make room, sorcerer," she said. "You can see anything I hand my uncle from a hand's span away as from a nit's."

Tamarisk gave her a sickly smile and backed away.

Gilly's attention swung to her uncle. Although free, her original plan was still worth a shot. Separate and conquer.

"How will killing Garren give you power, Uncle?" she asked.

The king nodded to Tamarisk. "Show her."

The sorcerer remained where he was.

"Show her!" The king's hand shook and the blade pressed against Garren's neck nicked the boy.

She began to question his hold on sanity. She had better get him to see things her way and fast.

Tamarisk reluctantly obeyed his king's orders. He rifled through the cupboard and fetched a sheet hidden in the back within a wooden box. His mood seemed to change then, and he handed the sheet to Gilly with a flourish, his ingratiating smile back in place.

She took the paper and read. It told a shorter version of the tale of King Tarrius and his curse. Gilly felt a telltale tingling in her fingertips as she read the writing. There was magic at work here. She cast a quick glance at Tamarisk. Did he think she would not notice?

The main difference between this tale and the one Jarrod had given her, resided in the last line. Tamarisk's version read, *in order to obtain the confined Light and claim that power, the gifted must be overcome by the cursed.*

She handed the sheet to her uncle who took it with a shaky hand, the other still pressing the dagger to Garren's neck.

"I am the cursed," he said. "I am the ungifted twin."

"Yes, Uncle, but the last line of the legend has been altered."

"You lie!" Tamarisk snatched the sheet back. "You have no proof."

Gilly reached inside her pocket and took out the sheet Jarrod had given her. Opening it, she showed the complete legend, which related the betrayal of King Tarrius and the reason he placed the curse on his brother's descendants.

In it, the last line read, *To release the confined Light, the gifted and cursed must join forces.*

"Uncle, you were duped. Killing your brother did not transfer his power to you. It prevented you from ever being able to cast a spell. The murder destroyed your potential to release your latent talent to use Light."

She gestured toward his mangled body with an open hand. "As Mam said, your actions have resulted in your present stature."

He eyed his curled hands, bowed knees, and clubbed feet. She could see his mind digesting her suggestion. Would he believe her? She almost felt sorry for him. He had been lied to, and led to this pitiful state by a man he called friend. Was he capable of seeing what had been done to him?

"Don't you think Tamarisk had his own reasons for wanting Keegan killed?" Gilly persisted, "besides you gaining the ability to use Light?" She was satisfied he understood her when his gaze flew from Mamosia and Tamarisk. "Who misled you into thinking you could gain power by killing your brother?" She didn't expect an answer. They all knew who had been behind the killing.

As she turned toward Tamarisk, her mother screamed a warning. The sorcerer tossed a binding over Gilly and she shrank to the ground cowering from the shafts of pain it shot into her.

Fool!

She'd concentrated so hard on turning her uncle to her cause, she'd forgotten to keep an eye on the sorcerer. Maybe she had accomplished her goal though. Would her uncle turn against Tamarisk? Her last hope died when she glanced at him. Uncle Ywen was a broken man. The dagger slack in his hand, he stumbled back.

Garren made a run for the door but Tamarisk caught him by the shoulder and tossed him toward her family. He adjusted the binding that held them to include the boy. Mam pulled her frightened son closer.

"You're clever," Tamarisk said to Gilly. "But not clever enough. Time I finished what I began long ago."

"Don't you touch my sister," Anna shouted.

"Tam, leave her alone," Mam pleaded.

He turned to her mother with eyes wide and a tentative smile. "That's the first time you've spoken my name in decades, Mamosia." He approached her and gently touched her cheek with a finger.

"Leave my daughter alone. Please. Don't harm her."

"Harm little Saira," he said in an offended tone. "Our little girl? Why would you think I'd do such a thing? We're going to be a family soon and as Ywen has just learned, it isn't wise to hurt each other, now is it? I don't want you to worry about a thing." He lifted her chin a little. "You and I were meant for each other. It was thoughtful of you to preserve your body in such a youthful state until we could be together. Now, don't give yourself worry lines, my dear. Once we're husband and wife, as we were meant to be before Keegan interfered, your children will be my children."

Mam's gaze spun to Gilly in fright.

Gilly shook her head. She hoped her mother would be wise enough to go along with Tamarisk. At least, long enough for Tom to get help.

The door to the corridor shook and wood splintered.

Tom hadn't gone for help. The foolish man had gone in search of an axe. Didn't he realize there was no way for him to kill Tamarisk? The sorcerer was too powerful. If only he'd gone to find Talus. With the King's Warriors, they might have had a chance to overcome the sorcerer.

"Well, the boy is persistent," Tamarisk said. "Must give him credit for that. This is like old times, isn't it, Mamosia? We shouldn't leave young Tom out of our reminiscence, should we, Saira?"

Gilly's heart contracted painfully when he gestured at the door.

"No," she shouted. "Leave him alone."

The hammering at the door ceased. The silence stretched interminably. Then Tom's footsteps retreat from the corridor, one step at a time, then faster and faster they flew.

"Cowardly boy grows into cowardly vean," Tamarisk said. "Comforting to know people don't change, isn't it, Saira?"

She watched his eyes and realized there would be no reasoning with the mad sorcerer.

"Yes," she agreed, still kneeling on the ground, unable to gain the strength to even stand. She was silently thankful that Tom had been removed from harm. "I was wrong about him."

"You were." He squatted in front of her and spoke softly. "You've been a bad little girl. Telling Ywen about my secrets. Now we're going to be one family, I'll have to teach you a lesson about interfering in your new papa's affairs. A lesson long overdue, I think. Spare the rod and spoil the child, I've always thought."

"No," Mam shouted. "Tam, no."

He grabbed Gilly by her hair and hauled her up. Her mother cried for mercy and Anna cursed Tamarisk. The pain of the binding enveloped her. She became aware the sorcerer lifted and carried her out of the room. As if still in a dream, the walls tilted and the floor receded. Through the open doorway she spotted her family.

"Let her go," Mam shouted.

The same words echoed from a lifetime ago. She had struggled then, as a little girl. *Tried to loosen Uncle Tam's hold on her as she was raised over the balcony. Mam's eyes wide with fear. Blood on her clothes testifying to the death of Papa at his brother's hands. Uncle Tam was going to kill her. Why? Uncle Tam said he liked her. That he was her friend. They'd played hide and seek and ten pin in the village. She'd sneaked the housekeeper's pies to him after Papa said he couldn't come to the castle anymore.*

Tamarisk had never been her friend.

Gilly shivered at the risks she'd placed herself in as a child. She struggled now but the binding shot pain into her body and she quieted. The walls wavered. Her head felt light-headed and her stomach heaved with fear. Beyond the railing, the ground called to her from far below.

In her dreams, she'd fallen over and over again, waking up in a sweat, heart pounding. The memory of past nightmares resurrected a true memory in vivid detail.

The ground closed in on her at an alarming speed. She screamed. Then the silent moment as bones crushed and twisted on impact on a rock hard floor. Shuddering, she instinctively reached out to Tamarisk for comfort but the binding bit into her, sending fire up her arms.

"Tam, please let her go."

Mam's sweet voice. Her beloved Mam. She'd disappointed her so many times. Despite all Gilly's faults, Mam still loved her. Her mother's words sounded far away, as if from a dream.

"I'll do anything you want. I'll...I'll marry you, Tam, I promise. Please, don't hurt Saira again."

Chapter 18

"**F**inally, you've come to your senses." Tamarisk still held Gilly as he brought them back to the doorway of the room where he had imprisoned her family. "Of course, I'll marry you, Mamosia. I love you. I have since the first day Keegan introduced us. We'll have the very best wedding. Every dignitary in the land will be present to witness our nuptials. I'll even invite Jarrod, as he's the new leader of Erov. Too bad about his father. He had a chest problem that led to his demise."

He broke into a crazy giggle and his arms shook. Gilly almost fell but he adjusted his hold until she fit securely. He was careful to stay away from the cord tied around her.

Her view of the ceiling shifted again as Tamarisk returned to the railing. A rush of cool air on her back suggested the floor no longer resided below her.

"Let's talk about the wedding, Tam." Her mother's voice retreated like a fading dream. "First, put her down."

"I intend to. Be patient." Tamarisk's raspy voice grated on Gilly's nerves. Why didn't he drop her and get it over with?

The railing butt into her side as he leaned over to look past her. "You've grown heavier, Saira. Almost too big for Uncle Tam to hold you up, even with the help of his magic. It's been a long day and my arms are tired."

Mam and Anna's shouts echoed dimly in the background.

Gilly's mind quieted. Uncle Tam was right. Better if she'd never lived. If not for her, Mam and her brother and sister would be safe, frozen by her mother's spell.

No! a voice screamed in her head.

Anna?

If not for you, I would have been trapped with mother. I wouldn't have met Marton. Skye and Bevan wouldn't be alive. What about Tom?

Tom! He had watched over her, her entire life. He loved her. She wanted to be with him. Her eyes opened wider. "I don't want to die! I want to live."

"Too late to wish that, Saira," Tamarisk said. "You've interfered too often with my plans."

Gilly suddenly remembered the game she played with her papa. It came vividly to mind, her moving things and her father blocking her. Like the binding blocking her magic now. Only it was painful. But it, too, was just an object, like the toys and bowls and pillow she moved about. She'd beaten her father at the game and moved those objects then, she could move this cord now.

Tamarisk's fingers loosened their hold.

She focused past the pain the cord inflicted, ignored the agony as if it were another of her father's irritating blocks, and flung the binding off her and onto Tamarisk.

He screamed and threw her away.

Gilly reached for the railing and her right hand connected with a bar. At the same moment Tom leaped forward, his sword aimed at Tamarisk's back. Tom hadn't fled. He'd beaten past Tamarisk's mind spell. What a clever brave man.

Her fingers slipped, sliding her downward.

It all happened as if in slow motion. Gilly caught the look of horror on Tom's face as Tamarisk's body, pinned to his sword, blocked his path to her. She reached with her other hand for the railing and her right slipped. Before she could get a secure hold, the banister rose past her.

"No!" Tom shouted, shoving the sorcerer's limp body aside to grab for her.

The world repeated itself.

She fell.

Her pregnant mother raced halfway down the stairs, two children in tow. Mamosia, eyes wide in horror, shouted with anguish, "Saira!"

The ground leaped up to meet her. She blinked in horror as her greatest fear came to life. The dream she could never wake up from fast enough. Only, this time she viewed it quite calmly.

Time to end this nightmare.

She held out her arms and commanded, "Stop!"

She hovered inches above the ground. Tears of wonder wet her lids. So easy. She looked up at Mam to show her what she'd done. The stairs were empty.

The world righted itself.

Her mam wasn't racing to safety with the children. Her uncle still held her mother prisoner upstairs. Tamarisk had fallen to Tom's sword.

A twirl of her finger and she rose through the air until she settled with her feet on the railings that had terrorized her for her whole life. The sorcerer was writhing beneath his cord.

Tom, laughing and crying, pulled her down off the railing. "Saira," he breathed in her ear, hugging her fiercely, "thank the Light, you're safe."

She looked over his shoulder. Tom's sword was still buried in the sorcerer's back.

Tamarisk's glance was brimming with hatred. He was dying and knew it. He couldn't draw on his magic to save himself. The desperation in his eyes reminded her of others who were also desperate. She'd made them a vow.

She pulled away from Tom and, pointing to the cord, flung it away from Tamarisk.

"What are you doing?" Tom asked in alarm.

Gilly held up her hand to still his questions. "For such a powerful sorcerer, you don't seem so frightening anymore, Uncle Tam. Perhaps that's why you confined all those guild sorcerers in the dungeon. If any had been free, I doubt you would have survived this long. Is that why you hated my father? Like Uncle Ywen, were you jealous of his powers, too? Isn't that really why you engineered his killing? Is that what ties you to Uncle Ywen? Your joint jealousies?"

Breathing harshly, Tamarisk stared at her balefully. Then the sword at his back slid out, leaving a gaping red wound in his chest. The air stirred and she sensed him reaching for the magic of the black cloud to heal his fatal wound.

Go, she silently bid. *Call on your last source of power.*

The cloud, instead of healing and energizing him, pulled him to them. His eyes widened in horror as understanding of the trap he'd walked into became clear and then his eyes went blank. His body slumped on the floor.

"What happened?" Tom asked.

"He's finally been forced to face justice."

Tom wrapped his arms around her and held her tight.

"My family. They're still trapped by the cord and Uncle Ywen is in there with them."

"Wait here." Tom rushed into the room where Mam was being held.

Gilly stared at Tamarisk's lifeless body. After all the deaths she'd witnessed in her journey to Tibor, this was the first time she felt complete relief and satisfaction. This man had been evil to the core. The atrocities he'd committed, planned to commit if he won, astounded her. Thank the Light for her father's teaching or she may never have fought past Tamarisk's binding.

A shadow stirred in the corridor. Uncle Ywen, dagger in hand, stepped forward.

She was about to call out to Tom when her uncle spoke.

"I'm sorry." his voice was barely audible.

An apology. She had not expected that.

"He fooled me, you see," the twisted and bent king said. "I thought he was my friend."

"Step any closer to her and it will be your last," Tom said from the doorway. Behind him stood Mam, Anna and the children.

Stomping footsteps on stairs announced new arrivals. Gilly breathed a sigh of relief as Talus ran upstairs, at the head of a group of King's Warriors.

"I see you've all started without me," he said as he stepped onto the landing. At the sight of Ywen looming beside Gilly with his dagger, Talus drew his sword.

"What took you so long?" Tom asked.

"Couldn't find a way to get past the dark cloud," Talus said. "Then suddenly, like smoke, it vanished." His attention remained trained on the king. "May I be of help, Missus Gilly?"

She took his hand and stepped carefully away from her uncle. "Thank you."

"Your Highness," Talus said to Ywen, "give Tom that dagger. This fight is over."

Ywen seemed to come out of a stupor. He raised the dagger to look at it as if he hadn't realized he still carried it. His glance slid from Talus to settle on Gilly.

"I killed Keegan. I would have killed your brother. All for nothing." He turned the dagger as if hoping it would clear his confusion. Then he glanced at her. "It was you, wasn't it?"

"What are you talking about?" Gilly asked.

"You're the Defender of the Light. It wasn't my brother who held the gift in the family. It was you. That's why Tamarisk wanted you. If he could kill you, he would have gained your immense power for himself."

"Uncle Ywen, have you not learned anything from these tragedies? Light cannot be stolen without paying a price. Tamarisk almost destroyed Ryca by draining the powers of sorcerers he captured. The legend of Tarrius shows you Light must be shared freely to reach its full potential. It did that when Anna and I shared our powers. Between you and Keegan, the Light could have been as powerful as ever it had been when King Tarrius wielded it."

He swung the dagger in an arc. "Keegan would never share anything with me."

"Did you ever ask?"

"I'm the elder twin, the heir to Ryca. Why should I grovel for a favor from my younger brother?"

She shook her head. What a reunion. Did this man not realize his only living kin surrounded him? She sighed. What was the use? He had never appreciated his own brother, how could she expect him to feel anything for his nieces and nephew?

She had nothing further to say to her uncle. All she wanted was peace. She was finally reunited with her family and it was the darkest moment of her life. She hated this landing. It added nothing but horror to her life. The sooner she was off it, the better. She headed for the stairs. Mam could handle her defeated brother-in-law.

"Don't turn from me, niece," he said. "I was duped by Tamarisk, just as you were."

She stopped. He was right about one thing. She must not turn her back on her family again. She faced him. As confused as he was, he was her uncle.

Tom sliced the air with his arm. "You chose your own path old man." There was no mercy in him for his king. "Your hand killed Keegan. Now give me that dagger."

He nodded and lowered his arm, the blade coming to rest by his knee. "Even an old man can learn from his error." He pointed to himself. "Do you not think I have paid for my mistakes, niece? Can you find it your heart to forgive me?"

"The one to ask forgiveness of is my mother."

"You were right all along." His glance fell to Mamosia and then swung back to Gilly. "All that bloodshed, when all I had to do was kill you." His hand snaked forward as he lunged toward Gilly, glinting steel thirsting for blood.

Tom pushed her behind him. At the same instant, Talus deflected the king's blow and in a fluid motion, struck his sword true at Ywen's heart.

Mam ran to pull Gilly toward her and huddled in her arms. Her mother was shaking as if winter had set into her bones.

Gilly understood that sense of sorrow. Even at the end, she had been unable to dissuade her uncle of his mistaken beliefs. He'd killed Papa, then her grandfather, and now tried to murder her to steal the power of Light. The moment he struck at her, his bitterness and frustration had licked at her like a scorching flame.

His friend, Tamarisk, casually casting spells must have also seared him with jealousy. His gaze, ever focused outward, had never perceived that Light could only ever come from within.

She released her mother and stood back. Tamara ran over to take her mother's hand, her face pale and terrified. Gilly couldn't think of anything to say to reassure her sister that their family nightmare was over. Was she capable of bringing peace to her land? Her people?

"What are you thinking?" Tom asked, retrieving his sword and coming over as he wiped it clean.

She shrugged, feeling the weight of responsibility. "The tradition of my journey east has continued. Another ruler murdered because I came to town. How many does that make? Vyan in Nadym, Aton in Erov, Hagan in Perm, Ywen in Tibor."

"It leaves the field open for a new regime across the breadth of Ryca," Tom said with a cheeky grin, considering he was the one who was responsible for Vyan's demise. But his infectious humor did lighten her mood.

She put a sympathetic arm around Tamara but her sister shrugged it off and huddled closer to her mother.

The queen brushed a strand of Gilly's hair behind her ear. "I knew if anyone could bring about a happy resolution, it would be you. So did your father."

"Papa would not have wanted me to be responsible for his brother's death."

"You did what was needed," Mamosia said. "Now it is time for the telling." She opened her free arm to Garren who ran over to hug his mother. "We three are orphans in time. Take us to where the scenery is less violent and recount what has happened since we last saw you."

"It will be a long telling, Mam," Gilly said. "I may not be up to it this night."

"You'll have me to help," Anna said, coming over.

"And I." Talus said.

"Don't forget me," Tom wrapped a supporting arm around Gilly's shoulders. She leaned into his strength, so very grateful to have him beside her.

Mam's eyebrows rose at the gesture and Gilly blushed.

Tom's grin widened and, if anything, his hold tightened.

"She always forgets us," Anna said. "You wouldn't believe the trouble we've had with her confiding in us. I have been in the dark almost as long as you have and I wasn't even trapped in time."

Her mother's stern look slid her way before Mamosia set the guards to clean up the carnage on the landing.

The senior staff was given instructions to meet with her later this morning, for a new order had taken over the castle and the land. Her mother then directed Gilly's group down the stairs and toward a wide chamber with tall windows on the third floor. Tamara still clung to Mam's hand as the queen glanced around the chamber with a fond look. "When we lived in the castle, this was my favorite place to sit and listen to a telling."

In moments, a cozy fire blazed on the hearth and servants brought in trays of sweetmeats and roasts, bowls of hot aromatic soup and fresh bread. Talus appreciated the jugs of ale most.

Tom settled in a seat next to Gilly, seeming reluctant to let her out of his hold.

"Marton has left with the children and the vessel full of sorcerers to Emba," Anna said, coming into the room. "I asked him to safeguard their journey. I want them far away until the changeover of rule is complete at the castle. In case we discover pockets of resistance." She sat on the spare arm of Gilly's chair, looking every inch the princess she was, as she addressed her mother. "Have you noticed yet that Gilly no longer limps?"

"I didn't think you had noticed," Gilly said.

"I knew the moment you sat next to me fully cross legged," her little sister said, with a smug smile.

Mamosia looked shaken as she stared at Gilly. "How could I have missed this change?"

"We have been a little busy, Mam," Gilly said with a tolerant smile for her overburdened mother.

"How were you healed? I tried every spell at my disposal and failed."

Gilly took Anna's hand and kissed the back of it. "We did it together. When Anna combined her healing powers with mine by a stream outside Tibor, the land around us was healed, as well as me." She glanced at her mother. "Mam, the land around the castle needs healing, too. The dark cloud did much damage to this city."

"Then let us take care of that problem right now," Mamosia said and jumped up.

••••

GILLY, ANNA AND MAMOSIA stood on the castle parapet holding hands and overlooking the city below. Tom and Talus stood watch a few feet behind them. All around, the land appeared dark and scorched. The first rays of sunlight painted details of the cloud's destruction.

Anna, who stood between Gilly and Mamosia, began a chant of healing. It had a musical quality that Gilly appreciated. She could easily picture her sister singing this song to her children at bed time. After a few repeated phrases, she joined in and fed Anna her Light as she had done in the dungeons. Her mother's sweet voice tuned in to theirs. Anna gasped and Gilly guessed that Mamosia's power had flowed into Anna as well. She held her sister's hand tight in support and encouragement.

A brilliant luminescence of a myriad of colors appeared. Darts of light sped ahead from it and then returned to report where help was most needed. The glow traveled slowly, its touch tender on charred ground, gently enveloping bruised trees and settling with infinite care over the city of Tibor.

• • • •

THE PEOPLE OF TIBOR awakened to a new day surrounded by lush plants, fertile fields and sparkling clean water in the streams. Several reports of spontaneous healing passed through the city.

News filtered out that Ywen and his sorcerer Tamarisk were dead and that until Garren, Keegan's eldest boy reached twenty-one, Mamosia planned to reign over Ryca as Queen Regent.

Heralds sped off to all corners of the land to announce the change in leadership. Minstrels gathered at the castle to learn of the manner in which Tamarisk and Ywen had died.

A day later, Mamosia held a ceremony at which she named the King's Warriors as the penultimate law of the land, second only to the queen. The Rycan Warriors were then thanked for their efforts in restoring Keegan's heirs to Ryca's throne. The men headed back to their families and friends carrying a satchel of gold coins each and the queen's promise of unlimited favors for them and their descendants for as long her family ruled.

The queen then bestowed on Tom and Talus a valuable parcel of land and gold each for their invaluable service. Tom asked for a further favor. He wanted himself and his descendants to again take up the role of Royal Bodyguards. Upon receiving a surprised royal assent, he left to continue his training with Talus.

Magic was reinstated in Ryca as a respected guild. Mamosia ordered all the netting recovered in the dungeons and in Tamarisk's quarters to be torched. Then news arrived that the sorcerers had reached Emba where they were treated as heroes and gifted places to live for the rest of their lives. On hearing this, Mamosia proposed a Light University be set up in Emba where the rescued sorcerers, once they were completely recovered, could teach young students how to enhance and focus their inborn magical talents.

The King's Horsemen were pronounced to no longer hold any authority in Ryca. A price was placed for the capture of One-Eye and his men. Within days, One-Eye's head was delivered to the castle and the bounty was sought. Gilly went to witness the delivery, wanting to be certain this Horseman would no longer be a problem to her family.

Invitations were soon issued to delegates from each region to attend the first joint meeting of the Council of Representatives to advise the queen on matters relating to their particular region. The first member of the newly formed council to arrive at the castle was Jarrod from the legendary city of Erov.

He was followed shortly by Marton and the children who were then introduced to their grandmother. Anna took her family in hand and showed them what life in a castle would be like. Apparently there was an opening for a royal blacksmith.

Gilly retreated into her room, into silence and into the past. Traveling back to Nadym to collect her goats dominated her thoughts. She missed the sound of their bleats. She didn't share her wish with her mother or Anna though, uncertain how those two strong women would respond.

Mam seemed different now. At the cottage in the woods, she'd been a mother who trained her children to hide and run from Horsemen. Here, she easily fell back into the role of monarch. Easier than Gilly settled into her role of Princess of Ryca. Her full memory had not returned despite the trauma of facing Tamarisk. She had felt more of a lady at Erov with Aton than she did in the palace.

Perhaps that was why she forgot about the Day of Celebration. Once a servant reminded her, she had to rush to get ready. By the time she entered the hall for the meal, the large wooden table set before the hearth was already full.

Anna sat between Marton, Skye and Bevan. Skye ran over to give Gilly a hug before returning to her seat. Tom was between Talus and Marton. That left a vacant spot between Jarrod and Talus. She was about to climb over the bench when Talus lifted her up and set her down.

"Thank you," she murmured. She had to have a talk with him about constantly lifting her off her feet without warning. A glance down the table suggested Tom hadn't cared for Talus' familiarity or where she'd chosen to sit. *Too bad.* He should have saved room for her.

Talus chuckled beside her and she sent him an inquiring side-glance. "You find something amusing in your meal?"

He held up a piece of roast dripping pink juice. "I was going to ask that this be roasted more. Now I've decided the looks you and Tom are sending each other should char it to perfection."

She decided to ignore him and turned to study the guests at the table. Her mother sat at the head beside Garren. Something struck her as odd about the placement around her. Then she realized Tamara wasn't nearby. Her elder sister, younger now since she was still thirteen summers, had remained glued to her mother after Gilly broke the time spell. Now she sat at the other end of the table, as far from her mother as she could have placed herself. By her hard expression, she seemed to hate Mam. Why?

"I wonder what's upset Tamara?" Gilly murmured.

"She needs time to recover," Jarrod said quietly.

Gilly glanced at him in surprise and was instantly swamped by the most terrible visions. While her mother, brother and sister were trapped by the time spell, only Tamara had remained awake through it, watching life go by, day after excruciating day. She had witnessed every moment of time's passage over her years of captivity. Listened to her Uncle Ywen's ranting and raving. Tamarisk trying spell after spell to free his Mamosia. Endless hours of being alone with nothing to relieve her but her thoughts.

Gilly shivered in horror. Mam had said it was as if they went to sleep one moment and awoke the next, decades later. Not so for her poor sister. The time spell had not stopped time entirely for Tamara. While she had not aged, she had remained awake.

"Jarrod, I must tell Mam about Tamara," she whispered.

His smooth dark hand landed over her light one in a firm hold. "No! I shouldn't have read Tamara's mind like that. Among my people, it is forbidden to read another's thoughts without permission. I hadn't meant to. But despite her silence, her thoughts were blasting out and I couldn't block them. If you heard them through me, you cannot betray her. She must speak of this on her own terms. It is her secret to keep or share."

The queen tapped a knife against her goblet, distracting Gilly. "Going forward, there will be changes to the way this land is governed," Mam said. "The first will involve the Erovians. Lord Jarrod, I wish Erov to play a stronger role in Ryca's development."

His head tilted sideways, gray-green eyes faintly inquiring, his dark ringlets swinging. "Such as?"

"Saira tells me that your people do an exemplary job of recording history. Yet you do not share your knowledge outside of Erov. The past several years have shown what happens if people are not aware of the true nature of events. Although our minstrels transmit news, over time, that information can become fictionalized."

"You wish us to share our historical records?" The idea seemed to intrigue him.

"We need good teachers," Mamosia said. "I want my people to learn how to read and write as well as learn about their past. The true past. Where our youths can learn both practical and historical information."

"You mean work with the other guilds?" Jarrod asked.

Mamosia nodded. "It is time Erov became a part of our world, Jarrod."

Everyone smiled and thumped the table to show their approval of this suggestion.

The conversation veered to other change her Mam envisioned. Gilly spent the rest of the evening dividing her attention between Tom and Tamara. Since neither seemed to warm to her, she excused herself.

Before she made it past the doors, Tom was by her side "Leaving so soon, Saira?"

"You seemed occupied with Talus," she said. "I had no wish to disturb you."

"Then you failed miserably, my love," he said gently kissing her hand, "for you have done nothing but disturb me since you kissed me several days ago."

Liking his words, she thawed a little towards him. He disturbed her, too, in many ways, and had for far longer than their first kiss. Since she had initiated their last embrace, it was his turn to kiss her next, surely. An embrace was long overdue. At least four days to her count.

"Will you come with me?" he asked.

"Where?" she asked coyly, hoping he would say to her chamber. Or his. She was tired of sleeping alone.

To her disappointment, with an irrepressibly devilish grin, he tugged her toward the front doors. "Outside."

He led her toward the horse barns and Gilly had a dreadful premonition he wanted to show her a new fighting technique while riding horseback. But he led her around back of the barn.

A bright elaborate green tent that screamed *Erovian* was set up in the field. What caught and enraptured Gilly's gaze were the goats grazing beside the tent.

"My goats!" she shouted in delight and raced to give each one a reverent hug, burying her face in their soft fleece. They bleated and gathered around her to give her head butts and wet face licks. She turned to gaze up at him with a contented smile. "How did you know?"

"That you were planning to leave me again? Because I know you better than you know yourself." He held out his hand. "Now come on. We're not finished yet. Not by a long shot."

She laughed and followed him as he led her toward the tent, thinking she would trail him anywhere. "Did Jarrod give us this? Why?"

"I told him finding a private place to be with you was virtually impossible in this vast castle with your mother's guards and hangers on around every corner.

"Are you calling my family hangers on?"

He chuckled and hugged her close. "I'm calling anyone who comes between you and me a nuisance. According to Jarrod, once we enter this tent, no one will disturb us until we're ready to leave it. I'm not thoroughly certain, but I suspect we may no longer be in Tibor once that tent flap closes behind us."

The tent was absolutely silent on their entrance. Her ears might even have popped. The inside seemed unusual for an Erovian home since she recalled every tent she entered in Erov being filled with a bevy of beautiful women and helpful men. In typical Erovian fashion, however, this one did seem bigger on the inside than out.

Tom opened a side flap and Gilly found herself in a room similar to the bathing one she'd last occupied in Erov. There was a giant pool in the center, with ointments and towels neatly set out along the rim.

"You owe me a chance to finish your leg massage," Tom whispered in her ear. "For all the days during which you tormented me by taking care of me."

"But I'm healed," she said, though she was thrilled by his turn of thought. She had been hoping he would remember. Since his last attempt, she had been dreaming every night about what it would feel like if she had allowed Tom to finish what he once began by the stream near Perm.

"Your lack of a limp is irrelevant." He turned her toward him and emphasized each word he spoke next with a kiss and the disrobing of one layer of her clothing. "Time. I. Repaid. You. In. Kind."

In short order, she was left as bare as the day she was born and too breathless to object. "I was hoping you would remember that debt," she whispered, and kissed him as thoroughly. Two could easily play this game.

THE END

• • • •

IN BOOK 2 OF THE TALES of Ryca series, **Hushed**, we learn more about Gilly's sister, Tamara, and how she reacts to being free of that time spell. She'll finally have a chance to grow up, and she'll have a special teacher on that adventurous journey. One that breathes fire. You can read more about **Hushed** here: https://www.shereenvedam.com/fantasy/

• • • •

IF YOU ENJOYED THIS story, please consider leaving a short review for this book wherever you purchased it. The review will help other readers decide if this book is worth their time.

• • • •

SIGN UP TO SHEREEN'S Newsletter to learn about her new releases:
    https://www.subscribepage.com/c9u7e6
Thank you for reading!

Don't miss out!

Visit the website below and you can sign up to receive emails whenever Shereen Vedam publishes a new book. There's no charge and no obligation.

https://books2read.com/r/B-A-POZG-YKEZ

BOOKS2READ

Connecting independent readers to independent writers.

Did you love *Hidden*? Then you should read *Hushed*[1] by Shereen Vedam!

[2]

Don't say a word!In one day, young TAMARA goes from being the king's firstborn and much-loved thirteen-year-old daughter to having her father brutally murdered. Then she's trapped by a time spell where no one hears her screams.Once she's finally free, she's determined to stay that way. So, when she turns eighteen and her mother attempts to marry her off for "her own good," Tamara is having none of it.However, is going on a quest across realms to find her lost nephew the best plan? She'll meet marauding giants and wily talking lizards. Face a fierce dragon on the run and spirits who should know better than to leave their graves.Most important of all, she'll have to come to terms with her greatest weakness, or strength, depending on her point of view. All the while, in the stillness a danger lurks that could destroy the rest of her family, and perhaps even her entire world.**WARNING:** *Wear your best chainmaille and carry a hefty sword before you flick open the first page of this adventurous tale.***Now hurry and pick up your copy today.**

---

1. https://books2read.com/u/b6MyME

2. https://books2read.com/u/b6MyME

Also by Shereen Vedam

Harrington Bay Mystery
Sage It Out
Missing You

Outside the Circle Mystery
To Capture Love
Death Takes a Detour
Death Shifts Gears
Death Smells Disaster
Death Swipes Right
Death Comes Up Short

Tales of Ryca
Hidden
Hushed

The Cauldron Effect
Coven at Callington
Warlock from Wales
Love Spell in London

Standalone
Tales of Ryca: The Complete Series
Torn
The Cauldron Effect: The Complete Series
Believe
Innocent

Watch for more at www.shereenvedam.com.